The first *favela* was created in November 1897 when 20,000 soldiers, mostly Afro-Brazilian, veterans of the civil war (1893-1897) in Bahia, were brought to Rio de Janeiro with no place to live. They were installed with their families on a *morro* (hill) outside the city, the *Morro da Providência*, which the former soldiers renamed *Morro da Favela* after the *favela* (fava beans) that grew in abundance in Bahia and the stem of which they wore in their hats as a campaign badge. It is estimated that up to two million people now live in Rio's 750 *favelas*.

THE LITTLE GIRL OF THE FAVELA

M.K. BATES

GILL CHICK PUBLISHING

*Life can only be understood backwards;
but it must be lived forwards.*

Søren Kierkegaard

Prologue

The four-year-old girl lay ill in the dark, shuttered bedroom. She had been running a high fever for days, with an aching head and body. The sounds of the *favela* (shanty town) where she lived, shouting, children playing, motorbikes, music, the occasional gunshot, had all become distant to her. Her grandmother was sitting on the edge of her bed, stroking her hair with bony fingers. The pair were normally inseparable, doing everything together, including sharing the same bed at night.

"I want some mango juice," the girl whispered to her granny.

"Yes, we will get some mango juice, only for you." The granny said it in a baby talk voice, a singsong way of speaking, still stroking the little girl's hair. She turned her head. "Fetch some mango juice," she shouted through the open bedroom door.

The little girl's mother entered with a glass of juice and handed it to her mother-in-law.

"Here, sit up," the granny said. The little girl sat up and sipped the juice, looking at her granny's wrinkly face and smiling. She knew nothing could harm her if Granny was there. She finished the juice and lay back down. "You look a little better. You look like you might be able to eat… I put a mango here." The granny rubbed the little girl's palm and put an imaginary mango in it. "I put a date here." She rubbed the girl's wrist. "I put a banana here." She moved up to her elbow joint. "I put an orange here." She squeezed her upper arm. "Where have they gone?" She tickled the girl under the arm. "They're here, aren't they?" She patted the girl's stomach and peered into her face laughing. The little girl dissolved into a mass of giggles. "You sleep now, little one."

The granny stood up and went to the door of the bedroom where the girl's mother was standing, looking anxious.

"Is she going to live?" the mother asked.

"Of course she is." The granny was known as something of a visionary in the *favela*, with quite a following of devotees, and even rich people from downtown Rio would sometimes come to see her. "She will have a charmed life and be adored by everyone who meets her, not because of her looks or wit, but because of the love she gives. She will live for love. She will be very successful and rich. She will perform an act of great courage in order to save the lives of others."

"Oh, please God let that be right." The mother put her hands together as if in prayer.

Meanwhile, a pristine, shiny black Mercedes had stopped on the road at the foot of the *favela*. The lady in the back took off her Rolex watch and handed it to the chauffeur.

"I'll be three quarters of an hour. If I'm any longer, send out a search party."

The chauffeur laughed. "Yes, *senhora*. I'll be here. I won't go home without you."

The lady stepped out of the car and looked at the *favela*, sprawling up the hillside in front of her like an enormous rubbish tip, but one made of compact, bunker type houses of all shapes, sizes and colour, randomly sited, squeezed in close together. She was wearing simple beach clothes: a white blouse, light blue cotton trousers and sandals. This

2

was in order to try and hide her wealth, yet any *Carioca* (native of Rio de Janeiro) would have looked at her and known, just by the stylish cut of her hair, her manicured hands, and her calm, comfortable body language, that she was a well-to-do, from downtown Rio or one of the coastal neighbourhoods. She took a handkerchief, doused in lavender oil, from her pocket and held it to her nose. She had prepared it earlier to protect herself from the stench of the *favela*, which was already invading her nostrils, even though she stood at the very edge of the slum. It was a mix, in variable quantities, of sewage, diesel fuel, nicotine and cooking oil, a noxious potion, like being downwind to a glue factory.

She left the safety of the car behind her and slowly picked her way across a piece of rocky waste ground, to a gap in a high wall, where two tough looking *bandidos*, in their early twenties and dressed in sportswear, were sitting on old wooden chairs. They were guarding a path that ascended into the township. A box of firecrackers was at their feet, to let off as a warning in the instance of a police raid, telling everyone to take shelter from stray bullets.

"Good morning, *senhora*." There was deference in the voice, despite the fact that it was the gangsters who had the guns on their laps.

She held the handkerchief discretely by her side. "Hello. I've come to see the fortune teller."

"Of course. You wouldn't visit for any other reason. Come with me. I will guide you. You will be safe. The cocaine baron of this township has granted safe passage to anyone wanting to see the old lady fortune teller. She brings honour and respect to our community."

The coffee coloured gangster, who had done all the talking, left his black companion behind to guard the *favela* entrance and proceeded to guide the lady up the

3

hill, up the narrow path, past the little houses, the piles of decaying rubbish and the little groups of children and teenagers who stood and stared. They turned off the main path and started to twist this way and that down a labyrinth of smaller alleyways. As they turned one corner, the gangster looked back at her.

"*Senhora*, don't look to your left."

Instinctively, the well-to-do lady looked to her left. The dead body of a mixed race young man, dressed in a white T shirt and navy blue shorts, lay face up on the side of the path. His feet were bare, and his face was swollen and bruised from a punishment beating, the skin broken in a few places and already attracting flies. The lady let out a gasp of shock. The body would stay there till the man's relatives came to take it away. No police or medical teams would be entering the *favela*, for fear of hostility or attack from the local gangs. If the police were to enter, it would be in a small armoured personnel carrier, and in order to capture drugs or shoot-to-kill gang members. The gangster saw the lady's distress.

"Aah youth!" He shook his head. "The things they get up to. Very bad."

Her face looked crumpled. "The poor boy…why?"

"Oh, for a reason," the gangster said enthusiastically, beckoning to the lady to continue walking. "I heard about it. He put baking soda in the cocaine he was selling, to make it go further. He brought a bad reputation to our *favela*. People will stop coming to buy cocaine from us. He kills our business, so the cocaine baron said, 'we kill him.'"

The lady looked down at the ground and sighed, as though overwhelmed and thinking her visit may have been a mistake.

After ten minutes, halfway up the hill, they reached the fortune teller's house. Inside, the old granny sat on the edge of the bed, watching her little granddaughter sleep and gently laying her healing hands on the girl's head.

"*Mamãe*." The little girl's mother called to her mother-in-law from the living room. "A lady has come for a reading. I'll stay in the bedroom until you've finished."

The granny gently stroked the little girl's hair, got up and went to the front door.

"Hello, *senhora*." The granny smiled, and then nodded, as though in deference to the visitor. She turned to the gangster. "Wait there." The voice was less respectful as she pointed to a chair, just outside the front door. "We'll be about half an hour." She turned back to the lady. "Please come in, *senhora*." She ushered the lady into the living room and shut the front door behind them. "Sit down." She indicated the place at the table where the lady should sit, fetched her fortune-telling kit from a sideboard and sat herself down opposite. She then spread a brown, velour cloth over the table, placed a crystal ball on a stand in the centre and put a pack of tarot cards in front of the visitor.

"Why I've come... " the lady started.

"I know why you've come." The granny's voice was definite, almost fierce. "You think your husband's having an affair, and you don't want to lose him. He's very wealthy, he's a good father to your three children, and you still love him."

The lady's mouth dropped open in astonishment as she took an inward breath. "Yes," she said softly.

"Shuffle the cards." When they were shuffled, the granny spread them face down across the cloth like a fan. "Pick ten cards." The lady hesitantly picked out ten from the pack, and the granny laid them out horizontally and proceeded to turn them over one by one to reveal the picture underneath. The first card said The Lovers, a naked man and woman. "Yes, he's having an affair." The granny nodded. "It's with his secretary."

"I knew it was her. The bitch. He always stays late at the office now. She's only interested in his money and glamorous lifestyle."

The lady sighed as the granny turned the second card. It said The Devil, ugly with horns.

"He could not resist the temptation." The granny looked up at the lady.

"She's very alluring. She wears very revealing clothes to the office."

The granny turned the third card, The Tower, a teetering inferno of mayhem. "You're worrying. Stop worrying! Everything will be okay for you."

"You think so?" The lady looked so sad, like she didn't believe things could work out for her.

The granny turned the fourth card, The Empress, a motherly looking queen. "You spend too much time with your children. Remember he needs your attention as well."

"I'm a good mother. Surely he appreciates that? Our children are so precious to me."

"Yes, you may be a good mother, but do you want them to have a father in the house too?" The granny's face had lots of lines, but it was still handsome, and she had piercing, dark eyes. They burned into the lady who flushed and held her head down as if in penance.

"Yes. You're right. I must make more time for him."

The granny turned the fifth card, Queen of Pentacles, a serene, homely woman on a throne. "You have become too much of a mother. In the bedroom, you must still be sexy. You can be the Madonna in every room of the house, except the bedroom." The lady continued to look down as the granny turned the sixth card, Two of Pentacles, a man juggling. "He will continue the affair for a while, juggling the two of you in his life." The lady sighed as the granny turned the seventh card, The Hanged Man, a man

6

suspended upside down against a tree. "You still have some difficult times to go through." The granny turned the eighth card, Three of Swords, piercing a red heart. "There will be three of you in this marriage for a while." The granny turned the ninth card, Ten of Pentacles, a domestic scene, but with the woman looking concerned at the man. "You feel everything is upside down in your world right now."

"Maybe I should divorce him." The lady said it in an empty headed sort of way.

"Don't run away. Fight for your man. Don't expect everything to be easy." The granny gave the lady another piercing look. She then turned the tenth and final card, Two of Cups, a happy, harmonious couple facing each other, looking like they were renewing their wedding vows. "See. Stop worrying! It will be just you and your husband together again. Everything will be good and happy for you." The granny gave a big chuckle.

The reading was finished. The lady smiled for the first time.

"Really? Is it possible everything will work out?"

"Of course it is. Stop worrying. Just do as I said. Do you have any more questions?" The granny looked at the lady.

"No. Thank you. Thank you so much. I feel much better." The lady had a relieved look and reached across the table to grasp the granny's bony hands. "How can I repay you?"

"Put a donation in the dish." She pointed to a glass bowl on the television in the corner of the room and the lady got up and put some notes in.

"But how else can I repay you?"

"That's enough. I don't need any more payment."

"No, really, I want to help you."

The granny looked distant for a few seconds. "I would never normally say this, and I don't know why, but okay, there is something. Come through here." The granny opened the bedroom door. "This is my granddaughter." She said it quietly, in order not to wake the sick little girl, who was sleeping. A chocolate coloured teddy bear lay in bed beside her.

The lady leant over the little girl and touched her hair. "Oh, she's so cute." The lady half closed her eyes and placed her hand across her chest, as though to contain her feelings. Some tears started to well up in her eyes. "She's so adorable."

"You can help her, when I'm gone."

The lady thought for a few seconds. "Yes. I can be her godmother. Here's my phone number." The lady took a card from her pocket and handed it to the granny. "Any time you need help, just ask."

The granny scrutinised the card. It said, "Maria Josefina de Alencar," which meant the lady was descended from Portuguese aristocracy.

"Thank you. God bless you." The granny bowed her head slightly, in deference.

The lady's tears were flowing more freely now. "I'm sorry. I don't know why I'm crying. I've been so worried. I think all the tension's being released."

"Come back to the living room and I'll give you some healing."

After the lady had left, the little girl's mother emerged from the corner of the bedroom where she had been sitting quietly. She went and sat on the bed by her daughter, who was still sleeping, and looked at her mother-in-law.

"What you said earlier, about her having a charmed life, is it true?"

"Of course it is. I can see it so clearly, but I won't live to see it happen. Your daughter will be the saviour of your family, but I will be gone by then. I will be with you in spirit only."

8

1

Hamburg Arrival

He had been travelling all day, and it was a January late Sunday afternoon and getting cold and dark, as Shaun Johnson arrived outside the apartment. In the one hand he was holding a weekend bag, which he put down beside him, and in the other, a bouquet of yellow roses, which he tucked behind his back. He stood for a few moments staring at the doorbell and the name 'Neddermeyer,' written above it in small, typed letters. He took a deep breath and puffed out his cheeks as he expelled the air. He twitched his mouth to one side.

The words of his friend Pete, down the pub in London the night before, were still ringing in his ears. Pete had been holding Shaun's shiny black iPod phone in the palm of his hand and looking at Christiana Neddermeyer's photo.

"Are you going to Germany, just to get into a tart's knickers? You're not, are you?" Yorkshire men often answered their own questions.

Shaun laughed and gave a big smile. "No, I'm going on business. But if this girl puts out," Shaun tapped Christiana's photo, "two birds with one stone."

Pete nodded. "Aye. I remember the beautiful Hamburger alright. I remember you raving about her." He studied Christiana's photo for a moment, peering through his black rimmed glasses, perched on his beaky nose. "Aye. She's a looker, alright. So she's invited you to stay in her apartment?" Pete's brow furrowed beneath his greasy black hair, as though he was put out. Where women were concerned, Shaun could get away with things that other men couldn't.

"Not exactly. I haven't been in contact since we met six months ago."

"So how are you going to stay with her?" Pete challenged.

"She gave me her address and said I could visit any time, so I'm going to turn up on spec, unannounced, just knock her up."

Pete shook his head and looked away, as though he needed a moment to take it in. "God, you've got some guts. I wouldn't have the nerve to turn up without any warning. What if she's got a boyfriend?"

"I beat a hasty retreat and find a hotel." Shaun mimicked a running motion with his arms.

"You're a lad, Shaun." Pete shook his head again. "Let me show you something I learned recently. Give me your hand. Hold it out straight." Pete took hold of Shaun's hand and examined the ends of his fingers. "Ah yes, I thought so. You see how your ring finger, your third finger is longer than your index finger?" Pete demonstrated by tracing a line between the two. "That means you're a risk taker."

"Maybe that's why I'm so attractive to women."

"But you've had a dry patch lately." Pete gave Shaun a quizzical look.

"Well at least I haven't had to spend any money on girlfriends."

"But I think you've spent quite a bit drowning your sorrows down here. You know what? I'm going to put money on't table." He opened his wallet and slapped a note down. He was a teacher of physics and maths, so not overly paid, but as Head of Department, he could indulge himself with a few extravagant gestures. "I'll give you fifty quid if you get her in the sack, and vice versa."

Shaun raised his eyebrows at the amount of money Pete was willing to risk, but they shook hands on it while Shaun laughed.

It wasn't so funny now he was actually standing outside Christiana's apartment. She had seemed like someone who might spread herself thin, everybody's friend, when he had met her in London six months previously. She had been talking and smiling to everyone in the bar near enough and plenty of men had been buzzing round her. But it was Shaun who had got to sit on the barstool beside her, making her laugh with a string of jokes. Did she take seriously inviting him to Hamburg? Would she remember him even? Was she at home or might some caveman of a boyfriend answer the door? There was only one way to find out. He took another deep breath and rang the bell.

The door flew open and there she was. Christiana didn't look particularly German, more a smouldering Mediterranean beauty with black hair down to her shoulders, a long face and a full sensual mouth, which she emphasised with red lipstick.

"Might you possibly be interested in buying a set of thirty six encyclopaedias, printed in English?" Shaun smiled at her.

Christiana blinked and looked down at Shaun's bag beside him. "No, thank you," she said softly in her beautiful, refined voice, and started to close the door.

"Christiana." He brought his arm round to reveal the bouquet of flowers. "Have you forgotten me already?"

She opened the door wide again and stood looking at him, like she was trying to puzzle something out.

Suddenly her eyes and mouth opened in astonishment. "I thought your face was familiar. Shaun, from London?" she said in her broken English. "What are you doing here?" She sounded more surprised than pleased.

"I've come on business, for a meeting tomorrow morning. You said I could stay." Shaun maintained his smile.

"Did I? Oh no!" She tapped her forehead as if to say, 'silly girl'. "How much had I had to drink? My apartment's very small."

"I don't mind squeezing up with you."

She laughed momentarily, but then looked serious, her face tense, like she was trying to make a decision. In the silence, he gestured for her to take the flowers. She hesitated, gave a nervous laugh and then accepted the bouquet. She gave the blooms a sniff, and then just stood there.

Shaun wrapped his arms around his body and pretended to shiver. "I'm not a polar bear, Christiana. It's cold out here."

She frowned. "You're a naughty man, Shaun, surprising me like this." But then she sighed and looked a little more relaxed. "Anyway, don't stand out there. I suppose it's okay for you to come in. It's not like I have a gorilla of a boyfriend lurking inside."

She gestured for him to enter and he felt like he was breaching a fortress wall as he stepped into the warmth of the little hallway and put his bag down next to a pair of ice skates and some football boots that had been thrown carelessly into a corner. He wondered who would be the owner of the pair of boots, but said nothing. She embraced him and gave him a kiss on both cheeks.

Christiana was wearing a green silk skirt, quite short so that it showed off her shapely legs and on top she wore a

12

thin white V neck jumper that did not leave the shape of her ample breasts to the imagination. The jumper had no sleeves and revealed her well-developed biceps and forearms.

"Leave your bag in the hall. If you're staying, I'll have to sort your bedding out later." She sighed, as though it was going to be some bother for her, and led him from the small lobby into her living room. "Sit down." She gestured to the sofa. "You must have been born under a lucky star. Twenty minutes later and you wouldn't have caught me." There seemed to be a touch of resentment in her voice, that he had just managed to catch her. "I'm meeting some friends tonight. We're going to see the Hamburg Freezers play the Berlin Ice Barons… hmm… so what would you do?" She thought for a few moments. "You like ice hockey, if I can get you a ticket?"

"Great. That would be the first time I've been to an ice hockey match. They fight with their sticks, don't they?" He gave her a cute smile, trying to turn on the charm.

She suddenly looked more relaxed and laughed. "I've never seen them fighting." She gave him an intense gaze, like when he had first met her in London six months previously. It seemed to promise quite a bit, that he might be in with a chance. "Let me put these lovely flowers in some water and I'll make you some tea."

With that, she disappeared into the kitchen and Shaun sat alone in the living room. He sank back into the sofa, feeling relieved, thinking she could hardly throw him out now he was in. The atmosphere in her apartment was easygoing. For six years Christiana had been an English teacher in a tough Hamburg School, but she had given up the well-paid job, she hadn't told Shaun why, for a life on social security, which she supplemented by translating English into German in her spare time. Sunday was her day of rest.

The living room was large and dominated by two book cases, facing each other from opposite sides of the room, both sagging under the weight of the hardbacks and paperbacks. There was a music system next to the book case on the right, with a pile of albums set beneath it and next to that was a small portable television tucked away, as though it was only occasionally watched. In the left hand corner by the only window, which overlooked the street, was her desk with a laptop, lamp and chair, and above was a cork notice board, covered in photos and yellow sticky notes. Opposite the window was the sofa on which Shaun was sitting, and apart from that the only other seats were large cushions scattered around the floor.

She popped her head round the living room door.

"Settling in okay?" she enquired.

"Fine, thank you." He pointed to the corner of the room, where there was a pile of knitting magazines and a basket of wool with knitting needles resting on top. "I've heard about the new craze for knitting and that you have your own website, 'StitchyBitch' isn't it?"

She laughed. "It's 'Stitch and Bitch'. It relaxes me... not StitchyBitch!" she said as she left the room again.

She returned a few minutes later with a plate of cream cakes and some tea on a tray. There was a coffee table by Shaun and she leant across it to put the tray down. He could see so much of her breasts as she bent down, he thought she couldn't have been wearing a bra.

She sat beside him on the sofa. "You've thrown me into a state of shock, Shaun. I still can't believe that you'd turn up after six months. Sorry if I was a bit off with you. Did you hire a car from the airport?"

"I did, but look, I can't eat all those cakes." He made a feminine gesture with his face and hands, "I have my figure to consider."

She suddenly gave him a hug. "Oh! It's a nice surprise to see you again."

He was a handsome man with fair hair. A broad forehead and a strong chin made him look confident, but his features were not too angular, so he had the more refined looks of a Hollywood leading man. She knew he was a businessman, she remembered that from their meeting in London. She had the impression he wasn't so successful at the moment, but he was young and there was always the chance that one day he might be wealthy.

Shaun was enjoying Christiana's welcome and her come-hither clothes. It seemed to him, alone with her in her little apartment, that he had her on a plate. He took hold of her hand.

"There's something I wanted to tell you."

She looked down at the hand holding hers and raised her eyebrows slightly in surprise, but she carried on smiling and leant her head forward in anticipation. She smelt of soap and freshly laundered clothes and quite a heady perfume which he hadn't noticed earlier, so he presumed it was freshly applied following his arrival.

"Okay…" She hesitated. "But I managed to get you a ticket for the ice hockey, so we'll have to leave soon, or we'll miss the start of the game."

He had intended to tell her he found her very attractive and that he hoped she might feel the same. But the moment had suddenly evaporated. "It'll keep. On a serious note, will there be food tonight? I've only had aeroplane food today."

"Well, there's lots of beer on sale, and you can get things like sausage and chips, not quite your," she put on an English gentleman's accent, "bangers and mash… but also there's an Indian restaurant, with live music. We could go after the match if you can wait that long."

"Great. Maybe I could make a quick sandwich? Would

you mind? Just to sustain life for a few hours? Don't want a corpse on your hands, do you?"

He made one from some ham Christiana had in her fridge and placed it in a plastic carrier bag which he stuffed into his coat pocket. Christiana put on a red, skiing puffa jacket over her skimpy clothes and they set off for the ice hockey match in Shaun's rented car.

* * *

They had streamed down the road with the crowds of fans, passed through the sports arena entrance and were now standing in the open space of the services perimeter. Christiana's friends, about twelve of them, looking well dressed and relaxed, were mingling with drinks in their hands. After a few minutes, one of them handed Shaun a plastic *stein* of beer.

"Hi, I'm Wolfgang. Good to have you in Germany. Where are you staying?" He was a large man with a long nose and muscular build, and stood smiling at Shaun.

"Cheers!" Shaun raised his glass. "With Christiana."

"Oh, her flat is very small. Mine is much more spacious, and in a more stylish part of Hamburg. You're welcome to stay with me if you like."

"That's kind. I'll see how I get on." Shaun took in the size of the man for a moment. "Wow, you look fit. How many times a week do you go to the gym?" He touched the man's bulging bicep. It was not something he would normally have done, but he was maybe tired from the travelling.

"Every day." Wolfgang lurched forward to move his head closer, invading Shaun's personal space and breathing beer fumes over him. Shaun backed away in an involuntary movement.

"So you can have all the beer, pizza and ice cream you

want?" Shaun looked uncertain as he said it and didn't wait for a reply. "Will you excuse me?"

He had glanced across and saw that Christiana was looking annoyed. She was talking to a long-haired young man, who was wearing a leather jacket. He had been holding a crisp above Christiana's head, like he was feeding a dog, but then he ate it himself. Shaun went over and the young man turned to him.

"Hiya. I'm Gunter. What brings you to Germany?"

"Hi, I'm Shaun, here on business, I'm an entrepreneur."

"Good for Christiana." Gunter looked at her knowingly and winked. She let out a sigh and looked away, as though exasperated.

Shaun was puzzled and was going to ask her if everything was all right, but at that moment her group of friends started to move, to go through to the auditorium to find their seats and Shaun just went with the flow. He sat next to Christiana, with Gunter on his other side.

"Here's a programme," said Gunter.

Shaun opened it and studied the team line-ups for a few seconds. "Hang on, all the players are Canadian."

"Correct." Gunter nodded. "They're mostly Canadian, with a few Czechs and Russians. The Canadians invented the game, you know."

"But why no home-grown players?" Shaun looked at Gunter.

"We don't have so much ice. Canadian babies have ice skates strapped to their feet as soon as they can walk."

Shaun laughed. "Good answer! Sold, to the man in the leather jacket." He turned his head at that moment to look at the players who had come out to warm up, the Freezers in white, the Ice Barons in red, and caught sight of Christiana pouting at him, as if annoyed that he wasn't paying her any attention. He looked back at Gunter.

"Excuse me," he said and then turned to Christiana. "Beauty is in the eye of the beer holder." He raised his *stein* of beer and took a sip. He leant towards Christiana. "Your friends are okay. I've already had one offer of a place to stay, if you were thinking of throwing me out."

She laughed. "No, you're okay." She put her hand on his arm and gave it a squeeze. "But who invited you to stay?"

"Wolfgang, the muscle man. He gave me this beer."

"He lives in the St. Georg district on the other side of the Alster Lake, it's the gay area… you're better off with me, Shaun."

"I'm sticking with you." He squeezed her arm in return and then held on to the material of her coat, tugging at it for a few seconds. "I thought Gunter spoke very good English."

Christiana frowned. She leant forward like a conspirator and whispered, "he's a hippy and a freak. I don't know why I bother with him. Let's ignore him."

Shaun was again puzzled. He wondered why Gunter evoked such a strong reaction in Christiana. "Of course. No problem," he said softly. "Look, I've turned my back on him." He angled himself round a little further so that he was facing Christiana square on.

She gazed at him intensely for a few seconds, like she was getting full on, and then put her face close to his. She whispered in his ear, with her soft, seductive voice, "you're not my usual type, but you're cute." With that she kissed his hair and then resumed sitting back in her chair. The match started at that moment and the crowd began to shout encouragement to the players, but Shaun didn't notice. He was numb. It was the first definite come on she had given him. He sat there in a haze, like he was drunk.

The game came and went without Shaun noticing much. In any case, he was not really a sporty kind of man;

18

he didn't play golf or watch football. He was more a music, theatre, stand-up comedy, artistic sort of person, but what he mainly cared about was making money. With time he settled down to nibbling his sandwich and sipping his beer to keep the boredom at bay. Nothing seemed to be happening, in any case. No side was able to slot the puck into the little area of the goal. That is, until about half way through the second session when the Berlin forward barged into the Hamburg goalie and pushed him over. The Hamburg goalie got up and punched the Berliner. A fist fight broke out, looking like a scene from a Laurel and Hardy film. Shaun chuckled and leant forward in his chair, at last showing some interest in the game.

"I told you they like to fight." He nudged Christiana.

"But they're not using their sticks." They both laughed.

After that, with the delinquent players placed in the cooler, Hamburg's substitute goalie, being more of a field player, started to let in a goal every five minutes. The game ended 11-0 to Berlin.

As everyone stood up to make their way out of the auditorium, Gunter was busy collecting up empty *steins*.

"You're not paid to do that." Shaun looked at him with mock seriousness.

"There's a euro refund on each one," Gunter replied.

"Wow. Can I help you?" Shaun gave him a thumbs up.

They went back to the hospitality and services perimeter and Shaun slipped away to the toilets. Suddenly he was aware of Wolfgang standing at the urinal next to him.

"We bought it here, so we may as well leave it here," Shaun joked, but the smile dropped off his face as he caught sight of Wolfgang's monster penis poking out from his trousers.

Wolfgang turned his head to look at Shaun. "The offer's still on for my place."

"That's really sweet." Shaun gulped as he fastened his zip. "See you around." He patted Wolfgang on the back as he walked off.

"Aren't you tempted then?" Wolfgang, still mid-flow, called out.

Shaun rushed back to the hospitality area. "Shall we go to the restaurant now?" He looked at Christiana. "Wolfgang's getting up close and personal."

"Of course, let's go."

They returned to the car and Christiana navigated the drive to the restaurant.

"Did you do anything to encourage him?"

"Not really… well maybe… I don't know."

At that moment, Shaun's mobile rang.

"Sorry, I'll take this in case it's my mother worrying if I'm alright."

"Have you touched base yet, you haven't have you?" Pete's voice boomed through the car.

"Hi Pete. I'm just driving right now. I'll catch you later. Give me an hour." Shaun switched the phone off.

"What did he mean, have you touched base yet?" Christiana asked.

"Oh, just checking up on me. Did the plane touch down okay, did I pick up the hire car okay, that sort of thing."

"He's a good friend. I would like to meet Pete. How do you know him?"

"We go to the same pub. It's our local."

"I notice he speaks differently to you."

"He's from Yorkshire in the North of England."

"Ave you tooched bayse yut." She imitated Pete's accent.

They parked and went in to the Indian restaurant that had advertised live music. The German waitress wore Arab style clothes, with red, baggy trousers, a blue waistcoat, a turban headdress that concealed all her hair and a little curly dagger hanging from her belt. She looked slightly embarrassed about being in the costume and her wan face peeped out from beneath the overlarge turban. They both gave her an order for *Thali,* which they could see from the photo on the menu would come as a selection of eight different dishes, served in small stainless steel bowls on a round tray. When it arrived, it looked and smelt delicious: rice, dhal, vegetables, chapattis, papadams, raita (yoghourt), chutney and pickle.

There was just the sound of appreciative chomping for some time, until Shaun broke the silence:

"Is it okay?" He looked at Christiana, who was sitting opposite him.

"Hhmm, except the vegetables are a bit oily."

"Yes, and they don't give you much either." Shaun held up the little dish of vegetables to emphasise his point.

"Indian food is so tasty. We have very few Indian restaurants in Germany, but I think you have four or five on every high street."

Shaun nodded. "India and Pakistan used to be English colonies. You would really enjoy London. There'd be lots of opportunities for you, and anyway, you can come and work for me. I have a little office and warehouse of ten staff. It would be a wonderful chance to improve your English." Shaun often got carried away when he was on holiday, offering attractive women jobs. No one had ever taken him up on it though.

"Thank you. That's really kind of you." She reached across the table and squeezed his hand. "I'll think about it."

Shaun was at last beginning to feel mellow and relaxed after his long day. A little wave of euphoria swept through him. "What made you give up teaching? That must have been a really good career." His voice was upbeat.

"Yes, it was." She hesitated. "I suppose you could say it gave me up. I had an affair with one of my students." She stared at him, like she was trying to read his face for a reaction.

"Wow!" He started to choke and took a sip of water. "Excuse me," he wheezed. "A bit of chilli took me by surprise… So," he thumped his chest and then gave a nervous laugh, "is there anything else you need to tell me, young lady?" He gave another nervous laugh while she continued to study him, unsmiling. "How old was he?" Shaun added in the awkward silence.

"Fifteen, but he had the body of a twenty-year-old."

"Christiana! You'd have gone to prison in the U.S. for that." Shaun's face had flushed slightly, but he hoped it was not noticeable in the subdued lighting of the restaurant.

"We are more liberal in Germany, not embarrassed about our sexuality." There was some anger in her voice and she continued to look at him like she was working out whether he was judging her. "Do you think I was wrong to sleep with him?"

"Hey… no, of course not… I'm a live and let live sort of person. Every youth develops at their own speed. The age of consent is a very generalised thing." He glanced at Christiana's bosom and sculpted arms. "I understand how it happened, obviously."

She gave a satisfied smile and nodded, like she was content with what Shaun had said, but he turned his head to look at his surroundings, as if trying to defuse the situation. It was by now late evening and the restaurant was quite full, the promise of live entertainment having attracted a large amount of diners. The band was on a break, but Shaun could see their set up in one corner, a sitar, tabla drums and a bamboo flute, arranged against a colourful backdrop.

22

"I'd give my right arm to be able to play a musical instrument properly." Shaun gestured to the little tableau when suddenly, the three musicians emerged from a back room, a tall man and two women. They sat down behind their instruments. The man, sitting at the tabla drums, picked up his microphone.

"Good evening ladies and gentlemen. Welcome to our final set of the evening. For those who missed the first one, we're Indigo Eye and we're from Brighton, England."

"Hey, I came to Germany to get away from English people." Shaun shrugged and turned to look at them as they started their first number.

They began with slow, resonating drone notes from the solo sitar, sounding like the Aborigines' didgeridoo. Then the flute entered with a few melodic snatches in a low register, also very slow. This became faster, higher pitched and more mellifluous as the minutes passed. The flute player looked like she was in a trance. After about seven minutes, the tabla entered, slow single beats to start with:

Dhaa Dhin Dhin Dhaa, Dhaa Dhin Dhin Dhaa, Naa Tin Tin Taa, Taa Dhin Dhin Dhaa

After a few minutes, the man upped the tempo to double time:

TaTe TeTa TeTe TaTa, TeTe DhaGe DhiNa GeNa, TaTe TeTa TeTe TaTa, TeTe DhaGe DhiNa GeNa

Everybody had warmed to the atmosphere and was either engrossed in conversation or watching the band. Two street boys, in their late twenties, wearing sportswear, had slipped in to the restaurant unnoticed by everyone except Shaun. There was a smaller one, talking on a mobile phone, and a taller one, quite muscle bound, carrying a shoulder bag. Shaun thought they looked out of place. He would have expected them to eat in a fast food joint. The muscular one disappeared into the toilet, while the smaller one waited in the corner nearby, talking on his phone but casually surveying the diners. After a few minutes, the muscular one emerged from the toilet and exchanged a few words with his accomplice. The smaller one started to talk more loudly on his phone and went up to a table of diners.

"Excuse me, speak English, speak English, you speak English, yes?" His tone was loud and emphatic, commandeering everyone's attention. Meanwhile, his friend had deliberately dropped some coins on the floor behind the table and was crawling underneath the chairs. He picked up a lady's handbag and dropped it into the shoulder bag he was carrying.

Having watched the whole thing, Shaun strolled over.

"Oi mate, that doesn't look like your bag, or are you getting ready for a sex change operation?" Shaun stood between the thief and the exit, grabbed the shoulder bag and removed the lady's handbag concealed inside. By now some of the diners had caught on what was happening and were looking round. The thieves casually walked out, but the muscular man shot Shaun an angry glance and raised his middle finger to him.

"Next time you wave, use all your fingers, pal," Shaun called out, waving goodbye.

"*Danke, danke schoen*," the lady, reunited with her handbag, shook Shaun's hand.

He shrugged off her thanks and returned to his seat.

"You're a hero," Christiana said, as Shaun sat back down.

"Ah, it was nothing."

The band had continued, oblivious to what had happened, the flute player still in her trance and the tabla player still absorbed in his rhythms.

Shaun settled the bill and they left and were soon back

at Christiana's cosy little flat. It was an unusual situation, in that they were virtually strangers in a small, intimate space, having only met six months previously for about half an hour in London in a hotel bar. Christiana went to make some tea and Shaun thought he would, in the meantime, poke his nose into her life. He went over to the notice board above her desk. There was what was obviously a family photograph of Christiana's mother and father, still young and in summer clothes, with their four children outside the door of their cottage. It had a freshness and simplicity of a bygone age. Shaun could see the young Christiana at the front of the group, down on one knee, and in a striking pose, shouting and waving simultaneously as though some electricity was flowing through her. She seemed to stand out from the photo in three dimensions. Everyone else was posing normally, but it was as though she wanted all the attention for herself. As if in confirmation, in each corner of the board, she had pinned a postcard of iconic beauties from the Golden Age of film: Marilyn Monroe, Ava Gardner, Hedy Lamarr and Marlene Dietrich, and superimposed at the bottom of the photo of Dietrich was a verse and the chorus from the diva's signature song:

Men cluster to me
Like moths around a flame
And if their wings burn
I know I'm not to blame.
Falling in love again
Never wanted to
What am I to do?
I can't help it.

Suddenly, Shaun noticed a photo of a very muscular

man, aged maybe late thirties, taken at a picnic, sitting there grinning. He was wearing a sleeveless vest and very short shorts, which seemed to contain an inappropriate bulge. It was a strange photo, incongruous amongst the family snaps. It was almost like a piece of soft porn beefcake. Christiana entered the room at that point and placed a tray of tea on the floor by the sofa. Seeing Shaun scrutinising the photos, she came behind him and put her hands over his eyes from behind, squidging her breasts, like sea sponges, into his back.

"These are all in my private collection… only joking, you like my photos?" She let go her hold and came to stand beside him, slightly in front, smiling. She pointed to the man at the picnic. "This is my boyfriend, Ralf. He's a cage fighter in Berlin. I was there over the New Year. I'm planning to move to Berlin to live with him. He was an old boyfriend from years ago. We've got back together."

Christiana did not notice that Shaun had turned his face to the window. He had hoped he might get a girlfriend out of this trip, even if she did live in Germany. Christiana was busy looking at the family photograph.

"This is my family outside our weekend cottage: my parents, two sisters and one brother. Look at me shouting. I was always climbing trees, cycling, playing football, always boys' things. I never sat playing with dolls or doing anything girlish." Only a minute had elapsed when she turned her head to look at Shaun. "Oh Shaun! I'm so sorry!" She put her hand on his arm. "You must have had a really long day. Maybe the ice hockey was a mistake. Or has Ralf being a cage fighter upset you? You look so tired."

"Yeah, all of a sudden, I've run out of juice. No, I'm not scared about Ralf."

"I spoke to him this afternoon. He's in Berlin! That's 250 kilometres away."

"Really, no problem. You've been a great hostess. Let's just drink our tea and then I must get to bed. My business appointment is at 11 a.m. tomorrow and I'll need to have my eye on the ball as we'll be talking numbers."

They sat on the sofa and drank their tea, Shaun at one end, Christiana at the other.

"So what's your usual type of boyfriend, if it isn't someone like me?"

"I didn't say I didn't like you. Don't take it the wrong way, but I usually date cage fighters, bodybuilders or footballers."

"So how come one of them hasn't tied you down, how come a beautiful, nubile woman has reached the age of thirty and is still unmarried?"

"Well, I've had lots of affairs, but I don't like to settle. I get bored easily and then I like to move on. Why do I need to be married? In fact, you know something?" She became a bit breathy, as though nervous. "I've had three abortions rather than get tied down to a man. The men wanted me to have the baby in every case. They wanted to marry me. But I wanted to stay free. I cannot be tied down."

Shaun was looking serious and trying not to frown. He was thinking Christiana was promiscuous and silly. She was more like a man, sowing his wild oats, and she had made the same mistake three times. She was not describing his ideal woman. He was normally attracted to girls who combined warmth with orderliness, someone who could support an ambitious businessman. He wasn't often wrong, but this time his instincts had led him down a false trail. He had been taken in by her glamour.

It was about midnight when they finally retired. Shaun's made up bed was in the living room, which had no door to the hallway. He was already settling down to sleep after his long day, when Christiana passed by as she returned from the bathroom to her bedroom. She came into the living room and knelt down beside his bed, so her head was right by his. She looked at him.

"Everything okay?" Her voice was soft and warm and he could smell the peppermint toothpaste on her breath.

"I'm fine, thanks," he said drowsily.

"I'm glad you came. I wasn't sure when you first turned up. I almost didn't let you in, but I've enjoyed your company. Goodnight, then. Sleep well." She kissed him on the forehead, got up and went into her bedroom.

He was confused as to why she was encouraging him. She already had a boyfriend, and in any case, they were not each other's type. He fell into an uneasy sleep, but hoped his business meeting the next day would lead to good things.

2

Hamburg Day 2

They had awoken late on Monday morning. Shaun was sitting in the kitchen eating some breakfast cereal. He was wearing a smart blue suit, cream shirt and red tie, ready for his meeting. The doorbell rang, which Christiana answered, after which she returned to the kitchen.

"Shaun, I have a surprise for you. My brother-in-law is in town for a business meeting, and has popped by beforehand...This is Hartmut. He's married to my elder sister, with three children."

A solidly built, fair haired man, a little older than Shaun, followed Christiana into the kitchen. He greeted Shaun and they shook hands. Hartmut glanced round the kitchen at the posters, mostly of football teams.

"You'll get used to my sister in law; football crazy, football mad, is that how the song goes?" He grinned at Shaun as he pointed to a poster by the window. "Did you ever have anyone to match him?"

Shaun looked at the photo of Franz Beckenbauer, the greatest German footballer of all time. "Well, not in England, but if we take the whole of the UK, then... "

"George Best, right?"

Shaun nodded. "The maestro."

"You two are going to get on well, especially as you're

both businessmen," Christiana interrupted. "Hartmut, Shaun has built up his own business from nothing, all by his own efforts and he's offered me a job in London. But I'll let you talk while I make some tea."

Hartmut sat down, across the table from Shaun and looked him in the eye. "I'm intrigued. What did you study at university to prepare you for your business?"

"I didn't. I went straight into the world of commerce to learn something useful. Everyone was telling me that the three years of university would be the best time of my life, but what would I do after that? Do you keep watching a DVD of your three years at university, and think what fun it was?"

"It's a good point." Hartmut laughed. "Unless you're going to be an academic like Christiana or some specific profession, you may be right. So what job did you get into?"

"I learnt the import export trade. I would be getting e-mails from old friends on their gap year, travelling round the world, latterly, looking at their photos on Facebook, now they're on an elephant in Thailand, now they're climbing to Everest base camp in Nepal, now they're bungee jumping in New Zealand, now they're surfing in California, and I would be stuck in London working away. But now I have a little company employing ten people and the old friends are back home in England, doing some menial task in an office or waiting on tables in a restaurant, or working in a bar, or you know, 'I majored in art and design. Will that be eat in or takeaway, sir?'"

Hartmut looked thoughtful for a few moments, as though taking in what Shaun had said, getting the measure of the man, sensing he was more powerful than he looked at first sight. He finally broke the silence. "So what is your company?"

"I have a little import export business, based in London, mainly importing from the Pacific rim: Japan, Taiwan, China. I bring in gadgets and gizmos; at the moment, air purifiers, iPod docks, luggage scales, digitizers, slide show picture frames, binoculars, karaoke machines, radiation blockers, travel adaptor plugs, key ring gameboys, a whole range of things, you just have to keep your finger on the pulse and capture the mood of the moment. But I'm working right now on something original, a brilliant new idea. I'm hoping it will make my fortune."

"What's the idea?" Hartmut asked.

"Well it's all under wraps really, but I want to patent a special MP3 player designed for insomniacs and tinnitus sufferers." Shaun had by now pushed his cereal aside and was leaning forward. His face had become flushed.

"What's tinnitus?" Hartmut looked quizzical.

"Have you ever held a shell to your ear and heard the sea in it?" Hartmut nodded. "It's like that," Shaun continued. "It's a ringing or hissing sound in the ear that has no external source. It's created inside your head. Everyone gets it when they go to a rave or a rock concert, but it usually goes away. But when people get to fifty, it can come back and stays for good this time."

"So what does the player do?"

"Well, I have to source it as cheap as possible, obviously and how it works, it has a lullaby effect for insomniacs and a sound masker for tinnitus sufferers. Did you know Bach wrote the Goldberg variations for a wealthy aristocrat, who suffered with insomnia? One of Bach's students was hired by the aristocrat to play the piano for him in the middle of the night when he couldn't sleep. What's clever about my idea is to provide a choice of different modes: nursery rhymes, lullabies, Chopin, Mozart, new-age ambient music and so on, for the insomniacs, and for the tinnitus sufferers: waterfalls, ocean waves, air conditioning, and so on, to mask the whistle in their ear. I could call the MP3 player 'Good Night' sleep aid. You can set the volume how high you want it and you can also time it to go softer and fade and then switch off."

"How do they choose which mode is right for them?"

"Well that's the beauty of the design. They can cycle through the different modes and choose one that suits them. If things change with time, they can select another mode."

"Have you tested it, done any trials?"

"Only on myself. It works for me when I can't sleep. I've got a crude prototype, but I need to get one designed by an electronics engineer and test it with other people. It's early days."

Christiana put some tea in front of them and joined them round the table. She could see Shaun was excited, his voice was louder than usual and his face had gained lots of colour. Talking business, the joker from the night before had disappeared. He had become very passionate, focussed and she perceived a steely determination in him. She thought the best of him would be devoted to business. He and Hartmut were getting on well. Hartmut was even leaning forward and nodding his head a little, as though in deference towards Shaun. That was not the brother in law she knew. He was normally a dominant, macho man.

"I like this English man, Christiana. Where did you meet him?"

"You remember I went to London last summer? We became friends then."

Shaun nodded and took a few sips of his tea. "I've really enjoyed talking to you Hartmut and you've got me all fired up for my eleven o'clock meeting, but I must leave now. Good luck with your business today." Shaun shook hands with Hartmut and left him and Christiana chatting in German, arranging with Christiana to return to the apartment late afternoon.

* * *

Shaun forgot about Christiana's little world, as he sat in the large, expensively fitted out meeting room of his prospective Hamburg supplier and as he ate the sumptuous lunch that followed. He was interrupted by a call from Pete, which he went out to the doorway of the restaurant to take, an icy wind blowing along the street and getting into the little gap between his trouser bottoms and his shoes.

"How you doing, Shaun?"

"Not so good mate. She's already got a fella."

"No! Bad luck."

"Looks like I'll be owing you £50."

"Don't worry about that now. Just enjoy yourself. Do you fancy her?"

"Well… she's highly attractive, no question about that. But there's something about her," Shaun sighed. "Can't quite put my finger on it right now. But I'm in the middle of a lunch meeting. Actually, I'm standing outside in a Hamburg street, shivering. Can I catch you later?"

"Okay, mate. I've got a class waiting in any case. Have a good day."

"Good luck with the little monsters. See you in a couple of days."

By late afternoon Shaun was back at her apartment, once more immersed in her world. He was sitting on the sofa and she was standing by her desk.

"Was your meeting good?" Christiana asked.

"Germans are clever, aren't they? They had some very well designed gadgets, like a laser you put against your skin and it analyses your health… a bit expensive, though. Their offices were really grand, so much space. I can't believe the square footage allocation per member of staff you have here in Germany. I'd have a riot on my hands if my staff saw the working conditions of Germans. We'll see if I can afford to carry the products, but it's always good to network in business, whatever the outcome."

"Did you tell them about your MP3 Player sleep aid idea?"

"No way… and let them steal it?"

"It's all dog eat dog, isn't it? You know Shaun, I think we should do some Pilates this afternoon, get relaxed, and you can work off that business lunch!"

"You're the teacher, then."

"I'll show you how to do it. Just follow me. I'm going to change into something more casual. You need to get out of that suit."

"Okay, I've got some jeans I can put on."

Christiana went off to her bedroom and returned a few minutes later barefoot, wearing tight black leggings, cut off mid-calf, and a tight fitting pink top with no bra underneath. In front of her, she was rolling two large inflated balls. She had two exercise mats under her arm and two stretch bands in her hand.

Shaun looked her up and down. "You look very athletic, really strong."

She smiled, like it was what she wanted to hear. "I work out a lot. I play in a women's football team once a week and train with them every Thursday evening. Eleven a side football takes real fitness, you have to run so much." She rolled one of the balls to Shaun. "Okay. Pilates session. To start, sit in the middle of your ball with your hands by your side." She positioned herself facing him, quite close, and demonstrated by sitting on her own ball. "Now just bounce." She started gently bouncing on the ball and Shaun followed suit. "Now bounce up and down off the ball." She started to bob up and down more vigorously and her breasts moved to the same rhythm. "Keep going, keep bouncing. Keep your back straight, so you work the abdominal muscles." She was smiling and looking at him intensely. She caught him sneaking a look at her cleavage and gave him an extra big smile, like she was proud of her body. After a minute, she said, "Now stop bouncing and centre yourself on your ball. Press your left foot down and raise your right foot." She demonstrated and Shaun copied her. "And then as a variation, raise your right foot, but this time straighten the leg, so we work the quadriceps… "

The session went on for half an hour and finished with gentle stretching on the mat.

"Okay, Shaun, that's enough for today. We can do it again tomorrow, same time, same place."

"I can see you're really fit and strong." He got up from the mat and sat on his large inflated ball.

"You bet. When I go to the leisure centre, I swim fifty lengths, and then I spend an hour in the gym on the weights. I can do sixty kilos on the chest press." She rolled her ball close to his and sat down on it, facing him, very close. She was staring right into his eyes, almost like a confrontation. She held her arms out to the side as if grasping the butterfly handles of a weight machine. Then she exhaled and slowly pretended to push the handles together in front of her chest, squeezing her breasts between her arms. Then she inhaled as she returned her arms to the start position out to the side. She repeated the movement, bringing her arms round to the front, staring right into Shaun's eyes and puckering her lips as she exhaled. She kept repeating it, staring at him all the time, and seemed to be getting closer, like she was rolling her ball forward or leaning into him. After six repetitions, their faces were almost touching. She had a slight smile on her face. Shaun just looked at her, his eyes wide open, his pupils dilated. It was as though he was hypnotised. She was about to kiss him when the door bell rang. She sighed, like she was annoyed and kissed him lightly on the lips as she got up from her ball to answer the door. There was a few minutes whispered conversation in German in the hallway, punctuated by silences in which Shaun could hear what sounded like kissing. Then she returned to the living room with a tall woman, in her mid twenties, by her side.

"Shaun, this is my best friend, Sandra. We're going to show you some of the Hamburg nightlife."

"Hi Sandra." Shaun smiled and held up his hand in greeting, but she didn't smile back, just nodding to him in a detached way.

* * *

Shaun, Christiana and Sandra walked through the Reeperbahn in the St. Pauli district, Hamburg's red light area where in 1960 the Beatles, still struggling to establish themselves, had a series of residencies that transformed them into a professional band. Christiana and Sandra were arm in arm, as the trio passed through the neon extravaganza of brothels and sex shops, Sandra leaning in towards Christiana, so that their heads touched and Sandra's long blonde hair fell on to Christiana's shoulder. Street walkers were standing around looking for clients, their minimal clothing exposing a remarkable amount of skin, considering how cold it was.

"Look Shaun, there's Herbertstrasse." Christiana pointed to a gated side street where prostitutes were sitting on display in windows like in Amsterdam. "Women are not allowed in there, or if we do go in, the sex workers might attack us because they don't like people who've only come to stare. But you can go in and have a look if you want. We'll wait here for you."

"I'm okay. Let's find somewhere for a drink." Shaun did not care for the harsh, cold world where sex was sold for money. He did not understand young men who paid good money to watch lap dancers. They walked a bit further.

"Look Shaun, 36 Grosse Freiheit, that's the Kaiserkeller where the Beatles played in 1960."

"Now you're pressing my buttons. I wouldn't mind going in there. That really is one of my 'must see before I die' places. I'm such a Beatles fan." Shaun held up his hands and made a bowing gesture in homage to the nightclub. "That's where their girlfriend Astrid Kirchherr first saw them. She became their stylist and gave them the mop top haircuts. Before that, they had teddy boy quiffs."

"That's right." Sandra interrupted him in her soft voice. She had a dreamy way of speaking and there seemed to be a time lag before she reacted, a little space where you didn't know what was happening in her mind. "You know what she said about first setting eyes on them... 'It was like a merry-go-round in my head, they looked astonishing. My whole life changed in a couple of minutes. All I wanted was to be with them and to know them.'"

Shaun grinned. "Like when I first saw Christiana."

"Yeah, right," Christiana retorted.

Shaun didn't notice Sandra's jealous green eyes glaring at him.

They arrived at a pub and went in. It was like being on the stage set of a 19th-century opera, old-fashioned furniture, bare floor boards, and cobwebs on the ceiling, where a big model toucan, with black body and yellow beak, was perched in the exposed rafters. The piped music was exclusively Beatles. The trio sat at a circular table with their drinks.

"A horse goes into a pub and the barman says, 'Hey mate, why the long face?'" Christiana laughed at Shaun's joke, but Sandra remained unsmiling. Shaun thought that maybe she couldn't follow his English. He spoke more slowly. "I tried to teach my dog poker, but every time he was dealt a good hand his tail wagged." Christiana laughed again, but Sandra just took a drink from her glass.

"Well did you like our Reeperbahn, Shaun?" Christiana asked.

"Thank you so much for that. As you'll have gathered, I really like the Beatles' music. What a magical partnership Lennon and McCartney had. To think their careers were launched right here. Mick Jagger said the Beatles weren't good performers, but John Lennon said in their Hamburg days, they were the best band ever... and John said, 'I was born in Liverpool, but I grew up in Hamburg.' They didn't have to pay the prostitutes. They could get it for free."

"Have you ever paid a prostitute, Shaun?" Sandra drawled as she fixed him with a cold stare. "Only, when you said, 'they could get it for free', there was a kind of a yearning in your voice."

"Why should I pay for it?" Shaun frowned and turned his face to her. "Girls usually come up to me, ask if I'd like to buy them a drink or if I'd like to sit down by them or if I'd like to dance."

"No I don't think so, Shaun. I think you must be fooling yourself." Sandra gave him a contemptuous look.

"Did you have parents or did you grow up in an orphanage?"

"What kind of a question is that? Of course I had parents." She looked indignant.

"Didn't they teach you how to talk to people?"

Sandra closed her eyes momentarily. "I'm sorry. I don't mean to be unkind. I just don't think lots of women would be queuing up to be your girlfriend, that's all," she said smugly, like she thought she had got one up on him. "And these girls that approach you Shaun, do you take them to bed?"

"I practise some discrimination and go with the ones where there's chemistry."

"Oh I don't practice any discrimination. As long as the penis is large; I really like to get my mouth round a big penis."

Shaun laughed. "Okay Sandra." He was smiling and held the palm of his hand up to her, as if to say, 'stop'. "Whenever women move the conversation onto this topic, I know they're having a tease at men's expense."

Christiana had remained silent, looking embarrassed and uncomfortable. "Shaun, I haven't seen Sandra for a while. Do you mind if we chat in German?"

She started to talk to Sandra in German, quite intensely and left Shaun to drink his beer and listen to the Beatles. As he discreetly glanced at them talking, they seemed to be having a lover's tiff as their exchange got heated.

As they made their way back through the Reeperbahn, Shaun, feeling a little excluded, walked slightly ahead of the girls. It was now much later, and the atmosphere had changed from touristy, to more seedy and menacing. Shaun felt uncomfortable. A small man was walking purposefully across the road, towards him.

"*Kommen Sie hier,*" he said, grabbing Shaun's shoulder. It was the smaller one of the duo of handbag thieves from the Indian restaurant. Shaun spun round and threw the man off-balance, so that he fell and hit the road on his back, his arms and legs flailing like an overturned tortoise.

"Speak English, short arse," said Shaun dismissively.

The little thug got up even more angry. "Do that again and I'll kill you," he said in a dark, thickly accented voice as he lunged at Shaun, who sidestepped and pushed the man to the ground once more.

"Yeah? You little runt."

However, Shaun could now see the far more muscular partner in crime a bit further down the street, rushing towards him at top speed. He knew a proper fight was looming fast and Shaun looked at the man's hands for a knife. There was none, so probably an uppercut was on its way. Shaun held his fists up as though he was also going to box, but just as his assailant went to punch him, Shaun, with perfect timing and range, delivered a powerful and assured thrust kick to the man's knees. As big as he was, the thug fell over as easily as his scrawny friend, and cried out in pain just as dramatically.

"Quick, run." Shaun looked round at the two girls, who had watched open mouthed.

They ran down a few streets until they thought they were far enough away to be safe. They stood there puffing.

"Wow!" Christiana put her arm through Shaun's and Sandra did the same the other side. "You little cage fighter! You show quite a bit of potential. You've got brilliant balance."

"Yeah! I suppose I could consider wearing blue tights and my underpants on the outside." Shaun laughed as he caught his breath.

"How did you know what to do?" Christiana gave him an adoring look as they started to walk on.

"Let's just say a little bit of the old *Yoko Geri Kekome*." He flicked out his leg in an action replay, but more as a caricature, as if he was dancing the Hokey Cokey. "I had a misspent youth practising karate in the *dojo*."

"Why did you run? My Ralf would never have run." Christiana was still wide eyed at how Shaun had handled the situation and could be so light hearted about it.

"Well those guys were ugly, with nothing to lose, but I'd rather keep my features as they are."

At that moment a car pulled up alongside them. The window rolled down.

"You look as though you're having fun." It was Wolfgang, the bodybuilder from the ice skating.

"We just escaped from some muggers." Shaun happened to look back the way they had come and to his horror, could just make out the two thieves turning the corner of the street, still in pursuit. "Quick, there they are. Let us in the back. Wolfgang, we need you to drive quickly."

They threw themselves into the car and Wolfgang pulled away just as the two thieves caught up with them. They banged on the side window menacingly, shouting obscenities. Shaun waved them goodbye, grinning.

"Your timing's superb," Shaun said, watching the two thugs getting smaller and smaller in the distance, still shaking their fists. "How can we repay you?"

"Just drop us off at Shaun's car, if you don't mind please. That will be fine." Christiana interrupted. "Sandra and I will cook you a meal next week as payment."

"No problem. Don't worry about it. I'm glad I could help you and any time you need some home grown Hamburg muscle," he held out his left arm and flexed it for emphasis, "it will only cost you a *stein* of beer." Wolfgang sniggered. "So you found our Hamburg street rats a bit intimidating, Shaun?"

"The trouble is I hope to live forever. So far so good."

Wolfgang relayed them to Shaun's car and Shaun in turn, dropped Sandra off at her apartment.

"Shaun, I'm so sorry about Sandra's rude behaviour in the pub," Christiana said as soon as they drove off. "She's my best girlfriend and she's very jealous and possessive."

"Well, I do believe I got that message, this evening."

The fight had bonded them a little and Shaun was feeling some attraction to Christiana, even if she seemed increasingly offbeat. The Pilates session was lingering in his mind. As they went to bed, he hovered at the doorway of her bedroom.

"So we had some fun this evening?" He stood and stared.

Christiana gave a big yawn. "I'm really tired now, Shaun. Too much excitement for one evening. Do you mind if we call it a day?" She sounded weary.

"Good night."

3

Hamburg Days 3 and 4

Tuesday morning, Shaun emerged from the bathroom to find that Christiana was especially happy.

"A publisher just phoned. I'd submitted a sample translation to them, on the sex lives of famous people. The editor said, 'I don't want you to get big headed, but the translation was really good. We're going to give you the work'… I'm happy." She sang it like a child and jumped up and down. "Look Shaun," she took a book from the shelf and opened it up at the title page and pointed to a line: "'*Übersetzer: Christiana Neddermeyer.*' That's me, a famous translator."

"But aren't you made redundant by all that translation software on the internet?"

"Not really, as you'll see by the amusing results when you translate a text into another language and back to English."

She sat at her desk all morning, working and singing snatches of song, particularly a German folksong that Shaun also knew in translation from Primary school:

Horch, was kommt von draussen rein? Ho-la-hi, ho-la-ho.
(Listen to the cheerful cry)
Wird wohl mein Feinsliebchen sein, ho-la-hi-a-ho.
(Is my sweetheart passing by)

Geht vorbei und schaut nicht rein?ho–la–hi, ho–la–ho.
(The voice fades down the street)
Wird's wohl nicht gewesen sein, ho–la–hi–a–ho.
(That was not my darling sweet)

"Well I'm going to get out of your hair today, and let you get on with your work. I want to go to the Kunsthalle Art Gallery to see Édouard Manet's Nana."

"You're going to leave the translator to continue her good work." She nodded in acceptance of the arrangement. "I'll see you later."

The Kuntshalle museum was fine and spacious with lots of marble walls and floors and Shaun enjoyed walking around it and looking at the paintings. At the very end of the gallery, where the director knew to save the best till last, was Manet's Nana, a beautiful woman with a twinkle in her eye, getting dressed. Shaun stood before it for five minutes and then went through to the gift shop at the museum exit and bought a postcard of Nana to give to Christiana.

"Well hello again."

Shaun looked round and to his surprise it was the long haired young man in the leather coat, from the ice hockey match.

"Gunter, we can't go on meeting like this."

"How are you enjoying your stay?"

"Yeah… great." Shaun laughed. "It's been a fun few days."

"How's it going with Christiana?"

"Well, she's gorgeous, isn't she?"

"There's something you should know about her… she plays both sides of the fence."

Shaun looked blank for a few moments. "She's bisexual? I suppose that doubles her chances of getting a date."

44

"She has a lesbian friend, Sandra."

"God, thank you Gunter. Everything's just become clear. I met her last night. She had a right go at me, jealous that I'm staying with Christiana."

Gunter smiled. "And you're not the only man in Germany, who thinks she's gorgeous."

"Hmm. Go on then. I could tell you had some secrets on her, because she seemed very nervous of you."

"When she was at university, she made a porno film."

"No!" Shaun stared open mouthed at Gunter for a few seconds. "I would never have believed it. A respectable academic is a secret porno queen?"

"She made it with Ralf Dobberstein. The largest penis in Germany."

Shaun gave a mischievous laugh. "God, what a tough act for anyone to follow! Hey, is that the Ralf she's moving to Berlin to be with, the cage fighter?"

"Petty criminal and gangster, more like."

"She said she'd gone out with him when she was younger. I didn't realise that those were the circumstances. I would never have believed it looking at her now."

"I have the film at home, if you'd like to see it."

Shaun looked at his watch. "Let's go. I'm up for it."

They drove back to Gunter's apartment, Shaun following Gunter's car. Gunter's road was quiet and tree-lined, but his block was grey and dreary, four storeys high, stretching much of the length of the road. The apartments had small balconies and in front of the block was a gardened area with a playground for children. What a nice and anonymous setting to watch a porno film in, Shaun thought to himself. They entered Gunter's apartment, which was sparsely furnished with a threadbare sofa, a table and some chairs. An old-style television and a sideboard finished the room. In a corner, there was a workout bench with a barbell resting above it and dumbbells on the floor.

"Come in. Sit down. Can I get you a beer?"

"Sure, beer and porno films go together. What more can I ask for?"

Gunter got two beers from the fridge, opened them and gave a bottle to Shaun.

"Here it is." Gunter held up a battered looking videotape. "The pride of my collection."

"You need to copy it, before it wears out."

The film flickered into life. It was obviously low-budget with not much of a storyline and had bland, ambient background music, right the way through. Ralf was dressed as a plumber who had come to fix a washer, with Christiana soon noticing a huge bulge in his jeans. She had a lot of beauty as a younger woman, with the vitality and freshness of youth, a clear complexion, a sparkle in the eye and shining, long, black hair that reached halfway down her back. She opened Ralf's zip, undid his trousers and pulled down his underpants, which was like an Indian snake charmer releasing the captive serpent from its basket. Then she led him to her bedroom, where he lay across her bed. She sucked and played with his penis till it was fully extended, at which point she could only manage to get about a third of it into her mouth, it was so big. She stopped for a few seconds and gave him a smile of approval. It was a moment of stillness, but only ten minutes after that, Ralf's enormous manhood was pounding her like a jackhammer, all the more vivid as the camerawork was graphic and close up. The atmosphere became electric as she said 'Aaah' at every inward penetration. Her passion seemed genuine and she was giving Ralf very intense eye contact. Shaun noticed she could take the entire shaft of Ralf's penis, right up to the hilt.

At the end, as Ralf came to a noisy, shuddering climax, they became locked in a muscular spasm, with Christiana helplessly impaled on Ralf's huge member. For the first time, her expression of carnal ecstasy changed to one of uncertainty. After thirty seconds, Ralf's violent thrusting movements subsided and Christiana suddenly rolled over on top of him and said in a loud raunchy voice:

"Jaaaa…du kanst meinen ass licking…deinen borsten kann dass genug sein." Then she dangled her breasts over Ralf's face and started slapping him with them.

"What did she say?" Shaun didn't take his eyes off the film as he asked.

Gunter laughed. "She said, 'Yeaahh…you get rough with me… these tits will sort you out.'"

Shaun gave a big belly laugh and when it had subsided, finished his beer. He discreetly hid the erection the film had given him and stood up. "Imagine when she's older and has a family, if she discovers her son has a porno film hidden in his wardrobe, and then she discovers she's in it!" Shaun grinned as Gunter started to laugh. "Seriously, you're a pal. Thank you. I wouldn't have missed that for the world."

Back at the apartment Christiana, who was still working, broke off on Shaun's return.

"Did you enjoy that?"

"Yeah… I met Gunter."

She grimaced. "Please no. I don't want to know anything about it. What a stupid man that guy is… and what about the paintings, did you enjoy those at least?"

"It was brilliant, and I got to see one of my favourites, Nana. It's always a thrill, when you see a great painting in the flesh. Look, I got you a postcard of her." Shaun handed it over. "You know you would make a good artist's model?" She shrugged at the suggestion. "Well, at least when your looks have faded, you know you will always keep your beautiful voice."

"But I don't worry about my looks, Shaun." Her voice was heated. "I know I already have a few lines on my face, but it doesn't matter. My mother has many lines on her face, but she's still very beautiful." She went over to the bookcase. "Do you like photos, Shaun?"

She took down a large pile of photo albums from the top shelf. It was her life story in ten instalments. Shaun puffed out his cheeks at the sight of them, but she didn't notice.

"Yes, of course. With digital, a lot of people don't bother with hard copies any more, but I like to see the old-fashioned albums."

They started at the beginning. She was very attractive as a child, with lots of fancy dress photos and picnics. As a teenager, she looked handsome but rather tomboyish, with short black hair. There seemed to be lots of parties.

"You were the *Dancing Queen*." He sang the Abba phrase.

"I wanted to be a ballet dancer when I was young, but I wasn't the right shape. I'm always dancing, even now."

As a university student, it was the beauty, her hair long now, that he'd already seen in the porno film at Gunter's. Shaun wondered how many hearts she must have broken, how many boys had been distracted during their lectures and essays with the sight or thought of Christiana.

Last was the album of her six years as a schoolteacher, but she rushed through it rather quickly.

"Show me the boy you lost your job over."

She darted him a hard look and without saying anything turned a few pages till she reached a group photo, herself seated in the middle at the front wearing gym clothes. "There he is." She pointed to the boy sitting right beside her, a young Arnold Schwarzenegger look-alike, with bulging biceps and an alert optimistic look on his face. She sighed and snapped the album shut. "It's all history. I've moved on now. I know you fly back to London tomorrow, but I've baked us some pasta for this evening and we're going to stay in after all the excitement we've had lately." She said it sweetly but firmly. "After food I want to watch the news in English and make notes on any words I don't understand. You can help me."

When they had finished their meal, Shaun disappeared to wash up, having offered, while she sat on a cushion, knitting while watching the news in English, which was a nightly ritual for her when she stayed in. As the news finished, she switched the television off and carried on knitting, giving her a domesticated look. Shaun returned from the kitchen and sat on the sofa.

"What are you knitting?"

"It's a pullover for Ralf."

"He's a lucky man… I'm glad we've got this moment together. I want to thank you for your kindness and hospitality during my stay. It's been great."

"You're welcome."

"Also, I'm just a bit curious… you never mentioned you had a serious boyfriend when I met you in London."

She didn't look up from her knitting. "Does it matter?"

"I suppose not."

"Do you have a girlfriend?"

"Not at the moment."

She suddenly stopped knitting and looked up. "Did you want me?"

He shrugged. "Maybe. You're very attractive."

She put her knitting on her lap. "Did you want these breasts?" She placed her hands on her breasts and squeezed them. "Because I find you very attractive and if you want to go to bed, we can."

"What about Ralf?" Shaun looked puzzled.

"I believe in open relationships. We both have other lovers. So, do you want to go to bed?"

"Well." He let out a sigh. "What you've described is the opposite to what I'm looking for. I'm looking for someone to love, who will love me back. What you're offering, if I start to give my heart, I just see myself getting hurt."

"Have you tried it?"

"I've had a few casual encounters, where desperate or drunk women have thrown themselves at me and I've gone along with it. I haven't enjoyed it at all."

"Come on. I'm not desperate or drunk. Try it with me. Let's go to bed." She raised her eyebrows at him. He shook his head in response. "Oh come on, Shaun, take a risk."

"No, let's just leave it that we had a fun few days together. Besides, I would feel intimidated. Ralf's a tough act to follow."

"What do you mean?"

Shaun suddenly realised what he had said. "I didn't want to say that, did I?" He gave a nervous laugh.

"What did you say?"

"Nothing. I lost concentration for a moment."

"You said you would feel intimidated, that Ralf is a tough act to follow."

She was staring at him, eyes wide open, like she was in a state of high alert. He hesitated, like he was weighing up whether to continue.

"Letting the cat out of the bag is a lot easier than putting it back in."

"Tell me what you know," she said loudly.

"I saw the film of you and Ralf."

"What film?" Her face had flushed and she looked intently at Shaun.

"You know what film."

50

"No!" She shouted it, throwing her knitting across the room and banging her fists on the cushion she was sitting on. Her face had become contorted. "That bastard. He promised he would destroy it. How did you see it?"

"He took me back to his apartment and showed it to me."

She started to sob and covered her face with her hands. "Why did you have to go back with him?" She said it through her tears. "I thought you were my friend. I've tried so hard to make a career as an academic, and that thing comes back to haunt me. Just one little mistake, when I was broke." She continued to cry.

"Why don't you get it withdrawn?"

"It is. Gunter has a version issued years ago."

She continued to cry, and Shaun, feeling guilty, went over to her and, kneeling down beside her, put his arm round her.

"It's okay. Everyone's got skeletons in the cupboard. There's no need to cry. Look what John Lennon said when he appeared naked with Yoko Ono on the album cover of Two Virgins, 'a lot of fuss to begin with, then it's all forgotten'."

"He got shot."

For once, Shaun had no answer. Still crying, she rested her head against Shaun's neck and shoulder. After a while the tears and emotions began to have an effect on him. He relaxed his body and started to stroke her hair a little.

"What must you think of me, performing in a film like that?"

"I thought you were very beautiful and passionate."

"Really? Are you just saying that to make me feel good?"

"No. You're fantastic."

"I'm so ashamed. What if my parents were to see it? I was always such a good little girl."

"Okay, you were Snow White and then you drifted."

She chose that moment to kiss him, softly, and they carried on for about five minutes. She started to massage his hair as they kissed. She was good.

"Come on. Let's go where it's more comfortable." She got up and pulled him towards the bedroom.

"I'm scared. I've seen what Ralf's got."

"Don't be silly." She whispered it. "It makes no difference to me. It's only gay men that like them big."

She lit a scented candle that suffused the room with a red glow and took him into her bed to make gentle love. After foreplay, she put a condom over his erect penis, and he lay on top and penetrated her. She kissed him throughout, her tongue deep in his mouth or his in hers. He reached a climax and rolled to one side.

"There. That wasn't so bad, was it?" She smiled and stroked his hair.

"It was lovely." He couldn't speak any further.

"Do you want to go again?"

He shook his head.

Next day, Shaun packed his car, while Christiana sat at her desk translating. When everything was loaded, he returned upstairs and sat on the sofa, with Christiana still across the room at her desk.

"I want to thank you again for your hospitality, Christiana. You've been so sweet, not least, taking me into your bed last night."

"You're welcome." She smiled at him.

"You've been so kind. I'd like to return your hospitality. You have an open invitation to come and stay with me in London. That's any time you like. My house is your house. Turn up unannounced even, like I did to you. Keep me on my toes."

"Oh Shaun. Thank you so much. *Danke Schoen*."

"Bitte Schoen." (You're welcome). Shaun gave her a little bit of the German he'd picked up during his stay and held up his card, which he placed on the sofa beside him.

A car door slammed in the street outside. Christiana, seated at the window, looked out. A blond haired, muscular man in blue jeans and black shirt had emerged from the car. Christiana's expression turned to one of horror.

"It's Ralf! Oh no, it's Ralf! Get out quickly."

"I thought you had an open relationship?" Shaun's expression reflected a little of Christiana's terror.

"But he doesn't like me having an open relationship, and sometimes he drives all the way from Berlin to check up on me. Get out now, unless you want a fight, and it won't be as easy as the one in the Reeperbahn."

Shaun didn't need any further encouragement and grabbed his coat and was out through the door. He passed Ralf in the entrance hall to the apartment block, stepping to one side as the alpha male swaggered through, a muscular, blond haired man, with a round face and a broad nose with a split down the middle. He looked tough and dominant and smelt strongly of tobacco.

"Morgen," (morning) he grunted as he passed.

"Gusse Got," (God's greetings) Shaun said softly, passing Ralf by like a shadow.

By the time the plane banked over Hamburg and headed out to the North Sea, Shaun's palpitations were a distant memory and he was able to look back at Hamburg in the distance and reflect that it had been a successful few days; good business, good socialising, good stories to tell Pete when he got back home. Christiana was not the girl he'd imagined her to be, but he felt proud that he had been courteous and invited her back to London, even if people, himself excepted, never really took such offers seriously.

4

London

Shaun was down the pub with Pete that same evening. "How did it go?"

"It was great. You know, a few fights, a few meals, an ice hockey match, a porno film… "

"Who owes who the £50?"

"Technically, you owe me, but it was a bit odd, so I'm going to let you off."

"What do you mean?"

"She was gorgeous, but," Shaun pulled a face, "she was a bit unhinged. She's got a boyfriend, and a girlfriend, but she took me as an extra. Not my scene. I felt she did it just to get the notch on her bed post."

"More like a man?"

"There was something masculine about her," Shaun nodded, "but apart from that, I got the feeling that, even though she really fancies herself, she's one of those girls that things never quite work out for. Some men might feel they wanted to protect her, but to me, despite her beauty, she seemed more of a lame duck. Does that sound unkind?"

Pete's forehead became furrowed. "It does a bit… so you're on your own still?"

"Yeah. I'm going to sell the memoirs of my sex life to a publisher. They can make a board game out of it."

He immersed himself in his business; money had always been hugely important in Shaun's family. He saw it as power. It seemed to him like the oxygen of the world that made everything happen. He decided he needed a project to occupy himself and the obvious thing was to invest some time in his MP3 player idea outlined to Hartmut in Christiana's kitchen. He found an electronics boffin willing to work on it for a fee rather than a royalty on sales. It was a family friend of Pete's, and Shaun drove up to the Yorkshire moors for a meeting. He passed through beautiful, green rolling hills, until at last he reached a large detached house, which was built in honey coloured local stone and perched above a valley, commanding a panoramic view of the surrounding countryside. The gold plaque beside the front door said 'Wingate Machine Electronics'. Shaun rang the bell, and the door was promptly opened.

"Hi, I'm Dick Wingate." He stood there with a big grin, a tall man with a long, narrow face, his head seeming to be stretched out to house his extra large brain. He gave Shaun a firm, masculine, hand shake. "Come in. Did you have a good journey? Would you like some tea?"

Shaun was ushered into Dick's workshop, which had discarded circuit boards, system boxes and wiring stacked untidily on shelving against two walls. Stacked against the third wall were large storage cabinets with multiple transparent drawers that held brand new components. Dick's large desk-cum-workbench was placed beneath a wide window that looked across the valley. Dick disappeared for a few minutes, then returned and shoved a huge mug of tea into Shaun's hand.

"There you go, the base stuff of life." Dick had a jolly expression on his face. "Many a project of mine has been fuelled by tea." He took some gulps from his own mug. "Aah! I feel a solution coming on!"

"Thanks. How can you work with that fabulous view of the valley in front of you?"

"You have to call it a dale up here in Yorkshire. Well... I find the calm vista helps me organise myself in an orderly fashion and it's brilliant daylight for when I'm soldering... I like your idea, by the way." Dick's eyes shone with enthusiasm and he smiled. "I should have thought of it myself as I suffer with tinnitus. The whirr of the computer hard disk sets it off," he pointed to the computer sitting on one corner of the desk like it was a pesky nuisance, "and when I play the piano."

"You're a musician?" Shaun raised his eyebrows.

"I'm a concert pianist in my spare time. Actually, I can recommend some music loops that would be good for your player. I could even record the piano ones myself for you. I would enjoy doing that."

"Brilliant. Knowing nothing about electronics, to me the idea seems very do-able."

"Everything's do-able. The actual electronics for the device would be fairly basic, well, for someone like me who's doing it every day. It's just a standard MP3 player with one or two extra buttons to select the different modes, and an inbuilt speaker phone."

"Could it be patented?"

"Yes, but people will try and get round it if your product sells. Best thing is to stay ahead of the game and be the brand leader. Someone might try to leap frog you with an iPod style touch-sensitive screen. So if your initial launch takes off, you need to look at upgrading. You could make a deluxe version with little, detachable external speakers, for people to place either side of their pillow."

"You're a spark plug. For now I just need twenty basic prototypes to try out on volunteer guinea pigs. We may need to refine the design in the light of their feedback."

"I just work on a fee basis. I'll charge you an hourly rate, plus materials at cost."

"Done." Shaun was quick to shake Dick's hand.

Dick's face went expressionless for a few moments, like he was in deep thought. He drained his mug for the last of the tea and made a final observation. "I'm stupid really. I should be going in with you. I've been in this business for a long time. I'd say you're going to make a lot of money from this. It's one of those simple ideas that can make millions."

* * *

A few months had passed since his return from Hamburg and Shaun was feeling very positive after his visit to Dick. He sensed he needed someone else to share his life with and a few weeks later he was at a party, leaning against a wall, sipping his beer. It hadn't registered with him that a woman had been staring at him all evening, but she finally passed by and fixed him with her beautiful brown eyes.

"You look dishy." Her words were slurred, like she had had a few drinks.

"Well," Shaun gave a nervous laugh as he took in her soft rounded features and the silky auburn hair that came down to her shoulders. "I am enjoying this party. You're more than dishy. You're divine. I love your hair. Is it your own?"

"No, it's a wig! Here, tug it if you like." She offered him a strand of her hair to pull, looking away as she did so, as though uncertain of herself.

He was touched by what seemed to be her vulnerability and he looked at her, quite seriously. "You're beautiful," he said softly.

The woman gazed at him and gave a hesitant smile. "Thank you, but I'm sure I'm not. I'm just another lonely middle-aged woman." Her voice had a touch of sadness in it.

"Shaun, by the way." He held out his hand and shook hers. "And no more of that talk. You're definitely not middle-aged."

"Angela. I'm thirty five."

"You don't look it, and thirty five is never middle-aged, particularly nowadays."

"If you don't mind, how old are you?"

He shrugged. "Why should I mind? I'm thirty one, cradle snatcher!" He grinned, but stopped when he could see she suddenly looked worried. "That was a joke," he added.

"Of course. It's nice to meet you, Shaun."

"Let me guess what you do."

"Let me guess you first… you look artistic, a bit cheeky, very charming. You remind me of someone who sells to the rich, say, an art gallery owner."

Shaun raised his eyebrows. "Not bad. I run a catalogue of gadgets and gizmos, certainly nice to have, rather than essential… you look professional, but there's something caring there as well. I'd say you're a very young head of social services."

She looked startled. "Someone told you."

"I'm right? Oh my God, how clever is that?" He did a little victory dance, like a sportsman who had just won something.

"Who told you?" She looked quite serious, like she was a work orientated person and this was a task she was performing.

He looked at her thoughtfully. "It was a lucky guess, but aren't you very young to be a head of social services?"

She nodded. "I sacrificed everything for my career. I could write a book, 'How to climb the greasy pole in ten years.' I'm trying to make up for lost time now, trying to be less focused, have more fun."

"You want to have fun?"

"Yes." She looked embarrassed as she said it, like it might be something shameful.

Shaun took out his phone. "Give me your digits," he ordered. "I'll show you fun."

She laughed at last, as she punched her number into his contact list and they had spent the rest of the evening together.

It was a few days later, and Shaun was relaxing at home and thinking about whether to phone Angela. She had seemed a little melancholy at the party, but she had a sincerity and openness that he respected. Also, she didn't live too far away, and that was always useful when meeting up for a drink or a meal. The phone rang.

"Shaun, I hope you don't mind me phoning you."

"Oh, hi Angela. How are you? How did you get my number?"

"Heads of social services can find you very easily."

"No, I don't mind you phoning. Actually, I'm quite impressed with your synchronicity as I was about to ring you, to ask you out for a drink."

"Really? Oh, let's do that. I can see you tomorrow, if you're free."

"Err... okay then. Great."

* * *

It was the next evening, and they were sitting in a cosy alcove of a quaint old 17th-century pub that Shaun used for his romantic encounters, not the pub where he would meet Pete.

"Was it okay phoning you? Did it make me seem desperate?"

"Don't be silly. Women are so passive, waiting for men to make the first move all the time. It was a nice surprise to hear from you. I like a woman who's got some go in her." Shaun took a sip of his beer and cleared his throat a little. "Tell me, I don't mean to pry, but I sense something slightly sad inside you, like something has happened to you." He looked into her brown eyes that always seemed a little watery.

"Ooh! I can see you're horribly observant. I'm not going to get anything past you! Yes, I don't like to mention it when I first meet people, so I didn't tell you at the party. I'm a widow."

Shaun closed his eyes and covered his face with his hand. "Oh I'm so sorry. How tactless. I'm stupid, at times." He looked at her again. "I had no idea. You're much too young to be a widow."

"That's okay. Don't beat yourself up. How were you to know? It happened a year ago. I'm over it now."

"That seems very recent to me. Is it okay to talk about it?"

"Yes, I'm moving on with my life now."

"You haven't mentioned any children?"

"We both put so much into our careers. My husband was a consultant gynaecologist, so he was seeing baby stuff all day, and as a social worker I specialised in children, so we just put off having any of our own."

"How did it happen, if you don't mind me asking?"

She sighed. "We were such fools. The Alps weren't good enough for us and we had so much money, so we went to Whistler in Canada to ski. It was our first day on the slopes, and some stupid snowboard instructor collided with my husband and killed him."

"I'm so sorry. That's awful. Why don't they have proper health and safety out there?"

"He was drunk. The snowboard instructor, that is."

"Did you get compensation? Sorry to ask, but I'm a businessman. I can't help thinking money."

"One million pounds."

"Whooh! Mrs Cash Cow. Get you!"

She pulled a face. "It doesn't go as far as you think, and people beg it off you."

"You would have returned it all to have him back?"

She closed her eyes, like she had gone into a swoon. "Shaun, I would have given all my worldly possessions to have him back. I would have walked to the end of the earth." Her eyes had become watery.

They were sitting side by side on a sofa. She had a solid build, a bit mumsy, and Shaun took her hand and put his arm round her. "Seriously, what matters now is that you're young enough to start again… and beautiful enough to get anyone you want."

She looked right into his eyes. "You think so?" She leant her head in close to him, with a serious expression.

He felt overwhelmed and would normally have recoiled at the intensity. But he liked her and respected her for all she had been through, and she came with her own money, and he did nothing to alleviate the close proximity. "Yes, you'll have men queuing up to marry you."

"So you think men will want me?" She held his gaze and there was a silence.

He looked uncertain, like he was caught out. "Oh, and me, of course. I'll be in the queue," he added, like it was a hurried afterthought.

She smiled. "Will you? I'd like that." She tightened her grip on him.

"Hmm. Definitely."

She suddenly became more sure of herself, and her voice swelled with passion. "I've changed so much now. I've become a different person really. What mattered to me got transformed that day my husband died. Now I just want a big family." She laughed at the thought of it. "Lots and lots of *bambini*… but time is not on my side. I want to start soon. Marriage and babies very soon." She looked right into his eyes.

"Yes, of course you do. I know what you mean. Italian families toss their *bambini* in the air and kiss them, don't they? Lots of babies being thrown around." He looked away.

* * *

It was just a few months later and they had become close. Shaun didn't know whether he loved her, but he enjoyed her company, and she was always very amenable. They were lying in Angela's bed, having made love.

"That was amazing." Shaun stroked Angela's back.

"Do you love me?" she asked softly.

He sighed. "I adore everything about you, right down to the way you smell."

"You know what liking my smell means?"

"It means you smell nice."

"It shows our genes are a good match. It means our children will be healthy. I feel it too. I didn't know whether it would be possible to love again and now I know it is… " She snuggled up to him. "How much do you love me?"

"Lots and lots."

"Tell me, where's our relationship going?"

"It's getting stronger and stronger."

"But where's it going?"

"What do you mean?"

"Where will we be six months from now?"

There was a silence before Shaun spoke. "Oh okay, this is your marriage and babies thing, right?"

"We love each other. We should be together."

He sighed and was silent for a while. Then he spoke. "Look, I understand where you're coming from. I'm used to a lot of freedom. I need time."

"Would you like a break, to think about things?"

"Not really. I would miss you."

She kissed him. "Good."

* * *

Dick Wingate had delivered the twenty prototype Good Night Sleep Aid MP3 players as agreed. Shaun had tested ten with insomniacs, who mostly refused to return them because they liked the player so much, and he had retained ten for testing with tinnitus sufferers. To this end, he had arranged to join a tinnitus support group in a town in Essex. They met on a Friday evening once a month. Shaun entered the church hall where the meeting was held and saw a semicircle of about thirty chairs, most of them occupied by middle-aged people, with a table and chairs across the top, where the group leaders were sitting.

"Welcome," a middle-aged lady had got up and came to greet him, picking him out as a stranger. "You must be Shaun? We spoke on the phone."

"Hi. Thanks for the opportunity to address your group."

"We're about to start, so I'll let you talk first. You'll find they're a very friendly crowd." She returned to her seat at the table. "Welcome everyone to this month's meeting of Whistle Stop, the mid-Essex tinnitus support group. We have a guest this evening, Mr Shaun Johnson," she gestured to Shaun who raised his hand in salutation, "and I'll let him explain why he's here. Ask any questions you have, Shaun, and tell us whatever it is you want to say."

"Thank you. First of all, I notice that none of you are

young. Does that mean that tinnitus only affects older people?"

"There are a few younger sufferers, but they tend not to come to the support groups," the leader answered.

"Do all of you suffer with the problem?"

"I don't." The leader spoke again. "My late husband suffered with it, so I carry on the group that he started, in his memory."

"That's a wonderful gesture on your part." Shaun paused, and some of the group muttered agreement. "Why I'm here, I haven't come to sell you snake oil to cure your tinnitus." He paused, thinking he might get a few laughs, but they were just staring at him, like they were wondering, who was this stranger in their midst. He had already learnt that you have to tell a joke or two, before people realise, 'he's telling jokes'. He continued, "I've come to give you something, really. I'm developing a sleeping aid to help lull insomniacs off to sleep, and I wondered if tinnitus sufferers can also be kept awake by the ringing in their ears. So that's a question to you all."

"Sometimes." A middle-aged lady spoke. "If you're anxious or worried, you might notice it as you fall asleep. Normally you won't."

"It bothers me sometimes," another lady added.

"What I have is ten little players for when your tinnitus is bothering you as you drop off to sleep." Shaun held one up. "They're programmed to give you a choice of sounds to mask your tinnitus: waterfalls, ocean waves, air conditioning, and more. You can adjust the volume, time it to fade and switch off, so you keep it playing just as long as you need it. You don't have to wake up to switch it off!" He paused again, and a few people laughed this time. "I'm looking for ten volunteers to try it out for two weeks."

"I'll try it."

"And me."

Shaun found more volunteers than available players and he had to prioritise, giving the players to those with the worst tinnitus. He made a breakout group of the final ten and showed them how the player worked, arranging to meet up with them two weeks later. He drove home very satisfied with his evening's work. The signs were that he was on to a winner.

* * *

It had been a very busy few months at the office for Shaun, introducing new products into the catalogue, a shipment of defective goods needing resolution and a trip to the Far East to get his Good Night sleep aid MP3 player into production. He had thought quite a bit about Angela and had wanted to phone her, but had resisted because he felt he shouldn't get distracted from his business.

The break had been much longer than he had anticipated. He was so busy he had even had to give up going to lunch, and now had to make do with sandwiches at his desk, sometimes even working as he ate them. He was just eating one when the phone rang.

"Shaun." Her voice was loud and excited. She never usually phoned him at work.

"Angela. Oh, it's so good to hear your voice. I'm so sorry. I've never been so busy. I was in the Far East, working on a really big new product. I should have been in touch."

She laughed. "Shaun, I've got some really big news too. I'm getting married."

Shaun's heart started to beat much faster. "Married? What do you mean? Who to?"

"I met him a few weeks ago. He's wonderful, and he's so keen to make his life with me."

Shaun hesitated. "Are you sure? Isn't it all a bit rushed?"

"I suppose he swept me off my feet. Shaun, he's so wonderful!" She giggled. There was a silence. "Shaun, you okay?"

He paused. "Yes, of course. But I'm shocked... I'm worried that you're rushing into something with your eyes closed, and... what about us?"

She thought for a moment. "Was there ever an us, Shaun?"

"You know there was an us! Don't ask silly questions."

"Oh, you're getting upset."

He exhaled. "Of course I'm getting upset. Didn't you feel anything for me?"

"You don't sound okay, Shaun. What's happening? You're usually Mr Smooth."

"Do you want to meet for a chat?"

"I've got so much to arrange. The wedding's next week."

"So it's a done deal? Do I get an invitation to the wedding?"

"Oh, it's a very small do, just a registry office, then we're off on our honeymoon to the Maldives and lots of baby making activity!"

"So that's it then?" She didn't respond to Shaun's question. "You're throwing me off like an old tow rope?"

"Oh, Shaun, don't give me a hard time. Aren't you happy for me? You'll find someone else."

He sighed. "Yes, of course. I wish you all the best... and lots of progeny." he said in an angry tone and put the phone down.

At that moment, Michael, his office manager, happened to come in to see him.

"You left a message for me."

"Did I? Oh, that's right. I'm fed up with eating sandwiches at my desk for lunch and working all hours. It's interfering with my leisure time. Put an ad on the

Internet for a personal assistant for me."

"Are you okay, Shaun? You look flushed and your eyes are watering."

"I'm fine." He coughed. "This sandwich just got stuck in my throat, that's all, a bit of crust, that's all." He thumped his chest a few times. "I'm fine now. Put that ad on and I can have proper food for lunch."

5

London – Part 2

Disappointment is the most negative human emotion, draining a person of hope and vitality. Shaun realised that he hadn't loved Angela, but had just enjoyed her company, and she hadn't loved him, but had been looking for a sperm donor. Even so, he was hurt and wondered if his soul mate would ever come along. His love affairs seemed to be so superficial. A shroud of pessimism enveloped him and he lost all appetite for relationships. It was just as well there was always lots to do at the office.

His import business was run from a yellow brick building on an industrial estate near his home, on the London border with Essex. From the outside, the ground floor was dominated by the bright red, metal roller shutters of the loading bay for goods in and out. Behind the bay lay the warehouse, where the gadgets and gizmos were stacked in orderly rows on shelf racking. Shaun loved to be down there with the pickers and packers, the aroma of the cardboard packaging always signifying work and wealth for him. On the left-hand side of the unit there was an entrance to a downstairs reception office, where customers could buy the products over the counter, although the majority purchased via the Internet or by phone. Behind the reception was a staircase to the main offices on the upper floor, where the clerical staff and Shaun worked.

"Michael, come in." Shaun called out to his operations manager as he hovered at the doorway.

Michael entered Shaun's office, which was relatively plush compared to the rest of the unit, with a director's style desk, swivel chair and board room table. There was also a display unit along one wall, carrying most of the company's gadgets and gizmos.

"Shaun, I caught Alan with a pair of binoculars in his bag as he went home last night." Michael was a clean cut, clean living young man, who had been with Shaun for eight years, from the very start of the company.

"Thieving git."

"We've had quite a lot of shrinkage lately and I had an idea it might be him. Do you want to talk to him?"

"I'll kick his arse if I see him. Just give him a letter of dismissal for gross misconduct and archive the CCTV of you searching him, in case he takes us to employment tribunal."

Michael had a disappointed look. "He's actually a very good worker."

"But that's secondary. We can't keep someone who's got their fingers in the till. Do the letter immediately and walk him off the premises. Are there any more at it?"

"I won't know until he's gone."

"Good catch, Michael, thank you. Let the others know why he's been dismissed. By the way, I've been looking at the resumes for my personal assistant vacancy. I've asked only two to come in for interview, Fiona Quigley and Ravinder Bansal. Can you join me to interview them? The first is Fiona, later today."

"Of course."

It was lunch time.

"Hello Fiona." Shaun smiled at the dowdy, middle aged English woman. "I see you're working at the moment.

Why do you want to leave your current position?"

"I want to be part of a growing company like yours."

Shaun nodded and looked down at the checklist he used as a prompt during interviews. "How do you get on with your team mates in your current job?" He looked up at her.

"Very well."

"Give me an example of that."

"If we're stuck on a problem, we'll help each other."

"What do you think of this definition of a boss: Someone who is early when you're late and late when you're early?"

"I wouldn't know about that. I'm always early."

Ten minutes later Fiona had answered well on all Shaun's questions. He had a final one. "Why should I hire you over the other candidates who have applied for this role?"

"I have relevant experience, I'm very hard-working, and I'll be very loyal to you and the company."

Shaun nodded. "Do you have any questions?"

"Not at this stage."

"Well, if there's nothing further, thank you for attending today. We have more people to interview and we'll let you know whether you've been successful."

When she had left the room, Michael spoke. "I thought she was very good."

"Yes, certainly good enough for what we're looking for."

Late afternoon, they had the second interview. Ravinder Bansal was a second-generation Indian, born and raised in London.

"Hello Ravinder." Shaun looked at the beautiful twenty five year old woman, who had eyes shaped like almonds, with long lashes and black silky hair falling onto the shoulders of her turquoise top.

"Hello." Her voice was soft and refined and accompanied by a beautiful smile, with perfect white teeth. She seemed a pampered person, not someone who was used to hard work. Michael imagined she had been her father's Little Princess.

"I see you're not working at the moment but, when you were, how did you get on with your team mates?"

"Very well."

"Give me an example of that."

"Well, we would have a nice chat as we worked."

"What do you think of this definition of a boss: Someone who is early when you're late and late when you're early?"

She laughed. "Yes, it's so annoying when that happens."

Shaun asked his usual closing question. "Why should I hire you, rather than the others that we are interviewing?"

"Well, I'm available immediately and I make a nice cup of tea." She smiled at Shaun and looked into his eyes for a few seconds.

"Well, that's always useful." Shaun laughed. "Please, can you wait outside while I talk to Michael?"

As soon as Ravinder had left the room, Michael spoke. "I think Fiona's the girl for this company."

"I thought Ravinder had the edge."

Michael blinked and looked at the résumés with his annotated notes in front of him, wondering what he had missed. "Really?" He looked at Shaun with a puzzled expression on his face. "Well, I suppose she's good eye candy."

"It's not about that." There was authority and slight irritation in Shaun's voice. "I think she has potential."

"Sure, of course Shaun, whatever. I'll call her back in and we'll offer her the job."

Ravinder, or Ravi as she was soon called, had her own

desk in the main office but, after a few weeks, spent more and more time in Shaun's office, sitting on a chair beside his, flirting with him and going to lunch with him most days of the week. After four months they had become much closer, but she was married and lived with her in-laws, so not too close. Shaun would often find an excuse to buy her flowers or chocolates and, when she took them home, her husband would say things like, 'What's that all about?' and she would say it was for some good work she had done, smiling to herself. She would often go and sit by Shaun's desk at about five o'clock, when everyone was going home, and chatter away for an hour or two in her soft, flirty voice, the close proximity of her feminine presence mattering more than the content of the conversation. A lot of the people in the company commented on the 'close working relationship' that had developed between Shaun and Ravi.

She came into his office one Monday morning.

"Cheer up, Ravi."

"Sorry." She yawned. "We went to Birmingham on Saturday evening to see one of my husband's old university friends and we watched a boxing match on TV that started at eleven p.m. My husband drank a bottle of whisky with his friend, so I had to drive home. We got in at four in the morning. Was I knackered!" She said the last three words with emphasis.

"I'm really annoyed with your husband. He shouldn't have done that."

"It's my fault. He asked if he could drink and I agreed to it."

"Let's go out to lunch today, get a smile on your face."

They went to one of their regular haunts, a local pub where Ravi liked the beer garden. Ravi had egg and chips and Shaun had a tuna salad. They sat in a secluded part of the garden, away from everyone, like a lovers' tryst, at the corner of a table, so they were side by side, but still able to look in each other's eyes. Ravi had seen Shaun's flair for business and she liked his confidence and good looks.

"I was thinking," she said softly, "why don't you book a hotel room, one lunch time?" She put her hand on his.

He sighed. He couldn't help feeling there was a parallel universe in which he would have taken her up on the offer, but something was cramping the old Shaun style. "I would love that more than anything. How long have you been married?"

"One year."

"I don't want you to do anything you might regret later."

"I thought you loved me." She said it very softly, eyes downcast.

"It's because I love you I'm saying that. I don't want to play with your life just for my own gratification."

"But I want you to book a hotel room. I'm asking you to do it." She leant in towards him so that her low-cut top revealed even more of her breasts.

"You should put your husband first."

"He's not as good to me as he should be. Like you said, you were annoyed with him for making me drive back from Birmingham."

"Nobody's perfect. You have to work at the relationship."

"At weekends he goes down the pub in the evenings with his friends and afterwards he brings them back to our house, all of them drunk and him in the worse state of all." She sounded like a child, telling tales. "Then he comes upstairs and wakes me up, so he can show me off to his friends and I have to make them drinks and, if they're hungry, *roti*."

"He should be doing things with you at the weekend, not going off with his mates." Shaun frowned.

73

"So you can do things with me instead. Pleeeease," she held his hand tighter and looked intensely into his eyes, "book the hotel room."

Shaun sighed and sat up straight in his chair. "Really, you have to try and make a go of it with your husband." Shaun shook his head. "With time you would regret cheating on him. If you were single, it would be completely different."

"You want me to get a divorce? Indians don't divorce. Please don't ask me to do that."

"It's just a passing fancy on your part."

Ravi thought for a while. "You're quite noble aren't you? I admire you."

"There's nothing to admire."

As it happened, Ravi fell pregnant by her husband a few weeks later and became more absorbed in family life and less interested in Shaun.

He would sometimes browse the high-class escorts on the Internet. He had never paid for sex in his life, but used to look at their pictures in the agency galleries just to pass the time. He was not taken in. He knew how much could be altered using Photoshop, because his office used it in his own business website, to make his gadgets and gizmos look more attractive. Most of the girls had a hard, cold look, as though they took themselves very seriously, and usually their photos looked well airbrushed, almost like paintings.

He looked but did not touch. His focus continued to be money. He could not fail to make money. He had a natural flair, focus and an ability to get on with his business partners. He had built up a large customer base with his catalogue of gadgets and gizmos, a combination of style, value for money, usefulness and *Zeitgeist*, and Shaun had cleverly printed a swish logo across each item, stating the catalogue and website name *VIVA* in red, so the separately sourced items became part of a brand and lifestyle. The *VIVA* logo had a Nike style swoosh going across it, but not similar enough to breach copyright. In addition, his MP3 player for insomniacs and tinnitus sufferers had also been hugely successful, mainly because he had sourced it cheaply enough for the retail price to be an insignificant factor in the context of getting a good nights sleep.

* * *

Shaun arrived at the warehouse mid morning one Friday to find three people sitting in his office, which doubled as the showroom. Michael intercepted him, just as he was entering the room.

"Shaun, I've been trying to get hold of you," he said in a confidential tone. "These people phoned from their hotel early this morning and wondered whether they could visit us today. They're over from the States, on a tight schedule, so I agreed. Ravi's just taken their orders for drinks."

"Good job, Michael. Thanks. I'll see to it from here…" Shaun stepped into his office. "Good morning," he said with enthusiasm, but looked at them as though uncertain of the purpose of their visit. They stood up, each one holding a business card in their hands.

"Hi. I'm Kathy Davis." She handed her card to Shaun with a friendly smile. "I'm president of Empire Manufacturing Incorporated. You may have heard of us." She was a plump, middle aged woman with a pale face and black hair in a bob cut. She was wearing a black two-piece jacket and skirt.

"I detect a bit of Scottish in the American accent."

"Good spot, Shaun. I emigrated to the US twenty years ago. The accent always gets much stronger as soon as I land on British soil. I'll be back up in Edinburgh in a few days."

"Hi. I'm Ted Broccoli, US operations manager." The middle-aged, balding man with black rimmed glasses and a loud voice handed his card to Shaun.

"I've heard about your family. Your grandfather introduced broccoli to America, I think."

"That's us. We're an Italian American family, and my grandfather used his Italian connections to build the business."

"Well, last but not least, I'm Bob Paisley, Europe operations manager." The small man with a bald head gave Shaun an enthusiastic smile.

"What a wonderful display." Kathy had moved over to the array of products on the shelving set against a wall. "Is this your entire range?"

"The major lines are there, but we're introducing new ones every month, and some drop off as obsolete."

"Do you go out to the Far East to source them?"

"I go three times a year, plus I have agents working for me, and also existing suppliers send samples of their new lines."

"Well excuse me asking so many questions, that's very rude. Shall we sit down and explain the purpose of our visit?" Kathy spoke with authority and Shaun thought she might be a despotic ruler of her company.

They sat down round the board table just as the door opened. Ravi entered with the drinks, coffee for Kathy and Ted, water for Bob, who had said he never drank anything hot.

"We're here in Europe with our buying boots on." Kathy put her glasses on and looked at Shaun to see his reaction.

"Okay." Shaun kept a neutral expression on his face.

"We like your range and what you've built up with your catalogue and website. It seems probable to us that you have a good customer base." Kathy paused. "I'll be honest."

She leant forward. "It's your 'Good Night' sleep aid MP3 player that we particularly like. My husband suffers from tinnitus and he loves it. Couldn't you go the whole way and bring out a cure for tinnitus? My husband would like that."

Shaun laughed. "The doctor who finds a cure for tinnitus will win the Nobel Prize for medicine."

"Might you be open to offers for your company?"

"I'm always ready to listen to opportunities."

"Can we go over some numbers?" Kathy listened attentively as Shaun gave an overview of volumes, costs and profit margin, like he was in the Dragon's Den. When he had finished, she said, "Subject to verification of your books by our accountants and subject to further discussions, we think we would like to make you an offer."

"How much?"

"It will be a very fair offer. How much do you think you'd want?"

"I would have to think about it. The 'Good Night' sleep aid may be my once-in-a-lifetime idea. I may not come up with anything as good again."

"How did you create it?"

"I developed it with an electronics professor."

"Does he get a cut on sales?"

"No, I paid him a one-off fee."

"Wise move." It was the first thing Ted had said, since they had sat down.

"Do you have the worldwide patent?" Kathy continued her questioning.

"I do, but I keep improving it in any case, to stay ahead of the game, and I have a scrappage scheme where customers can return an older model for an upgrade."

"Would you like the weekend to think about how much you're looking for?"

"Sure." He looked at her business card. "I can e-mail you."

"Well, how about some early lunch? We just about have time in our busy schedule." Kathy looked at the others. "Good idea?"

"Well we have a pub, a short drive away, where I sometimes lunch with Ravi."

"This is a very attractive young lady." It was the first thing Bob had said.

"Bob, can we stay focussed on the purpose of our meeting?" Kathy gave him a stern look.

"But if you want something really quick," Shaun continued, "there's a little cafe on this estate, does English breakfast fry ups, sandwiches, that sort of thing. You can get bacon and eggs, a day's work for a chicken, a lifetime commitment for a pig."

Ted smiled at Shaun's joke. "Do they do burgers?"

"Okay boys, we'll go for speed," said Kathy, cutting them both off.

They had a quick lunch in the cafe on the estate and then Shaun ordered a taxi to take them to their next appointment. He waved them goodbye, wondering if this was the watershed of his life, if he should savour the moment.

That evening, he discussed the day's events with Pete, down the pub.

"How much do you think they want to pay?" Pete looked thoughtful as Shaun suggested a sum. "Then double it. They might just pay it. You don't know how cash rich they are. The worst thing that can happen is that they say they can't afford it. Do your profit projections and ask them double what you think it's really worth. You won't get this opportunity again."

Shaun followed the advice and put in an inflated

amount for the sale of his business. It was millions, but his price was accepted in full, with no arguments or bantering, just a simple, 'That looks okay.' in an e-mail from Kathy. 'Hmm. Americans and money.' thought Shaun.

The ensuing weeks working on the contract were fraught for Shaun, in case everything fell apart. He was in his lawyer's City of London office sitting across the polished table from his lawyer, who was wearing a bold pin striped blue shirt, ostentatious red tie and gold cufflinks. It was in stark contrast to the no frills and dress down style of Shaun's industrial unit.

"Do you wear a red cloak and a pair of horns? This is a whopper of a deal you've pulled off." His lawyer's plummy tones echoed round the office.

"Yes, it must be unusual for you to have a client that smiles more than you."

"Oh, so cruel… and I'm working flat out to help you. I see they're releasing you with immediate effect and just want you to be available for consultancy if required. To all intents and purposes, you're completely free."

"I'm a bit surprised, even hurt, they haven't tried to tie me in for longer, but then Michael knows all of the operations and he was trained by me, so he is very good, of course."

"What will you do with yourself?"

"I suppose I'll retire."

"Don't be ridiculous." His voice boomed with all the confidence and authority of a middle-class professional. "You're much too young to put your feet up and let the world go by. You don't want to end up just playing golf or pushing a trolley round the supermarket, like you're a back number."

"Maybe I'll look for a wife."

"You don't have a wife and four children like me?"

"So that's why you have to work so hard."

"Seriously, it's time for you to settle down, now you've made your fortune. What a catch you'll be! Watch out for gold diggers. They'll be fighting over you when they know what you're worth! They'll be camping outside your door! 'Let us in! I want to have your baby!'" The lawyer looked at the clock on the wall. "Do you want to try for more money?"

"I don't want to kill the deal by being greedy. Let's just play it cool and hope it goes through as it is."

"Well in that case, I think it's in the can. I'll remove 'without prejudice' from this draft and submit it as the final version for signature."

The money was in Shaun's bank account one week later. Shaun had to celebrate very quietly as he knew not to tell anyone, except his parents, of his massive windfall. He had already made enough money to know that revealing how much you had would only lead to jealousy and resentment from those who had less and contempt and pity from those who had more.

The first few weeks were pure euphoria at having pulled off such a big deal, as Shaun realised that he was free to do whatever he wanted for the first time in his life. He had some relaxed lunches in his local High Street bistros, went to the West End for a few art exhibitions, caught up with old friends he hadn't seen for years. He read a few books and saw some films, all things he hadn't done before, because he had been too busy working, building his empire. He tidied his home office and got a new computer system. He kept himself busy. He did some refurbishments around the house. They made him feel good. He considered going on holiday, but realised he didn't have anyone to go with and that he might feel lonely. Not playing golf or going to watch football, being without hobbies, having always shunned relationships in favour of work, he started to realise his life was rather empty, like a dark tunnel with an unknown destination waiting at the end.

It was about one month after his departure when Michael called him from the office.

"Shaun, you okay?"

"Hi, Michael. I'm fine. Do you need my help with something?"

"No, actually I was just clearing out your desk and found a few of your belongings. I wondered if you'd like to come in and pick them up or shall we post them to you?"

"I'll come in. I'll see you for lunch, if you like."

"I'm booked up for lunch this week, business meetings. Sorry, but you'll remember how it is. If you come in before twelve or after two, that'll be okay."

Shaun arrived at his old warehouse before lunch, in order to catch Michael, who was now ensconced in Shaun's former office and was sitting in Shaun's director's swivel chair. He stood up to greet Shaun, who noticed from the upward incline of Michael's forearm as they shook hands, that Michael was now very much the boss.

"Hi Shaun. Sorry I have to rush out. Here's a box of stuff I've collected from your drawers and cabinets." He handed Shaun a sealed cardboard box. "I'm off out now, but do take a tour and have a chat with everyone."

Walking round, saying hello, Shaun suddenly realised how much he missed the excitement of the office, the thrill of the business deals, the banter with his staff and not least the flirting with Ravinder, who was by now on maternity leave and had been replaced by none other than Fiona Quigley, the dowdy middle-aged woman whom Michael had favoured at interview over Ravinder.

Shaun felt quite sad as he drove home, a sense of loss,

with nothing to replace his old life. When he got into his home office and opened the cardboard box, he found it also quite empty, just a few desk ornaments, souvenirs from his buying trips abroad, and his desk diary. He flicked through it, finding the date of his departure, seeing how the appointments and reminders suddenly stopped and gave way to blank pages. As he went to throw it in the bin, a piece of paper, which had been tucked into the back cover, fluttered out and dropped onto the floor. He crouched down to pick it up. He had quite forgotten it was there. It was a little note from Angela, handwritten on perfumed, love letter paper, at the height of their affair. At the top of the page, she had plagiarised a piece of Haiku and re-written it especially for Shaun.

To ask how deep is my love for you
Is like asking how fierce is the torrent of water
When the snows melt
And the river flows East in Spring.

She followed the poem with some tender lines, and he suddenly remembered how much he had enjoyed their relationship, the silkiness of the skin at her neck, its sweet smell, the way her hair got caught in his mouth when he went to kiss her. He was so lonely. He started to cry.

6

The Favela Girl comes to London

Shaun was bored and browsing the high-class call girls on the Internet one evening at home, his eye jaded with the hundreds available, when his attention was caught by an escort who stood right out from the other girls. A little sticker flashed on her photo frame, 'New'. She was a small girl with a cheeky, impish face. Her smile was infectious and Shaun gave a little laugh at the sight of her. He clicked on her photo to open up her profile. At the bottom of the screen there was a long strip of miniature frames which, when he hovered the mouse over them, expanded into a full-screen picture. It was an extensive photo shoot, a professional glamour portfolio, showing off her shapely body and long dark hair. On one shot, she had her back to the camera and was looking over her shoulder, grinning. Her features were cute and innocent but her dark eyes were quite intense, piercing. It said her name was Gabriella, which Shaun realised would just be a working name. He read her vital statistics. She was just five feet two inches tall. 'What a sweetie', thought Shaun. Then he read the little blurb that described her.

Newly arrived from Ipanema beach, Rio de Janeiro, is this magnificent Brazilian beauty who is full of life, energy and charm. She will welcome you into her luxurious apartment with courtesy and will treat you with the utmost respect. We guarantee her photos are genuine. Why travel all the way to Rio to experience that Latina passion? She is here in London and waiting to give you a genuine Brazilian GFE. Highly recommended!

'What's a GFE?' Shaun said to himself. He googled it.

GFE [Girl Friend Experience]: The Holy Grail of the man who pays for sex is to find a prostitute who offers the physical and emotional intimacy associated with a girlfriend, even though the relationship is essentially commercial. In practice, this means kissing, cuddling, foreplay and friendly conversation, in a 'no rush' atmosphere and giving the client the full advertised time, or even longer, rather than trying to finish the session once a climax has been achieved.

She didn't come cheap, pitching herself at the very top end of the market, but that was not a concern for Shaun, whose hands were trembling as he phoned her agency from his home landline, withholding his number. He tried to control his shaky voice.

"Hello, I'd like to book an appointment with one of your girls."

"We don't answer withheld numbers." The woman's voice was brusque. "Phone back on your mobile, and don't withhold the number. You'll receive her address as a text on your mobile."

He fixed up a meeting with the little Brazilian for the next evening. Her apartment was in a stylish part of the West End, just off Oxford Street. Shaun rang the bell. She opened the door and was wearing a silk dressing gown over lingerie. Her skin was tanned, like she was just back from holiday and her face was fresh and innocent, more like a student than a call girl. She looked up at him, her dark eyes exuding passion. She put her hand on her chest and winced slightly, in a gesture as if she was overwhelmed.

"Hello Darling. Come in. You okay, baby? Oh, look at you. Come and sit down." Her voice was pleasant and smooth, a bit girlish in its pitch. She brought him across to the sofa and sat down beside him. "I'm used to sweaty, balding, middle-aged business men who smell of beer or whisky and want to be my daddy. You're beautiful. How come you have to pay for it?"

"Well, paying for sex up front is much cheaper in the long run."

"What happened to you?" She frowned slightly as she said it.

"Well, it's a bit early in our relationship to go into that, don't you think?"

She stroked his hair, looking deep into his eyes for what seemed a long time. "Oh, I get it. You need a lot of love." She looked at him full on. "I have lots of love." With that she kissed him passionately, then looked at him again. It felt like her eyes were burrowing into him.

"Are you really Brazilian?"

"Of course I am, why shouldn't I be? I'm from Rio."

"It seems a long way away, that's all."

"There are lots of South Americans in London. You just have to look out for us."

"What are Brazilians like compared to the English?"

"You want me to give you a stereotype?"

"The interesting thing about stereotypes is that they're ninety per cent accurate."

"Well, I suppose we're very warm and friendly, and we kiss a lot… and we mean it. Nothing's fake and we're not shy about our bodies." She looked him straight in the eye.

85

His pupils, already dilated, opened up even more. "Anyone who's depressed with life should go to Brazil. They would soon be cured... But I have to charge you, baby, cute as you are. I need the money, and I'm not doing special offers this week."

"No buy one, get one free? It's okay, don't apologise."

"I'm not apologising. I'm just explaining."

"Hmm! Youth doesn't come cheap." Shaun handed her an envelope he had prepared. "There's the paperwork then."

She disappeared into another room to hide it. After a minute, she returned.

"So your heart belongs to Brazil, but your body's international?" he asked.

She looked sideways, less certain of herself suddenly, and sighed. "Well," she paused. "My body belongs to handsome English men." She kissed him. "You like my little dog?" She referred to the Chihuahua that had just run into the room. "I've only had him a few days. I hope you don't mind dogs."

"They're more like cats than dogs, those little things," Shaun said.

She picked the puppy up. "You're not a cat, Chimbo, you're a proper dog, aren't you?" She kissed him a few times and then turned to Shaun. "You want to get started? You can have a shower first and there's some mouthwash." She led him through to the bathroom and set the shower running. "Here's a clean towel, and then come through to the bedroom." she said in an encouraging tone.

Five minutes later, he was in the bedroom, with just a towel wrapped around him. He dumped his clothes in a pile on the floor. A chocolate coloured teddy bear, battered and worn and with only one eye, lay between the pillows of the bed. Shaun presumed it had been hers since childhood. 'How sweet,' he thought, 'how innocent to share such a personal thing with an unknown person off the street.' or maybe that was what he was supposed to think.

She started kissing him, short pecks to begin with, but then becoming slower and more drawn out. It carried on for about five minutes, until she stopped.

"What you want to do, baby?" She looked at him. "You want to play a little?"

"Some massage."

"You want me to massage you?"

"No, I want to massage you."

"Good, I need a massage."

"Take your clothes off then." he ordered.

"You want me on my front or back?"

"Lie on your front, it's easier for me to start with your back."

He knelt beside her on the bed and glided the palms of his hands up her back, either side of the spine, using moderate pressure. At the top, he brought his hands across her shoulder blades, squeezing the muscles to release tension, and then brought his hands down the edges of her back using a lighter pressure to return to their original start position. He repeated this five times and then started gliding his hands in opposite directions, like a push-pull technique, up and down and across her back.

This carried on for about five minutes. She was completely silent. Shaun then got to the real target from his perspective and started to knead her butt, alternating with stroking it in a circular movement. All of this was a genuine massage technique that he had learnt years before. She remained silent. Shaun then got to where he really wanted to be. He put his head down to her butt and started kissing it, more like it was her face. After a few seconds, she started giggling hysterically. He carried on. She craned her neck round off the bed and looked at him.

He went back to stroking for a few seconds, but then resumed kissing her butt. She started giggling hysterically again and looked round at him.

"Okay, okay, looks like we're going to have to leave your bum." He made do with spanking it mildly and watching the ripples travel across her flesh.

He continued down her legs, kneading and stroking the thigh and calf muscles, and then reached her feet, which were another fetish area for him. He started kissing them, but she started giggling hysterically again.

"Okay, let's have you on your back now."

He repeated something similar on her front to what he had done on her back and, when he started to kiss between her thighs, she started the hysterical giggling once more.

"Okay, that's it. Your turn to massage me."

As he was fully erect, she opened a condom and rolled it over his penis.

"Small, but perfectly formed."

"You're a nice size baby. It's cute. You're better off. Those big boys kill me."

She started to suck his penis, not looking at him as she did it. This carried on for a few minutes.

"Okay." He put his hand on her arm. She knew what this signalled.

She automatically climbed on top, Shaun's least favourite position, but her vagina was tight round his penis and she had a nimble movement. He understood why she chose not to go underneath and thought she must have got crushed in the past. It was over very quickly, and she collapsed down beside him, smothering him in kisses. Her face was very close to his as they lay together.

"So that's it?" She giggled, "You've finished with your Brazilian wife in three minutes? Now you're going back to your English wife?" She couldn't stop giggling.

Shaun didn't answer, but smiled. As they lay there, the puppy ran in and curled up on Shaun's clothes that he'd left in a bundle on the floor.

"I think he likes my shirt."

"I'm sorry, put him out."

"I'm not bothered about it." Shaun sounded mellow. It was almost a family scene.

He looked thoughtful as he was about to leave.

"What are you thinking?" she asked.

"I normally make jokes with people, but I notice with you, I don't feel a need to do it."

"Maybe, because you're paying me, you feel you have no obligations." She nodded her head, as if for emphasis.

"That might be the case with some people, but it feels different to that."

She looked at him intently for a few seconds. "So you don't need to wear your clown's mask with me? You can let me see your true self?" He didn't answer, but just looked at her as she led him to the door. She stood between him and the exit, putting her arms round his neck. "You liked your time with me, didn't you? You were hungry." She started to peck him and nibble his lips. "You like me, I can tell." She looked at him, but he said nothing. "Come and see me again. Make it soon." With that, she opened the door and let him go. Her perfume stayed with him for the rest of the evening.

* * *

He thought about the encounter for a long time afterwards. Technically, it was far from the best sex he had ever had, but there was something about her closeness and innocent charm that was capturing him. She had shared herself with him, like the girlfriend experience promised on the website. He had to consciously shut his feelings off,

89

because falling in love with a prostitute was a ridiculous notion. It was such a cliché, the little whore with a heart of gold. Even so, he couldn't get her out of his mind.

He left it three weeks, but finally succumbed and booked with the agency to see her again. As she opened the door, she immediately embraced him. Her body seemed to go limp, somehow yielding, submissive. It felt like, 'I'm yours'.

"Oh heeelloooo." It was drawn out. "Where you been, darling? You been okay?" She said it as though she really cared. He looked surprised.

"You remember me?" He sounded nervous.

"Of course I remember you." She laughed. "You came on a Sunday evening. You were wearing blue trousers and a yellow shirt. You gave me a massage. How could I forget you? I'm only twenty two years old. You think I have dementia?"

"Well, the good thing about Alzheimer's is that you make new friends every day."

"Mr. Joker."

He looked shocked. "You really remember me, don't you? You're scaring me. People don't always want to be remembered in this kind of situation."

"You scared of me?" She pulled a cute face.

"No I'm not scared of you. I really like you."

"And I really like you."

The sex was largely a rerun of the first time, except she didn't take any money up front, and afterwards she lay in bed, stroking his back and didn't make any move to end the session.

"Do you have a boyfriend?"

"What a question! Of course I don't have a boyfriend. How could I have a boyfriend, doing this kind of work?"

"So you don't think it's good work?"

"Don't take this the wrong way, you're a very nice man and very charming, but, every night, I pray to God to forgive me for what I'm doing. Sometimes it goes on for ten or fifteen minutes, I can't stop talking to God."

"So why do you carry on doing this work?"

"Why do you think?"

"For the money, obviously, but what I mean is, why do you need the money so much?"

"I have to get my father out of the *favela*. He's not well and I'm scared he'll deteriorate, and that he might even die."

Shaun frowned. "What's his medical condition?"

"He has a bad heart."

"Oh, I'm so sorry to hear that… that must be really worrying. I'm lucky, both my parents are well." He turned so he could see her more clearly and propped himself up, on his elbow. "Tell me more about the problem, then. What's a *favela*? I've never heard of it."

"They are the shanty towns, the slums. The rich live in downtown Rio and in the coastal neighbourhoods, the poor live on the surrounding hillsides. It's like an ant hill. Everything is irregular and random, just what people have built for themselves. No proper roads, just walkways and paths up the very steep hill, and our house is halfway up, so my father has to climb a thousand steps to get in and out, and I'm worried that it's going to be too much for him." Shaun looked at her as though she was a puzzle. "Why are you looking at me like that?"

"So you grew up in the *favela*?" He frowned.

"All my life, up to one month ago, when I came to London."

"Hmm." He sounded suspicious. "But we have something similar to the *favela* in London even, sink estates, and I know what kind of girls come out of that

91

environment. They're street girls, loud, emotional, and volatile. They talk rough. But you seem very together, quite calm, and your English is very pure, grammatically."

She rubbed her nose against his like an Eskimo kiss and then started kissing him. "Oh look at you! You're clever aren't you?"

"Have you only just noticed?"

"Yeah, okay… I was the most famous girl in the *favela*. I was in all the newspapers." Her voice seemed to swell with emotion as she said it, like an evangelical preacher. "They had a photo of me on the first day of term, wearing my school uniform and backpack. '*Menina da favela*…Little girl from the shanty town wins scholarship to top Catholic school of Rio'. During the day, I was mixing with the richest and most well-to-do girls of Brazil. For some of the lessons I was taught by nuns. At night, I was in the slums."

"If it was such an unusual thing for a slum girl to go to a school for the rich, how did you know to arrange it?"

"I had a fairy godmother, like a rich auntie, she did it all for me."

"Couldn't she help your father now?"

"No. We've lost touch. She became too involved with me. She wanted to adopt me and take me out of the *favela* forever. She would send her Mercedes to the edge of the township and a messenger would come to the door, that I was to come and stay with her for a few days. I didn't have to take anything except myself. I had my own room in her mansion."

"What an opportunity!"

"My parents were scared I would become a target for kidnapping, so they broke off all contact."

"They were scared they would lose you." Shaun's delivery was pompous.

"Of course." Her face flushed and she looked annoyed.

"I realise there was that side to it as well."

"Does it make you angry?"

She shrugged. "There's no point in being upset. I understand my parent's decision. I love them very much."

"Are you still in touch with the rich auntie?"

"I haven't seen her for eight years, when my parents told her to stay away." She went quiet for a few seconds. "Her daughter went to the same school as me, but it was always the chauffeur who picked her up. But, as soon as Auntie knew she couldn't see me again, she came to the school. She made the chauffeur and her daughter stand outside, while I sat in the back of the Mercedes with her. She wept and held my hand and said one day she would explain everything to me. She gave me some money, and they dropped me off at the *favela*. I cried all the way home."

"You should go and see her next time you're back home."

"Maybe. She would be easy to find, her name is so unusual… Maria Josefina de Alencar, descended from Portuguese aristocracy."

Shaun sighed and thought for a few seconds. "So where did you belong back then, rich auntie's mansion or *favela*?"

"I'll always belong to the *favela*."

"How bad is it?"

"If you were to walk down the street in England and see a dead rat in the gutter, you would tremble with shock. In the *favela*, you can see a dead body and people will be stepping over it as though it's not there." A look of shock came over Shaun's face. "Oh… don't think we're bad people. We're honest and good. We watch out for one another, we care for our children and we know the true value of things in life and," she put Shaun's hand against her breast bone, "my heart is an open door. Feel." She gazed at him intensely.

93

He looked thoughtful and held his head down. "You make me feel so humble."

"Humble?"

"I feel a bit ashamed that I've had such a privileged life and I've never valued it… so, if you're born in the *favela*, how do you get out of it?"

"Most *favela* children have no opportunity for a good education so, to make it big, there are only three routes out: become a footballer, become a rap or hip hop singer, become a samba dancer."

"Four routes; become an escort girl."

Later, Shaun got dressed and made a move towards the door.

"Hang on." He looked at her with a surprised expression. "You say you're only in this for the money, but you haven't asked me for any."

"It's okay. You don't have to pay."

"But I want to pay. That's our contract."

"That's our contract." She mimicked him. "It's free to you."

"So really, I'm like a boyfriend then?" Shaun smiled, like he was suddenly very sure of himself, like when he made a conquest in a club.

"Don't get big headed." She slapped him on the arm, but only playfully. "Yes, you're my boyfriend and, from now on, phone me directly, and my real name is Pilar… Pilar Fernandes." She wrote her name and mobile down on a sticky note and gave it to him.

He thought about her a lot and arranged to see her one week later, when much the same thing happened. Again, they lay in bed talking, afterwards.

"When you come to Rio de Janeiro with me, or" she adopted a more formal tone like a tour rep making a presentation, "the *River of January* as the Portuguese named the bay when they first saw it in 1502… we will go to Ipanema Beach. It is silky white sand, and all the beautiful girls wear thongs and bikinis made of string. You will see lots of nice butts." She pulled open the sheets and showed him her backside, smiling and got him to slap her.

"I know a song about that." He sat up and sang:

Tall and tan and young and lovely
The girl from Ipanema goes walking
And when she passes, each one she passes goes "a–a–ah!"

Pilar had also sat up, and swayed to the music, like she was dancing. But then she pushed him over, back down onto the bed.

"I sing it better than you:"

Olha que coisa mais linda, Mais cheia de graça.
É ela a menina que vem e que passa,
num doce balanço a caminho do mar.

He felt some cramp in his stomach. He was getting scared; he didn't want to get hurt again.

"And we will take the cable car up to *Pão de Açúcar.* You know what it is?" she asked.

"You said sugar, so it's the Sugar Loaf Mountain. I saw James Bond fight Jaws there in the film Moonraker."

"And we will dance samba or tango in the *gafieiras,* they are the old fashioned Samba Halls."

Shaun had tried quite a few salsa classes, hoping to meet women. He could never quite get that wiggle of the hips. "Are you any good at those Latin American dances?"

"Am I any good? I was *rainha,* Carnival queen of our samba school."

"Couldn't you have done it as a profession then?"

"My body's too small. Shame isn't it? Because I'm really good."

She jumped out of bed and started dancing her way round the bedroom, a mix of samba and a kind of carnival shuffle.

"Come here." Shaun beckoned her to join him. "Hey you, steady on with the charm. I'm only made of flesh and blood."

"You're scared I will hurt you?" She had the knack of seeing into his soul. "I won't hurt you baby. Let me look after you." Shaun said nothing in reply. "I have a surprise for you this evening." She said it softly.

"Give it to me then." Shaun closed his eyes and held his hand out, a mischievous look on his face.

"I can't give it to you like that." She put her hand in his. "I've made some Brazilian food for you, if you feel like eating it and if you've nothing better to do."

"Just put it in front of me and see how quickly I eat it."

It was traditional Brazilian *Feijoada*, originally an African slave dish, a casserole of black beans, sausages, smoked pork and salt beef, served with rice. It was very filling, a little too heavy for Shaun, as an evening meal, but he liked the sentiment and Pilar's light, bubbly personality as they ate.

"It's lovely and very thoughtful of you." Shaun said as the meal came to an end. Then he said something very bold. He couldn't believe he was saying it. "I would like to reciprocate and invite you to a meal at my house."

"Oh! Thank you so much. Invitation accepted." She flung her arms round him and giggled.

The next week, Pilar made her way out East to Shaun's on the underground railway, which surprised her when it came over ground at Stratford, the 2012 Olympic complex lying on the left-hand side. Many passengers alighted at

Stratford and the carriage was noticeably emptier as it continued its journey eastwards. A young man and his girlfriend were sitting opposite Pilar, and he took out a cigarette and lit up.

"Excuse me. There's no smoking on this train." Pilar looked at him.

"It's my birthday. You don't mind me having a cigarette on my birthday, do you?" He stared at her with a satisfied, smug expression on his face, as if he knew she would not be able to counter his retort.

"But I want you to have many more birthdays. My father smoked all his life and now he has so many smoking-related illnesses, I may lose him soon. Don't you look at the information they give you on the packet? Do you think it can't happen to you?" She looked him straight in the eye.

The boy took a final puff and threw the cigarette on the floor, stubbing it out with his foot. He looked at Pilar, a bit puzzled at how this little girl had put him in his place. She smiled at him. He smiled back.

She carried on out to Shaun's station, which was in a leafy suburb of London, on the borders of Essex. He collected her and she was soon standing in front of his Georgian style mansion. He had already owned it when the Americans bought him out, but the sale of the company had allowed him to pay off the huge mortgage. The double front doors opened on to a large entrance hall, which had a spiral staircase that started on the right-hand side and curled up to the left. It was the most magnificent feature of the whole house.

"Wow." Pilar giggled, overcome with the unexpected grandeur of the interior. "Wow."

"And this is just the servants' entrance."

"My God." She grabbed his arm. "You are *muito rico*

(very rich); my boyfriend is *muito rico*! I didn't know. I had no way of knowing you had money. Are you a gangster?"

"Don't be silly. Whatever I have, I've worked very hard for. I'm a businessman."

After a tour of the house, they sat down to the meal Shaun had prepared.

"If you like *feijoada*, I thought you would like this… Shepherd's Pie. It's my mother's recipe."

"Smells good. How do you make it?"

"It's minced beef, onion, a gravy made with flour, thickening and stock cube, seasoned with salt and pepper, and when cooked add mashed potato on top and bake in the oven till brown."

She tried it. "Hmm. It's fantastic. It's so tasty." She ate it without saying too much, as though she didn't want anything to divide her attention. "Hmm, I feel so nourished, kind of satisfied deep inside."

"What do you mean?"

"How can I explain it? It's like when my mother feeds me. It's like, comforting." She got up and kissed Shaun.

"We have a saying in England: the way to a woman's heart is through her stomach."

She laughed. "You're kidding me." She pulled his head into her chest and kissed the top of his head. "I think it's meant to be the other way round."

Afterwards, they made love, and then they lay in each other's arms. Pilar took the palm of Shaun's hand and rubbed it.

"I put a mango here." She said it softly, like a mother to a child and put an imaginary mango in his hand. "I put a date here." She rubbed his wrist. "I put a banana here." She moved up to his elbow joint. "I put an orange here." She squeezed his upper arm. "Where have they gone?" She tickled Shaun under the arm. "They're here, aren't they?" She patted his stomach.

"Where did you learn that? You haven't got any children."

"That's what my grandmother used to do to me when I was small."

"Is she still alive?"

"She died when I was thirteen." Pilar looked sad, and her eyes started to water.

"I'm sorry to hear that. I can see she meant a lot to you because it still upsets you. What was she like?"

"She was the most beautiful person in the world. She was a spiritual healer and psychic. Even the rich people from downtown Rio would come into the *favela* to see her. That was how rich auntie came into our lives."

"Have you inherited your granny's gift?"

"You can see I have. I don't normally like to talk about it, in case it scares people."

"I had a psychic girlfriend once before, but she broke it off before we met… why should it scare people?"

Pilar looked at Shaun, like she was weighing up the situation. "Because often it's like she's here with me."

Shaun looked puzzled. "What, you mean you think about her a lot?"

"No, she talks to me from the spirit world."

"Yeah, right… so what does she say about the work you're doing?"

"She says I don't have to do it much longer." Her mobile rang at that moment. "Excuse me." She leant across to her handbag and took out her phone, sliding it open to take the call. It was obvious to Shaun that it was her agency. "No, I'm not working today… no, you can't make me take clients if I don't want them… I don't care how long ago they booked up… okay then, take my profile off your site,

99

I don't care…" Her face was flushed. She slid the phone shut and looked at Shaun. "I've just lost my job, my income." She started to laugh, which became hysterical after about thirty seconds, and which had turned into crying after one minute.

"You okay?"

"I've just sent all my money to Brazil. My apartment's so expensive. I can't pay my rent."

"Why don't you…" He hesitated.

"What?" she said in between her tears, which she was dabbing with a tissue.

Shaun looked at her for a while. He had been about to say, 'why don't you join another agency?' But he realised he didn't want to say that. He took a deep breath.

"What?" she repeated.

"Why don't you move in with me?"

She stopped crying and looked at him. "Are you serious?" He nodded to her. "Oh Shaun." She put her arms round him.

7

The Favela Girl settles in London

"Is this all of your stuff? Your puppy seems to have more paraphernalia than you."

It was a few days later and Shaun was standing in the living room of Pilar's luxury apartment, about to move her and her Chihuahua to his house. The dog, who she had grandiosely named Chimborazo Cotopaxi after South American volcanoes, was standing devotedly at her feet, looking up at her with an adoring expression.

"Of course my little darling has more than me." She picked Chimbo up and kissed him. "I've just a few clothes and shoes. The flat was fully furnished."

Shaun loaded her suitcase and Chimbo's boxes into the boot of the car and Pilar closed the door on her old life, posting the keys through the letterbox before walking away for good.

"That's all in the past now, okay?" said Shaun in a soothing tone as they drove off and with tacit agreement her former line of business was forgotten and not to be mentioned again.

She settled in and at last he had the live-in soul mate he craved. Up till then, the atmosphere of the house had been one of lonely emptiness, which always hit him when he came home from the pub. It was replaced with Brazilian music, cocktails, excited phone calls, dancing, fun and laughter. She played quite a lot of Caetano Veloso on the CD player, a singer-songwriter often called the Bob Dylan of Brazil.

"Kind of bland, don't you think? Isn't it all being sung on the same note?" Shaun sat on the sofa beside her in the living room. "Reminds me of João Gilberto."

"He was Caetano's inspiration when he started out."

"I wouldn't play an album that much, even if it was my all time favourite piece of music."

"He opens the door to my soul." She ignored Shaun's rebuff and placed her hand across her chest and half closed her eyes. "He's my hero. Such poetry when he sings of love and he writes songs about poverty, racism, homelessness, corruption. He cares about real people."

"I can't understand any of it."

"But I can teach you Portuguese. Come on…" She made Shaun repeat each line after her.

Eu sou Brasileiro – I am Brazilian

Voce é alto – You are tall

O céu está nublado – The sky is cloudy

Eu estou sentado – I am sitting down.

"From now on, we do half an hour every day and you must learn to say Rio de Janeiro the way we say it: HEE-oo dye Zhan-AY-ro."

Her big personality seemed to be present in every room of the house, whether she was there or not. It was only a few days after she had moved in, that he called her into his home office. A mad thought had overtaken him.

"I've been looking at properties in Rio." He pointed to the computer screen in front of him.

Pilar peered over Shaun's shoulder at the photo of a villa, taken in glorious sunshine, with a turquoise sea in the distance, stretching to the far horizon. "You want us to buy a holiday home in Rio?" She hugged him from behind.

"Well actually, I want to buy a home for your parents, like you had in mind when you came to London."

"Oh, you would do that for me?" She came and stood to the side of him. "You haven't known me very long." She looked at him surprised, like she was seeing him anew.

"I want you to be happy."

"That's so sweet of you." She put her arms round him and started kissing him.

Pilar's ecstasy lasted the rest of the day. They had a celebratory lunch in a bistro in the local high street and then they did the weekly shop. She danced to the piped music up and down the aisles of the supermarket, while Shaun focused on the shopping list and stopped their trolley at the fish counter.

"Do people from Río like fish?"

"I love fish." Pilar looked at the large display, laid out on ice. "Are you going to cook it for me?" She grinned.

"Can do. Do you like sea bass?"

He pointed to the silvery skinned fish, their eyes staring blankly out at him, their bodies cut open in several places, with pats of herb, lime and chilli butter protruding. Shaun knew this would make them tasty, without him having to do much work.

"Don't buy them. They're not fresh." She shook her head for emphasis.

"How do you know?" Shaun had a puzzled look on his face.

"I know everything." She gave him a little smile.

"Seriously, how do you know?"

"You tell the freshness of fish by the eyes. Look, the eyes are cloudy. That means the fish is old. The eyes should be clear. Blood on the gills is another good sign. The sea bream look okay. Take those."

"Okay, but I'll need to make a sauce to go with it. We

need white wine vinegar, double cream, butter and lemon."

"Sounds delicious." She squeezed his arm. "You're spoiling me!"

As they arrived back at the house, Pilar went in while Shaun put the car in the garage and got the shopping from the boot of the car. Immediately, she could hear a chinking of pans and utensils from the kitchen.

"Hello," she called out. "Who's there?"

She stealthily edged round the open door to the kitchen and looked. A small, middle-aged woman with blonde hair was standing at the worktop, pouring a packet of powder into a mixing jug. Pilar could see the packet read 'Cottage Pie'.

"Oh hello." The woman looked up. "Shaun told me about you. It's all so sudden. I've done your cleaning and now I'm making Shepherd's Pie for your dinner."

Pilar gave a little sigh of relief. "Hello… thank you so much. But Shaun likes his mother's recipe for Shepherd's Pie. We don't use a packet. We use flour, gravy thickening and a stock cube to make the gravy."

"Oh." The woman had a surprised look. "I didn't know that."

"No problem. I'm Pilar, by the way." She held out her hand for the woman to shake. "And you are?"

"Sylvia, Shaun's mother."

Pilar closed her eyes for a moment, as if taking in the situation. "Oh *Mamãe*." She went and hugged the lady. "I'm so sorry. Shaun didn't warn me you were coming. I think he's playing one of his jokes." Shaun came in at that moment, heavily laden with the shopping. "Shaun, why didn't you tell me I was going to meet your mother for the first time today?" Pilar scolded.

"It slipped my mind, sorry… Pilar, this is my mother and she cleans the house every week, does the ironing and makes a meal if she has time. If my father's around, he does the garden. How's that for a deal? Mum, this is Pilar."

"Yes, we've just met. She's beautiful, Shaun. You've found a nice girlfriend at last... now, you two out of the kitchen please, and let me carry on with this pie."

"Okay then, and you dine with us when it's ready," said Shaun, "and chat to Pilar a bit more."

Later, they sat and ate the meal together in the adjoining dining-room, by which time the smell of home cooking and rich gravy permeated the house.

"Hmm. It's delicious, Mum." Shaun was scoffing the Shepherd's Pie at considerable speed. "Everyone thinks their mother's a good cook, but mine really is."

"So what was Shaun like when he was young?" Pilar looked to Shaun's mother.

"I didn't know I had him really. He would be reading or playing in the garden, absorbed in himself."

"So he was an introvert?"

"Maybe. But he was athletic. When he was older, he was out on his bike or on his skateboard a lot of the time... and as a teenager, he reached black belt with his karate. But he was very picky who he was friends with. He didn't have many friends, through choice, and he always kept his own counsel. You couldn't tell him what to do."

"What was he like as a baby?" Pilar continued.

"This is getting a bit embarrassing," Shaun interrupted.

"He slept most of the time. But when he was first born, I had postnatal depression for a few months. He would cry and I knew I should pick him up, but I couldn't bring myself to. I knew it was wrong of me, but I couldn't help it. He would just cry and cry."

"Oh no! Poor Shaun! That's why I have to give him so much love."

"You should marry this girl, Shaun. Listen to your

mother and remember I'm waiting for some grandchildren. It doesn't look like your sister's going to produce any… and I want your father to meet her. He's out on a men's day with the church today. I'm going to send your sister round as well, to take some photos of you both. You make a nice couple." She looked at Pilar. "My daughter's a professional photographer, got her own studio."

After the main course, Shaun's mother served an apple pie, which she had prepared at her own home, and Shaun made some custard, which he brought to the table in a jug.

"What happened when then apple pie got arrested?… he got put in custody." Shaun looked for a reaction, but the women ignored him.

"Oh *Mamãe*." Pilar had taken a mouthful of the pie. "You're such a good cook. You must teach Shaun more of your recipes."

"That's right. You make him help around the house, not like his father, who doesn't lift a finger."

Shaun muttered, "You can learn them too," but the women didn't seem to hear him.

The next morning, Pilar opened the door to a middle-aged man, who looked a lot like Shaun, but older, taller and more muscular.

"Hello, my wife's sent me round to meet you." He was wearing a baseball cap and old clothes. "I'm Tony, Shaun's father. I tend the garden once a week."

"Oh, *Papai*." Pilar held out her arms for a hug.

Tony kissed her quite passionately on both cheeks and squeezed her hips as he did it. Then he rubbed her butt a few times, finishing off with a slap. It was done in such a spontaneous, natural way that it took a while for her to register what had happened.

"Would you like a drink, *Papai*?" She walked through to the kitchen with Tony following.

"Thanks, but let me earn it first. You can make me one later." He hovered at the back door, leading to the garden, as if he wanted to hang round her for a while. "So, how do you like London? Are you missing Brazil?"

"Well, the sea and sunshine I miss, yes, but London is very nice also, and Shaun is a wonderful man."

"You think so?" He said it as though he was surprised and didn't believe it. He was standing quite close to her and staring into her eyes. Suddenly, he was reminding her of some of the middle-aged men who had been her clients when she was working as an escort.

"Yes, I do. Don't you?" She flushed slightly and frowned, feeling awkward with the situation, but Tony was not at all put off and just stood staring.

"You must come round to a dinner party, soon."

"Thank you. We'd love that and your wife is such a good cook."

Later, when Tony had gone, Pilar and Shaun were eating the sea bream together at the kitchen table.

"Hmm… it's delicious, Shaun. Listen… "

"I'm listening."

"Your father, was he a bit of a lady's man in his time?"

"Why do you ask?"

"He just seemed a bit… forward, for an English man, a bit cheeky, quite tactile."

Shaun nodded. "Oh, he was a terror in his time a sheep in wolf's clothing nowadays though. When I was young, he was always having affairs. My mother says he would take me out in his car to meet his mistresses, but I don't remember. I was too small."

"Where did he find the women?"

"He had a large business. Often he would have an affair with his secretary, but sometimes he would take one of the girls from the office or the factory."

107

"So that was the business you sold?"

"No, I did my own thing, but he lent me the money to get started. Banks only lend you money if you've already got it."

"But didn't his affairs hurt your mother?"

"Yes, of course, terribly."

"Why didn't she leave him?"

"Nowhere to go, I suppose. Lots of women stay in unhappy marriages. It's such an upheaval to leave, almost certainly a downshift in lifestyle."

"You look like him. Are you like him in your ways?"

"I've never two timed a girlfriend, never ever." Shaun sounded annoyed. "I'm a very loyal person. Don't blame me for my father's behaviour."

"Oh, Shaun. I'm sorry." She put her arms round him. "Of course, I trust you." She kissed him. "Your father slapped my bum, that's all." She said it thoughtfully, as though reluctant to mention it.

"You should have slapped him back."

"No, he would have enjoyed it."

* * *

Later that week, Shaun told Pilar they were on a mystery tour as they drove into the West End of London, and queued to get into a nightclub. From the outside, it was just an ordinary glass building with frosted windows, except that it had the name Guanabara written above it, which Pilar knew was the indigenous Indian name for the bay of Rio. She had heard about it, a place where Brazilians in London liked to meet up, but she gasped as she entered the main auditorium.

"It's Rio. They've made Rio in the middle of London."

The floor had been copied from the patterned swells of black and white marble of Copacabana beach and a panoramic backdrop created the bay of Rio with Ipanema beach and the hillside *favela* rising behind. The Sugar Loaf Mountain lay to one side.

"It's so clever, what they've done." Pilar laughed and gave Shaun a squeeze.

They went over to the bar and ordered two C*aipirinhas*, a citrus-infused cocktail made with *cachaça*, (a spirit made from sugar cane), fresh lime, sugar and cracked ice. The bar staff were Brazilian and Pilar chatted to them excitedly in Portuguese.

"I never take sugar in anything," Shaun said when she turned her attention back to him, handing him his drink. "It's my number one health rule. I'm only consuming this for your sake."

"The Africans were brought to Brazil to work the sugar plantations. Now fifty per cent of Brazilians have some African blood. You could say Brazil is built on sugar. Drink it and tell me how you feel afterwards. Tourists to Brazil sometimes find it too strong. They prefer *Caipiroskas*, where vodka is substituted for the *cachaça*."

Shaun took a sniff of his cocktail. "Hmm, quite a floral smell," he muttered.

At that moment, the distant sound of carnival drums became apparent, getting louder and louder over a few minutes, until the doors from the entrance lobby flew open and ten female carnival dancers, wearing skimpy costumes and elaborate headdresses, entered, edging their way forward with the carnival step, wiggling their hips and butts and waving their arms. They were followed by about thirty drummers, wearing green and yellow T-shirts and white trousers, with white Panama fedoras on their heads. It was a formidable sound, very loud and immediate, and such a definite, assured rhythm.

"Oh, that is so African; the whole thing is completely

African." Shaun turned to Pilar to find she was in a state of shock, with tears welling in her eyes. "What's wrong?"

She didn't answer, but the tears came more and more until she was sobbing uncontrollably. Shaun took her over to one corner out of the way and made her sit down on a leather sofa, but it was like the sluice gates had been opened and a force of nature so strong had been released, it could not be stemmed. She cried for a quarter of an hour, while Shaun sat with her, feeling helpless. One of the Brazilian girls came round collecting glasses and spent five minutes with Pilar talking to her in Portuguese.

"*Todos estão na mesma situação... Não se preocupe, as pessoàs estão felizes...Você toma outra bebida?*" (We're all in the same position. Don't worry, people are happy. You want another drink?)

In the end, her tears started to subside. Shaun finally broke the silence.

"I'm sorry, Pilar, I thought you'd really like it here."

"I didn't realise," her voice was shaking with emotion, "how much I missed my family and Brazil. I miss them so much, my parents, my sisters, my friends." She continued to cry.

"Maybe you should go back for a holiday."

"No," she shook her head. "If I go back, I may never return, and I don't want to lose what we've got." She grabbed Shaun's arm.

She cheered up after an hour or two, and they finished the evening with some dancing. As they left the club, the waitress who had been comforting Pilar pressed a note into her hand, telling Pilar to phone.

"It was an emotional catharsis. It was very good for you, like a cleansing of the soul," said Shaun as they drove home.

"You're right. I feel great. I feel brand new."

"Hmm. I wouldn't mind feeling brand new." Shaun looked at her, envious that he could not be more open with his feelings.

* * *

"Look at my finger." The voice was high-pitched and sugary, almost like a child's. "Wherever I put my finger, you look... but don't angle your head too much, Shaun. Move your eyes, but not your head so much." Shaun and Pilar was sitting side by side in the bay window of their living room, in the middle of a makeshift photographic studio set up by Shaun's sister, Olivia. Every few seconds she was clicking a trigger attached by a cable to the camera. "That's it. Just relax. We want natural poses. I'm only going to use the best of these."

Shaun was wearing a blue shirt and grey trousers. Pilar had a cerise lace top, revealing her midriff, and a short black skirt. Her glossy hair came down to her breasts. Olivia kept snapping while she chatted.

"You two are a very attractive couple. Where did you meet?"

"Internet dating site." Shaun was always circumspect on this topic.

Sensing he had become tense, Pilar pulled her hair right back in a bun, which she tied with a band.

"Wow!" Olivia gasped. "You have to be really beautiful to still look good, with all your hair scraped back like that... Shaun, can I take some shots of Pilar on her own?"

"Of course. If Pilar is willing."

Olivia started snapping Pilar, who seemed to fall very easily into the role of model, looking this way, then that and putting different expressions on her face each time.

"You've done this before, haven't you? I can always tell when someone has worked with another professional."

"Not really." Pilar was relaxed, but Shaun looked tense. "I think I'm just a natural."

"No." Olivia stopped snapping. "I've been a photographer for ten years. You've definitely worked before on a professional shoot."

"It's probably being Brazilian. We all pose and show off on Ipanema beach, like we're supermodels even if we're not."

"Not Copacabana, then. Barry Manilow got it wrong?" Olivia sniggered.

"Copacabana's awful; the water's like sewage. Ipanema has class."

"Do you miss Brazil?" Olivia put the trigger down, as if she found this topic engaging and she had had enough of photography.

"For quite a few things, yes."

"What sort of things?"

"You get invited to some really nice parties, with *churrascos*, charcoal barbecues, with delicious meat. The weather is a lot sunnier, although it can be sweltering in the summer. People are much more passionate… they hug and kiss you."

"Hmm! I'd like to visit. Are there any bad things?"

"Rio is more dangerous than London. There's always a feeling that violence isn't far away, with lots of guns… traffic is a nightmare… and I think there's a lot of pressure on older women to stay looking young and sexy. If a woman has grey hair, she has to dye it. If she's rich, she might get liposuction or a bum lift, or a tummy tuck. They even die getting it done… and it's a very noisy city. Everything is very loud; everyone talks very loudly."

"It sounds as though there are some things you like about London."

"Of course. It feels much safer, more civilised here. I like the way people tell you the truth. In Brazil, they tell you what you want to hear. It doesn't seem to matter that they can't do what they promised, or they don't really know the answer to something. But Shaun is what I really like about London…" She reached across to touch him.

Olivia delivered some prints back to Shaun a day later. They had come out in rich, dark colours, classic shots capturing a couple at the height of their good looks and with a future full of promise ahead of them. Shaun made an album of them and framed a few, displaying one in the entrance hall and one on the mantelpiece in the living room, making it seem like they were a married couple. Pilar e-mailed some of them back to Brazil and put them on Facebook.

* * *

A few days later, Shaun had been out alone and returned to the house to find Pilar with a friend in the kitchen. Shaun recognized her immediately. It was Luisa, the Brazilian waitress from Guanabara, who had comforted Pilar when she was crying. Pilar seemed distant, in a trance, with a kind of atmospheric haze round her, like when heat shimmers in a desert. The kitchen table was covered with a brown velvet cloth, on which was placed a crystal ball in the centre and a pack of Tarot cards spread out like a fan.

"Sorry," Shaun whispered. "I'll get out of the way." With that, he withdrew to his home office.

Half an hour later, the girls opened the door of his study to find him sitting at the computer.

"Shaun." Pilar gave him a hug. "Sorry about that. I should have warned you."

"No problem. Hi Luisa. So you came for a séance?"

"Hi Shaun. She's brilliant."

"You didn't tell me you read the Tarot cards." Shaun looked at Pilar.

"My grandmother taught me. I still use her cards, tablecloth and crystal ball."

"Well, how about giving me a reading, while you're all set up? Luisa, you can play on the computer here for half an hour?"

"Sure. I can look at my e-mails."

Shaun and Pilar sat down opposite each other at the kitchen table.

"Did you give Luisa a good reading?"

"I don't know. I go into a trance. I don't remember one word of what I've said, afterwards. Even if I did, I couldn't tell you... client confidentiality."

Pilar was sitting with her back to a work surface and Shaun suddenly noticed a photo, in a frame, placed behind her head. It was an old lady with a wrinkly face and very piercing eyes. It startled him and gave him instant goose bumps.

"Wow! Who's that? She made me shiver. She looks a bit austere."

"That's my granny. She's my spirit guide during the reading."

"Spirit guide?"

"She's my helper in the spirit world, communicates with other spirits for me. If you ever find me sitting quietly, whispering, don't mind. I'm just talking to Granny."

"Right... okay." Shaun sounded hesitant. "If you're so professional at this, couldn't you have made your money doing this, instead of what you did when I met you?"

"And would you have come to see me doing this? Would we have ever met?"

Shaun nodded. "No. You're right. I believe in making your own fate. That's why my business was so successful."

"Tell me," she leant back in the seat, as if aware she was digressing from the Tarot reading, "how did you get to be so determined and focused? How did you make all this wealth by yourself and so young?"

"Well I asked God to give me a clear sign that he existed, by making a large deposit into my bank account."

"Don't joke about God, Shaun." Pilar stared at him.

He held her gaze for a few seconds, "You're serious, aren't you?" He frowned.

"I'm very serious, Shaun." She was giving him a hard look.

"I'm sorry." Shaun held his head down.

"Do you go to church, Shaun? You don't seem to."

"I'm a hatch, match and despatch church goer."

She gave him a haughty look, while she worked it out. "Christenings, marriages, funerals. I thought as much." She nodded. "Well, we're going to start going to church every Sunday... so how did you make all this wealth by yourself?" She repeated her question.

"Well," he gave a big sigh, as though he needed think time, "I may have been born that way. But I do remember changing a lot at the age of sixteen. I saw a film that transformed me. I don't know why it had such a powerful effect."

"What film?"

"*La Strada*, by Fellini."

"I've seen it."

"How can you have seen it? A girl from the *favela*? How can you have seen an obscure art house film like that?"

"Don't get shitty with me, Shaun, just because I've had a good education." She flushed. "I've seen it, okay? It won an Oscar. Anthony Quinn plays the strongman. It's a sad film. They're like *favela* people, living on *La Strada*, the road, existing hand to mouth."

"I know what *La Strada* means," he snapped. Then he took a deep breath and sighed. "I'm sorry. You have seen it. Yes, it's very sad. It made me cry and I hadn't cried since I was about three years old. It made me realise, make your own destiny or others will make it for you... so are we having our first argument?"

"No, we're just talking, like couples do. Let me give you your reading now. Luisa is waiting on her own."

Pilar again went into a trance, with a kind of aura round her head, like when he'd first walked in on them. He didn't take much notice of what she said, he was more absorbing her ambience. In her normal state, she came over as passionate, energetic and fearless. It was as though he was now seeing a deeper level of her. She seemed very gentle, calm, as she turned over the cards and looked at them. Then she just sat patiently, motionless, with time suspended, as she waited for the clairvoyance to come through. He was thinking how much he adored her, even her feistiness, and how lucky he was to have found her, when suddenly she turned over a card that loomed out from all the others on the table. It was the Queen of Swords, a stern looking lady sitting on a throne, holding a long, large sword. Shaun was not superstitious, but he felt nervous at the sight of it. Pilar spoke immediately.

"You think you have your life sorted out, but you haven't. An aggressive woman is coming, a masculine energy, manipulative, selfish and self serving. She will wreak havoc in your world. She will try and destroy all that you hold dear. She will bring death and destruction in her wake."

He shuddered.

The séance continued and after about half an hour, Pilar suddenly awoke from her trance.

"Was that good? Do you have any questions?" It was the old Pilar he knew back in the room.

"It was wonderful. You look so attractive when you give a reading, you can give me a reading any time you like… do you know what you said to me?"

"No idea. It's my granny speaking, not me."

* * *

Shaun soon forgot the whole thing, although after that Granny's photo took pride of place next to their own on the living room mantelpiece and he would sometimes find her sitting on the sofa with eyes closed, quietly whispering to herself. 'Just talking to Granny,' she would say, when she came round.

It was a few days later.

"Pilar, get your bikini, flip-flops, and some towels, and I have a surprise for you."

"Oh, we're going to a beach party at Guanabara!" She screwed her face up and closed her eyes. "I'm so excited." She jumped up and down. "I won't get upset this time."

"No, it's not that, but you will feel brand new again, like last week."

"So what is it?"

"We're going to some Russian baths."

"I've heard of Turkish baths, but not Russian."

"Turkish baths use dry heat. Russian baths use steam. It's a steam room. The Jews brought them to London in the 1890s when they fled persecution in Russia. It's how they kept clean."

"You think I'm dirty?"

"You'll see. It's a fabulous experience. Think of it as a pamper session."

Half an hour's drive later, they were standing in the vapour suite in the East End of London. Wearing just their swimsuits and with their locker keys round their wrists, they slipped through the polythene strips hanging from the steam room doorway and were in a white tiled room, with benches on all sides. The steam hit their nostrils immediately and reduced visibility to an arm's length. It hissed out from beneath the benches with a low rumble, like waves crashing on a stony beach. The room smelt of a mixture of stagnant water and soap.

"Hmm." Pilar took a deep breath through her nose. "It's nice. I like it."

Shaun grinned. "I've arranged for you to have a traditional *schmeiss* bath with Ritchie."

Pilar looked uncertain. "What's that?"

"You'll like it. Here he is. Ritchie, this is Pilar." Shaun introduced them through the steam. "Ritchie is the *schmeiss* master. He can do ten people, one after the other."

The stocky, middle aged man with long black hair smiled at Pilar and shook her hand. He reminded her of a dashing Spanish bullfighter, brave and strong. "Let me hose you with some cold water before we start."

Ritchie sprinkled her with water from a shower fitting on the wall. She shuddered with the contrast between the steam and the icy water, but it was refreshing. She lay down on her front on the bench and, standing above her, Ritchie twirled the *schmeiss*, a yellow raffia brush, full of hot soapsuds, the handle of the brush like the head of a squid and the long strands of the brush like the squid's tentacles. When her back was sufficiently lathered, he suddenly smashed it down at the base of her spine and started moving it up her body, leaning in to create a substantial pressure. It combined the relaxation of a traditional massage, with the heat of the soapsuds and the abrasive feel of the raffia against the pores of the skin. All her tension dropped away. Ritchie did her back, neck, arms and legs, and then she turned over and he did her front.

"How was that, Pilar?" he asked ten minutes later, as the massage came to an end.

"That was lovely. Thank you, Ritchie."

"Any time. Just ask. But we're not quite finished yet. Sit up, with your back against the wall."

She was still covered in soapsuds and sat against the white tiled wall, as instructed.

"ONE!" Ritchie boomed, pouring a bucket of icy cold water over Pilar's head. It seemed to be a long time emptying as it passed across her face and the cold water on her chest took her breath away. She didn't like it, but started to recover as she gasped for air.

She could hear Shaun chuckling. "You've had your fun. Now you take your punishment."

"TWO!" Before she could tell him to stop, Ritchie delivered a second bucket of cold water, rather more slowly. It reminded her of swimming off Ipanema beach in the winter, when a storm had brought in cold water and big, rough waves from the Atlantic and the sea was so fresh and bracing that only the European tourists would swim. She again gasped for air, but Ritchie didn't notice.

"THREE!" With the third bucket, the water seemed to be pouring over her head for a very long time, during which she couldn't breathe and the iciness seemed to momentarily paralyse her lungs. It was like drowning, and she suddenly had a vision of herself trapped under the water off Ipanema beach, drowned. Ritchie put the empty bucket down and walked out of the steam room to cool off.

"Did you like that? Shaun asked, as Pilar came to sit beside him.

"Not the buckets of water at the end. I hated them."

"But the contrast of hot and cold is very good for the skin. It keeps it young."

"I hated the third bucket. It was like someone was treading on my grave. I felt like I was drowning. Ughh! What a horrible way to die."

At that moment, another man with short grey hair came into the room. He was muscular, but wiry at the same time. He looked alert and fit, like he could jump into action at any moment.

"Hi Freddie," Shaun greeted the man.

"Hi Shaun. Who's the young lady with you today? Haven't got friends outside of us lot, have you?" Freddie's voice was three times as loud as most people's. He was like a London cockney barrow boy, shouting his wares.

"This is Pilar, my girlfriend."

"Your girlfriend? What's she doing with you? You're no David Beckham, mate."

"He's Beckham to me." Pilar said.

"You're a very sweet girl. Much too good for Shaun."

Shaun laughed.

"I'm happy with him," Pilar continued.

Freddie suddenly smiled. "Nice to meet you, Pilar," and with that he walked back out.

"Who was that rude man, Shaun? Was he being serious?"

"He's always confrontational. I was quite scared of him when I first met him. He's okay when you know him. He's called Freddie the forklift. He has a yard where he buys and sells forklift trucks."

"He seems a hard man"

"His father worked for the Kray twins. They were the toughest London gangsters ever. You've probably seen the film with the Kemp brothers." Pilar nodded and Shaun continued. "I wouldn't like to be on the wrong side of Freddie. I know he's been in and out of prison quite a bit. He'd be useful if you had any security issues."

They drove home two hours later. Pilar's face looked

fresh and toned, and her eyes were sparkling. Shaun looked at her.

"So do you feel brand new again? The buckets of icy water did you good."

"It was great. Let's do it every week, but without the cold water."

"See, London's not so bad."

They lay in bed that night, having made love.

"Weren't you annoyed at what Freddie the forklift said to you?"

"No, I don't take men's banter seriously... just a little *badinage*."

"But I think women have hurt you in the past, haven't they?" She had softened her voice and was looking up at the ceiling and she said it.

"Yes, I think women can easily hurt me."

"I don't think they meant to hurt you. You don't show your feelings, much. They don't know where they stand with you."

"Yes, you're right. What about you? Does it matter to you?"

"Maybe. But I can see inside you. I can see that really, you care."

* * *

They were sitting at the kitchen table. Pilar was eating a typical Brazilian breakfast of fruit salad with fresh home made yogurt, followed by toast and black coffee, and Shaun was eating an English breakfast of porridge, followed by tea with milk.

"I've been thinking, why don't we start a business connected with Brazil? I'm much too young to do nothing and we'll get bored with each other's company, if we don't have something else to occupy ourselves."

"Well… " Pilar was crunching her way through a piece of toast and looked at him sideways, hesitant, as though he was giving her indigestion and spoiling her life of luxury. "I suppose, theoretically, you might be right. But it's hard to do things when you don't have to. You just think, what's the point?" She took another bite of toast, as if that was the end of the matter.

"But you have to do something in life. Even Shakespeare said it, centuries ago: 'If all the year were playing holidays, to sport would be as tedious as to work.'"

"Henry IV, Part one."

"Yes." Shaun ignored her tangential comment. "What can we do connected with Brazil? Could I import Brazilian artefacts or products? I know all about importing."

"Maybe samba and carnival instruments would be good."

"I'll take a look on the Internet. What else can we do? Could we arrange travel tours?"

"But I can just do Tarot card readings."

"No. What can we do together, maybe related to Brazil? We're a team now."

"Okay. I could teach salsa and samba. I'm a really good dancer, and I enjoy it."

"Wow! That would be brilliant. I can do all the administration and marketing, keep the books and drive you there and back. Let me see if I can get you some classes set up."

"Okay. Let's see if London is ready for me." Pilar laughed and shimmied her shoulders.

It only took a few weeks to get Pilar's salsa classes started, with Shaun buying her some sound equipment, setting up the venues and doing the advertising. He arranged for her to teach samba, salsa, merengue and lambada in dance studios, halls, and rooms above pubs, and it was just one month after she had given the first lesson, that Shaun was handing her a glass of champagne.

"We're showing a reasonable profit after only one month's trading. Carry on like this and I'll have another business empire to sell off."

"We, Shaun, we."

"Of course, we."

"*Saude!*" (to your health). She chinked her glass to his. "I'll be a millionaire soon, like you. My granny always said I would be, multi, multi."

"Well, you think you're going to get somewhere. Let's see."

She glared at him. "Sometimes your little jokes aren't appreciated, Shaun."

8

London has its Dark Side

It was five weeks since she had given her first salsa lesson, and Pilar arrived for an afternoon class in a spacious community hall, where she could divide the group into two, if necessary. Shaun had advertised for beginners to start that day, but Pilar wasn't expecting that many, as it was the evening classes, after work, that attracted the large numbers. Shaun had dropped her off early and she had set up her music system, which was a speaker on a trolley with a slot for her iPod. Fabiano arrived soon after, a scruffy looking Afro Brazilian, whose jeans always looked like they were about to fall down. He helped Pilar with the teaching, although he wasn't that good a dancer, but she needed him to demonstrate the turns and he did at least always show up.

Pilar looked at Fabiano. "When we're near enough ready to start, five minutes before, we'll demonstrate the salsa, to give the beginners a bit of inspiration."

"So many of them drop away after the first week or two."

"There's nothing we can do about that. We cast our net wide, and the little fish swim out. Be positive."

Pilar was wearing a short black skirt, black high-heeled shoes and a short, white blouse that exposed her midriff. Her long hair fell on to her shoulders and she was wearing red lipstick. She looked every inch a salsa teacher. People drifted in and soon there were about twenty new people in the room in addition to the regulars. When they were ready to begin, Pilar put some music on and demonstrated how the salsa should be danced, her movements precise and perfectly executed, with Fabiano as her relaxed and rather sloppy partner. He always seemed slightly behind the beat to her. She stopped the track after about five minutes.

"Welcome everybody. Can all the improvers go down that end of the hall," she gestured to the far side, "and Fabiano will work with you. We'll come back together as one group towards the end of the session." The regulars moved off and she stood in front of the beginners. "I'm Pilar and we're going to learn the basic step of salsa today. Salsa originated in Cuba and Puerto Rico amongst the Spanish community, and you may know salsa as a spicy sauce, and I think you can see that it's also a very hot dance." She scanned the group as she spoke and noticed a white boy, in his early twenties, quite tall, wearing a baggy T-shirt, tracksuit bottoms and trainers, who was staring very intently at her. When she held his gaze, he looked away. "Now I'd like you to stand in two lines and as we progress with the teaching, I'll from time to time ask the line at the front to go to the back, so that I can get a good look at what all of you are doing." They arranged themselves into lines and Pilar continued. "I'm going to show you the basic step of salsa. To start with, I'll face you as I do it."

She stepped forward on her left foot, balanced her weight back on the right foot, then returned the left foot to its start position, and gave a wiggle of the hips together with a shimmy of the shoulders. She then did it in reverse, stepping back on the right foot, balancing her weight on the front foot and then returning the right foot to its start position, again doing the wiggle of the hips and shimmy of the shoulders.

"So this is the forward basic and the backwards basic and the two together make the basic step." She repeated the movements, this time counting, "one, two, three, rest; five, six, seven, rest. Quick, quick, slow; quick, quick, slow… now you copy me." She turned to face the same direction as them and they repeated the step over and over. "So now I'll put some music on and I'll start you off with the step, but then I'll come round and see how you're doing."

She walked around, like a conscientious teacher and every time she looked at the street boy he was staring at her intently, but he looked immediately away with a guilty expression, when her eyes met his. She hadn't noticed that while she was helping other students, he had been sneakily taking photos of her on his phone.

The session went off okay, and afterwards Fabiano and Pilar took the money from everyone and packed up the sound equipment. Most of the students had by this time left, but Pilar noticed the street boy hanging around in a far corner. Pilar gave Fabiano his cut of the money and put her jacket on.

"See you tomorrow," she said to Fabiano, as she walked out, pulling her speaker on its trolley, behind her.

She stood on the pavement outside the hall, where Shaun would normally pick her up.

"Looks like your taxi's not arrived." It was the street boy, standing quite close to her. His words came out awkwardly, like someone who wasn't confident talking to beautiful women.

"My boyfriend picks me up. He's usually here by now."

His face became tense. "Oh, right," he blurted.

"He'll be here in a minute." Pilar could see the street boy

126

had an erection, protruding on the inside of his tracksuit bottoms. "What's your name and where do you work?" She looked at him straight faced as she said it, like a policewoman asking for ID.

"Jay. I don't have a job," he mumbled.

"What does the J stand for?"

"I'm just Jay."

"Look, there's my boyfriend now. You'd better go."

Shaun pulled up in the car alongside them. Pilar kissed Shaun as he came round to the boot of the car to stow her sound equipment. She got in and did not look back. She didn't think any more of it, but told Shaun off for being late.

The very next salsa class Pilar taught was an evening one, in the upper room of a pub. She was surprised to see Jay there.

"Hello." She went over to him. "Is this time more convenient for you?" she enquired, not smiling.

"I wanted to see you again." His manner was more confident than before. It was as though he was assuming there was a familiarity, a connection between them, like he had been fantasising over her.

Pilar walked away with no comment. After the session, Jay loitered in the room, and then walked down the stairs behind her as she made her way out.

"Want a drink in the bar?" His manner was still bold.

"My boyfriend's picking me up." Pilar didn't look at him.

"I'm rock hard."

"Don't be silly."

"I know about you."

Pilar stopped, halfway down the stairs, rested her sound equipment on the step and looked back at him. "What do you know?"

"You're a prostitute."

"I'm a salsa teacher."

"I saw you on the Internet."

"It couldn't have been me." She didn't miss a beat. "I've never been on the Internet. I have a very typical South American look. You're mistaken."

"No. It was you. I recognize your face… and your big butt."

"Oh!" She smiled and looked relaxed suddenly. "All South American women have big butts. We are famous for the *bunda*. We're like Jennifer Lopez. Excuse me." She turned away, picked up her sound equipment and started to carry on down the stairs.

He stood thinking for a while, like he was working something out. "Aah!" He gave a big grin of sudden enlightenment. "No they don't. You're kidding me."

"Have you been to South America, sweetheart?" She stopped again and looked back up the stairs at him.

"I've never been out of England. I don't even have a passport."

"Well you should visit. Then you would know more what you're talking about."

Pilar carried on down the stairs, hoping her air of adult authority mixed with charm had put an end to the matter. She didn't mention it to Shaun.

After that, Jay started turning up to all her sessions, till one day he turned up at the house. Shaun's car was not in the driveway, so Jay maybe knew there was a chance Pilar was on her own. He knocked and Pilar answered the door. Her mouth dropped open in surprise.

"What do YOU want?" Her voice was raised and angry.

Jay smiled and pulled down his tracksuit bottoms, took his erect penis out from his underpants and started masturbating. She slammed the door shut and ran for her camera, but when she returned to the bay window by the front door, he had gone. She left the camera on the windowsill, in case he returned.

That afternoon, when Shaun came home, she let him settle in before broaching the subject.

"Shaun, could one of my dance class students find out where I live?"

"Potentially, if they're clever and they've got connections." He was reading the newspaper and didn't look up as he said it.

"How?"

"Well, for example," he stopped reading and looked at her, "if they knew I was your boyfriend, they could take my car registration number when I pick you up, and if they know a private clamping contractor, they can get them to apply to the vehicle licensing authority for the car owner's address." He looked concerned suddenly. "Is there a problem?"

"No." She sounded hesitant. "Just wondered."

"You sure?" Shaun frowned. "You'll let me know if you need anything? I realise you're a long way from home and your support group, but you've got me instead."

"Thank you." She came to sit on the arm of his chair and rested her hand on his neck, giving him a gentle massage.

He took her free hand and looked her in the eye. "You realise how much I love you? Am I embarrassing you?"

"No. But you might make me cry."

* * *

The next day, Pilar got up and went downstairs to make a drink. She picked up a letter that was on the doormat. It felt squidgy, as if there was something soft inside, like the sachets of hair shampoo that come as free samples in women's magazines. It was too early for the normal postman's delivery, and the envelope had no stamp and said just one word, 'PILAR' in handwritten letters. She opened it and took out a little scrap of paper, on which was scrawled a poem:

I'll do you hard,
I'll do you good
I'll pump you
With my solid wood

She could see a condom in the envelope, tied in a knot at the top, to hold in a few teaspoonfuls of white fluid.

She pulled a face. "Ughh! That's disgusting." She opened the front door and threw the whole lot into the wheelie bin and then went to have a shower to wash off the dirtiness she felt. But the notes became a regular thing, and Jay sometimes knocked on the door, but Pilar always looked to see who it was and never answered him.

A few weeks had passed and it was a sunny day, late morning, and Pilar was sunbathing in a secluded spot in the back garden, lying on a lounger and listening to her iPod. Jay arrived outside on the quiet, spacious road. Shaun had left the garage door open, which meant Jay could see that the car was gone and guess that Pilar might be alone in the house. He moved the wheelie bin, which was standing in the front garden, to the side gate. He climbed up on the bin, then over the gate, and stealthily jumped down into the alley, which led to the back garden. He tiptoed forward along the side of the house and peeped round the corner.

The garden was a lush green with grass, shrubs and trees, lovingly maintained and watered by Shaun's father. In a secluded corner, Jay could see Pilar, completely naked, lying back with her eyes closed, soaking up the sun while listening to music. Her yellow bikini was hanging over the top end of the lounger. It seemed to Jay that he had dropped into a paradise, so different from the grey, concrete council estate where he lived. It reminded him of the settings for the porno films he liked to watch on the Internet, the ones shot in Miami or Los Angeles in poolside landscaped gardens. His heartbeat quickened and his face flushed as he removed all his clothes. It felt good to be naked, like Pilar, and he started masturbating while looking at her. He imagined they were connected in their nakedness, like they were in a porno film together. He slowly made his way across the garden to her and reached a frenzy of excitement as he stood above her. He started to pant.

Pilar had floated off to Ipanema beach listening to her playlist but suddenly came back to reality with what seemed to be heavy blobs of warm rain falling on her face and breasts, like the first drops of a monsoon. She opened her eyes.

"Aaghh!" She screamed. "Get out!" She jumped up off the lounger. "I'm calling the police."

She ran inside, still naked, locking the back door behind her. Breathing heavily with shock, she got some kitchen towel and wet wipes and started cleaning herself up. Then she put some clothes on and went to the kitchen to peep out of the window into the back garden. There was no sign of Jay. She entered the living room and looked out of the bay window onto the front garden. At that moment, Jay, fully clothed, jumped down from the side gate and raced down the road. Pilar could see her yellow bikini strap spilling out from his jeans.

She sat on the sofa for some time, thinking and biting her lip. She decided not to phone the police, but realised the time had come to tell Shaun. He was back later that afternoon.

"Look, Pilar," he called her to his computer. "I've found a brilliant set of samba instruments, I can import from Brazil. I've exchanged e-mails with the company, and it's looking good. I think they'll sell really well, because a music teacher can get an instrument for everyone in the class when they buy the thirty piece set."

Shaun made her look at the whole range of instruments, comprised of the *surdo* (samba bass drum), the *repenique* (side drum), the *malacacheta* (snare drum), the *timba* (conical, African style drum), the *tamborim* (tambourine) and the *pandeiro* (small tambourine).

"Hmm. That's great, Shaun." Pilar seemed to be viewing it from a distance, down a tunnel, and had a flat tone in her voice.

"You okay?"

"Shaun, I've got a problem."

"I knew something was wrong. You haven't been yourself lately."

"Some guy from my salsa class is bothering me."

They sat down in the living room, and she told him the story of Jay. Shaun listened with a concerned look on his face. When she had finished, he shook his head.

"I should have realised. I've noticed him when I pick you up, a skanky looking street boy."

"What's skanky?"

Shaun smiled. "Dirty, rough. He always seems to be hanging round, there in the background like in some surrealist movie. Why didn't you tell me?" He put his arm round her. "Don't worry." He started to rub her back. "We'll sort it out. None of this is life-threatening."

Pilar smiled and looked more relaxed. "Who deals with this sort of thing in your country? Do you call the police?"

"Certainly." He nodded. "But they tend to move rather

slowly. First of all, you should've kept a log of every incident, its date and time, any witnesses and any backup evidence, particularly the spent condoms for DNA."

"I binned everything. I just wanted to forget about it."

"The police might be willing to do something straight away if you could hand over a log."

"So what do I do?"

"Well," Shaun thought for a moment. "Not a lot will happen going through the police and courts to begin with. He might just get a caution, which he wouldn't take seriously. He might see it as a game. We may do better to deal with it ourselves."

"That's how things are done back home. The cocaine barons are prosecutor, judge, jury and punishment, all in one."

"I don't think this boy is much of a threat. If we deal with it ourselves, he'll stay out of prison, and he'll get the idea of what's acceptable and what isn't. We can probably nip it in the bud for him."

"How do we do that?"

"I'm thinking Freddie the forklift. You remember him from the steam room?"

"How could I forget him?"

"I'm going to visit him in his yard."

Pilar couldn't sleep that night. Shaun was aware of her wriggling around far more than usual.

"You're restless," he said in a drowsy voice.

"Sorry, I can't sleep."

"You need my sleep aid."

"What's that?"

He always kept one on his bedside cabinet, mainly for sentimental reasons as he was so relaxed he rarely needed to use it nowadays.

"Here." He put his bedside lamp on and picked up the

MP3 player sleep aid. "What mode do you fancy? We've got nursery rhymes, lullabies, Chopin, Mozart, new-age ambient, South American panpipes, Indian sitar night ragas…"

"Nursery rhymes." She cut him off. "Reminds me of the happiest time of my life, when my granny was alive."

"Okay, I'm setting it for half an hour. It will get softer and softer and then switch itself off. Put it on your bedside cabinet and let your thoughts be with the music rather than your problems."

She was asleep within fifteen minutes.

The next morning, Shaun was wearing his dressing gown and had already shaved and showered when he came back into the bedroom.

"Hey, that sleep aid was good," Pilar said as she got out of bed, stretching herself. "Where did you find it?"

"I designed it. The fortune you're enjoying is based on that device."

"Really? You designed it?"

"Well, not the electronics, but it was my idea and I did the prototyping and all the work to make it happen."

"Wow! You should have told me."

"Why? What would you have done, if you'd have known?"

She hesitated. "I'd have treated you with more respect."

Shaun's face showed surprise, even some hurt, but then he saw a little grin appear on Pilar's face and she started giggling. He picked her up and put her over his shoulder, twirled her round a few times and flung her down on the bed. He started tickling her and bouncing her up and down. She giggled like when she was a little girl, with her granny.

Later that morning, Shaun drove into rural Essex, having obtained Freddie's address from a mutual friend,

Ritchie. As he drove up the narrow lane leading to Freddie's yard, an orange dumpster lorry approached and Shaun pulled off to the side to give way to the larger vehicle. As it shot past, it hit a pothole in the road, making a loud thundering noise. Shaun pulled back out and entered the yard. Its forklifts were yellow and red in colour and parked in rows around the edge of the compound. Shaun stopped and was about to get out of the car.

"Freddie... skip!" one of the workers bellowed.

Shaun watched as Freddie came running out of the Portakabin office and went up to the newly delivered empty skip. He put his hands underneath the rim and started to inch the skip to one side. Shaun got out the car to take a closer look, when a pack of six white Jack Russell terriers, which he hadn't noticed previously, ran across to him and circled him, sniffing his ankles. Though small dogs, Shaun knew them to be a brave and tenacious breed. He could see their long rows of teeth. They followed him over as he walked across to Freddie.

"I knew you were strong," Shaun said when Freddie appeared to have finished, "but I've never seen anyone move a skip before"

"Hello young Shaun. They always put the empty one in the wrong place. What can I do for you?"

"I've got a security problem."

"Really? Come into the office and sit down." He sounded enthusiastic, like he welcomed something to break the monotony of the forklift trade.

They entered the Portakabin, which had a large desk, covered with an untidy mess of paperwork, like it wasn't Freddie's strong point, and a large leather, swivel chair, in which Freddie sat himself down. Shaun perched on the sofa that was to one side.

"Pilar and I are having trouble with a stalker, Freddie.

Pilar teaches a salsa class. One of her students, a young lad, has found out where we live and comes round and exposes himself. He even ejaculated over her."

Freddie pulled a face and his expression became serious. "Dirty dog. Leave him to me. What's it worth?" He wagged his finger at Shaun. "I'm going to make some money out of you for this."

Shaun opened his wallet and counted out some notes. "This now, the same on completion."

He leant across to hand it to Freddie, who looked sideways out of the window as he took it and slipped it into his pocket, almost as though it had never happened.

The next salsa class Pilar held, Freddie was waiting outside as the students emerged. Jay still had the gall to turn up to her classes, not doing much out of the ordinary except rubbing his penis from time to time. Everyone else thought he must have an itch. Freddie watched as Pilar came out onto the pavement, with Jay hanging round her, and saw her get into the car with Shaun and drive away. He casually strolled up to Jay.

"Hello mate." Freddie smiled as he said it.

"What do you want?" Jay seemed suspicious of the stranger with the loud voice.

"I understand you like to get your dick out in front of my friend, Pilar." Freddie continued to smile. "She's a cute little thing, ain`t she?"

"Yeah!" Jay gave a salacious grin.

"She's really nice, isn't she?"

"Yeah." Jay grinned and nodded.

"Come here a minute."

Freddie seemed conspiratorial as he said it, like he had a secret to share, and led Jay to a quiet doorway of the pub. Once there, out of the way, he put his hand on Jay's bicep, patting him a few times, but then suddenly tightened his grip at the same time as he put his hand down Jay's tracksuit bottoms and grasped his testicles. Jay stopped grinning.

"You do it one more time," Freddie's voice was even louder than usual, "and it'll be the last, because I'll rip the bollocks off you and ram them down yer throat, understand?" Freddie's face was very close to Jay's and he had sprayed Jay with saliva, as he shouted at him.

Jay was looking terrified. "Okay, okay... I'll stop," he whispered.

"Make sure you do!" Freddie tightened his grip on Jay's testicles. "You're not just saying that are you?"

"I'll stop, I'll stop, I promise."

Jay was grimacing with pain, as Freddie gave a final squeeze for good measure and then relinquished his grip. Freddie looked over his shoulder as he walked away. Jay was crouched on the floor in agony.

"Don't think I won't do it either, muppet." Freddie yelled.

Shaun and Pilar lay in bed that night, after making love.

"So it's all over with, the Jay stuff?" Pilar turned her head on the pillow to look at Shaun.

"We won't be seeing him again."

"I hope Freddie didn't hurt him."

"Why are you bothered? Look what he did to you. Doesn't he deserve a beating?"

"I am bothered. I can't change the way I am... and anyway, it wouldn't have happened if I hadn't been working as an escort."

"I would never have met you if you hadn't been doing that sort of work."

"You've never spoken about it, that time of my life."

"What would you want me to say?"

"Don't you want to know what I had to do?"

He hesitated. "Tell me then."

"Mostly it was middle-aged, married men. They were the only ones who could afford me. I had to do them with my hand."

"I know why that is. They wouldn't feel any guilt, with just a hand job. They wouldn't feel they were cheating on their wives. Did some have difficulty getting up?"

"Sometimes, the older men, and sometimes the younger men finished just looking at me."

"So what was I like, when you first opened the door to me? What did you think?"

"Oh! You seemed very alone." She said it in a matter of fact way, like a doctor giving a prescription. "It's good that you're discussing these things. Don't you feel bad about it? Aren't you angry that I did that?"

"If I was younger, I might have been. I'm old enough to understand. Anyway, I've had lots of disappointments in the past, and I promised myself if ever the right person came along, I wouldn't let them get away."

"So you're on the rebound from your disappointments?"

Shaun started to laugh. "You're no rebound to anyone. You're my whole world."

Pilar took Shaun's hand and twined her fingers around his. "Nothing can come between us now, Shaun. It's like our two souls have merged into one. We were made for each other."

9

All Roads Lead to London

It was a mid Thursday afternoon and Shaun was pottering around the house, while Pilar was out teaching her salsa class. He saw a taxi pull up outside and not having much else to do, peeped out of his bedroom window to see who it was. He had become a bit of a curtain twitcher since the Jay episode and had even bought himself a pair of top of the range binoculars, with x10 magnification and often surveyed up and down the street and the wider panorama.

His mouth dropped open in astonishment. It was Christiana and a little girl stepping out of the taxi, with the driver unloading a large suitcase and a pushchair from the boot. Christiana was wearing a white top and black trousers and the girl had a child's version of the same outfit. Shaun crouched down on the floor, like an infant thinking if he could make himself invisible, the problem would disappear. What could she want? Why was she here? He hadn't seen her since Hamburg, three years ago. The doorbell rang as he sat on the floor. It kept ringing. He just sat there.

Suddenly, he remembered. Over the three years they had kept sporadically in touch, with e-mails and phone calls, but, significantly, she had phoned him from Berlin about four months previously, after a year's silence.

Initially, her call was probably to show off how well she was doing. He recalled that conversation quite clearly:

"Hi Shaun. You okay? I thought I'd let you know we're moving again, to a really fabulous apartment. I'm not sure where Ralf is getting the money from, but he says we're rich enough to afford it."

"I'm so pleased everything has worked out for you. I really mean that."

"Hey, you sound really happy Shaun, and confident. What's going on? Have you just started another love affair? Not forgetting the good times we had in Hamburg, are you?"

"Well that's perceptive of you. I'm very happy. I've pulled off a big business deal. Actually, it was the idea that I put to Hartmut in your Hamburg apartment. So you maybe played a part in it. It's all come together for me in the most spectacular fashion."

"Hmm, Shaun, you're so clever at business. So how much did you make?"

"It's all part of a confidentiality agreement."

"Millions?"

"It was good."

After five minutes, it had gone quiet and Shaun ventured to look out from one corner of the window, curious to see what was happening below. But Christiana was sitting on his front garden wall, which was quite low, and she was looking up at him. She waved.

"Shaun. Let us in, quickly," she shouted.

Shaun waved back and went downstairs and opened the front door, holding his hands behind his back so that his tremor didn't notice.

"Christiana, sorry, I was in the bathroom. What a surprise! I'm in shock." He looked down at the mini Christiana. "Who's this sweet little thing?"

"Oh, Shaun let's get inside quickly. I've got so much to tell you." She brushed past him, ignoring his question, the little girl in her wake. They sat down, not even stopping to take their jackets off. "Shaun we're in big trouble, the biggest possible." She hesitated and looked at the little girl. "Sorry, I should have introduced my daughter first. This is Lisa."

Shaun looked blank for a few seconds. "You have a daughter? You never mentioned it in your e-mails. You never sent me any photos."

"Didn't I? I'm sorry, life in Berlin got a bit crazy. Yes, this is my daughter. She's two years old... anyway, back to my point, we got into money problems with our fabulous new apartment." She raised her eyebrows and took a deep breath then puffed it out. "And Ralf got re-involved with his criminal friends and then had a misunderstanding with a major Berlin drug baron. We've had to flee from Berlin; there's a contract on our lives."

Shaun looked stunned. "God, no! Where's Ralf?"

"I don't know."

"You don't know?" Shaun shook his head and looked puzzled.

"I don't know."

Shaun was thoughtful for a while. "So what are you going to do?"

Christiana looked at him, quite intensely like she was trying to hypnotise him. She smiled and then widened her eyes and raised her eyebrows, as if to say she was open to suggestions. She was still a beauty and she had the cutest of daughters, who was playing on the floor with Chimbo, in between staring at him. He was wondering if his cash windfall might have some bearing on Christiana's arrival at this particular moment. It might even have been a scam concocted with Ralf.

She finally answered his question. "I just need somewhere to stay outside of Germany, till things blow over."

Shaun frowned. "I have a girlfriend now, Pilar. I've fallen in love at last. I can't make any decision without her... look, I have to go and pick her up from her salsa class. She's the instructor. I'll be half an hour. You relax from your journey, make yourself a drink and we'll talk about things more when I get back. I can't promise anything right now."

When Shaun pulled up outside the dance class venue, Pilar was already standing on the pavement, arms akimbo and looking peeved. The sound equipment was beside her.

"You're late," she snapped, as Shaun got out of the car to stow her equipment in the boot, "I thought we agreed after the stalker trouble, you'd always be here early?" Then she sensed Shaun's tension. "What's wrong?"

"Get in the car," he mumbled, and as they drove off, he started to explain. "We've got a little surprise back at the house."

"What kind of surprise? Something bad?... Oh no, it's not Jay back, is it?"

"An old friend from Germany is visiting with her little girl."

"Well that sounds fun. Why are you so tense? Is it a girlfriend?"

"Don't be silly, you're my girlfriend." He took her hand and squeezed it.

"Don't play games, is it an ex-girlfriend?" she squeezed Shaun's hair at the nape of his neck.

"Was she my girlfriend? Her boyfriend is an ex porn star. Do you think she would be interested in me?"

"Oh, Shaun." She squeezed his arm, looking relieved. "So who is she?"

"She's just an old acquaintance who's in some kind of trouble."

"What kind of trouble? Shouldn't she have gone to the police?"

"I haven't got the details. She came just as I was leaving to get you. That's why I'm late."

"Okay, let me meet her." She was curious to meet Christiana and she knew all about trouble.

In the half hour that he had been gone from the house, Shaun could see that Christiana's suitcase had disappeared from downstairs, so she must have occupied a spare bedroom. She must also have unpacked, because she had put her albums by the sound system, pushing his own out of the way and Lisa's toys were spread out in a corner of the room that had previously been empty. Her herbal teas and special foods were on the work surface in the kitchen and she was on the landline having a conversation in German. It was like squatters had moved in on him. Christiana brought her phone conversation to an end.

"You've unpacked?" Shaun sounded annoyed.

Christiana ignored him and stood up and embraced Pilar warmly. "Hello Pilar, I'm Christiana. I'm so sorry to intrude on you like this, with no warning. My husband went back to his criminal ways. I've had to flee Berlin in fear of my life, and my daughter's."

"Don't apologise. It's not your fault. Men are so stupid. Where's your husband now?" Pilar asked.

"I don't know." Christiana sat back down on the sofa and started to cry. "I'm so scared. They're ruthless. They won't hesitate to kill him."

"Come here." Pilar sat down beside Christiana and cuddled her. Lisa seeing it, ran across the room and flung herself on them, like it was a rugby scrum. Pilar put her arm around Lisa also. "Don't cry. Let's see if we can get you sorted out. How did it all come about? What did your husband do?" Pilar looked at Christiana.

"I only spoke to him for a few minutes after it had all

happened, but he killed the younger brother of a major Berlin drug baron, Russians."

"Whoah, hang on. I didn't know this involved murder." Shaun had watched in silence up till that point.

"But it was only self defence. I know my Ralf would never kill someone other than in self defence. He's a good man."

"Shaun," Pilar had a look like she was in control. "Can they can stay with us for a while?"

"Well, drugs and good men don't go together in my world," he said, but Pilar was looking at him as if waiting for an answer of, 'yes'. He silently nodded agreement.

"Oh thank you, Pilar." Christiana hugged her again.

By the evening, Shaun had calmed down a little about Christiana's arrival. They were in the living room, which was stylishly furnished and had a patio door the whole length of one wall, overlooking the back garden. Lisa was lying on the carpet next to Chimbo. Christiana and Pilar were sitting at each end of the sofa.

Shaun was sitting in an armchair. "So Christiana, on more mundane matters, how's the translating going?" he asked.

"I dropped all that. I haven't translated for two years now."

"No! That's hard to believe. You were so enthusiastic about it when I was in Hamburg. What happened?"

"I got very lonely in Berlin; I missed my girlfriend Sandra. Ralf was down the gym all day, and I was left alone in the apartment with nothing but words going round in my head to keep me company. I became a personal trainer instead."

"You've reinvented yourself. Maybe you can give us a workout," Shaun suggested, but then he noticed Pilar, who was sitting on the far side of Christiana, shaking her head.

"Well, when we've sorted your problems out, of course. That's the big priority." Shaun gave a nervous laugh.

Christiana settled in over the next few days. She had dance in common with Pilar, and Shaun would catch them mid session, with Lisa running around also. They did some cooking together and Christiana helped Pilar with her English vocabulary. Pilar also seemed to hug and comfort Christiana and Lisa a lot, as they would often get concerned over the welfare of Ralf, of whom there was never any word.

Shaun remained aloof from and tense about the whole arrangement. He could feel Christiana discreetly trying to exert some power over him, but she would only do it when Pilar was not there, odd lingering moments when they were alone together, on the stairs, in the kitchen, on the landing or in the hallway, trying to revive some of the old intimacy they may have shared, talking to him in her soft voice,

"That was really nice the way you were playing with Lisa… maybe we can take Lisa for a walk tomorrow, while Pilar is giving her dance class… we can feed the ducks… what do you think?… Hmm?"

* * *

One week after Christiana's arrival, the villa to get Pilar's parents into Rio's coastal neighbourhood and out of the *favela* was ready for legal completion. It wasn't the original one that Shaun had found on the internet, but through some of Pilar's contacts in Rio, they had found a perfect villa, which didn't come on the market that often, most of the property sales being apartments. They had already transferred a deposit to Brazil, but now the time had come to sign the final paperwork, complete the payment and move house. As her parents had only daughters, of which

Pilar was the eldest, and as Pilar was registering the property in her own name, she had to return to Brazil to do the legal side and to help with the physical move. Pilar handed her teaching schedule over to Fabiano, her Afro Brazilian teaching assistant, including the sound equipment. She booked an open ticket as she wasn't sure how long it would take to complete all the business.

Shaun saw Pilar off at Heathrow. He parked in the short stay car park. She did not get out immediately, but took his hand.

"Shaun, I'm going to miss you so much. Look after yourself and see if you can get Christiana sorted. I'm only a phone call away. I love you to bits!" With that, she gave him a big hug and a passionate kiss.

"I love you too! Have a safe journey. Say hello to your parents for me. Text me so I know you've arrived in Rio safely."

"I'll be back as soon as possible. Three weeks at the most. We'd better go now. I don't want to lose the plane."

"Miss the plane!" Shaun laughed at Pilar's mistake.

"Huh! *Perder!*" She tapped the palm of her hand against her forehead. "I've been so busy packing and buying presents, it must have got to my brain."

* * *

It was later the same morning and Shaun, Christiana and Lisa got out of the car by a lake local to Shaun's house, the rather dank smell of stagnant water and rotting vegetation hitting them immediately. The ducks were waiting for them at the edge of the car park, the Canada geese waddling around on the path, the Mallards and Goldeneyes bobbing up and down in the water by the shoreline.

"Here you are," Christiana handed Lisa a few pieces of

bread. "Don't eat it; it's stale. Anyway, you haven't had your lunch yet, so don't spoil it."

Lisa took the bread and broke off little pieces and started to throw them to each goose, the dominant ones pecking the subordinate ones to shoo them away. She chased the geese that got too near to her.

"Lisa, don't bully them. They won't hurt you." Christiana smiled and put her arm in Shaun's. "Isn't this nice, Shaun? Like when we went around together in Hamburg."

"Hmm."

A little further along, a man was coming towards them with a large, fawn coloured dog on a lead.

"*Hund.*" Lisa pointed

"Dog," Christiana said. "Now we live in England, you must learn English."

As they passed, Shaun spoke to the owner. "He's an impressive sight, more like a horse. What breed is that?"

The man stopped. "Bullmastiff, bred to catch poachers and trespassers on country estates."

"He seems to be unhappy." Shaun looked at the huge head, with its wrinkled brow and sad looking eyes with black rings round them.

"They're Stoics. Like war veterans, they soldier on."

"Does he guard you?"

"Yes, but they're clever at working out who's a threat and who isn't. That's why he's looking so calm with you." The dog was sitting patiently beside his master, completely passive.

"Are they good fighters?"

"They won't start a fight, but they'll finish it."

"If you wanted to put him in fancy dress, like the Americans do at Halloween, he would look good in a tuxedo... or failing that, gladiators' armour from Ancient

Rome... cheers." Shaun held up his hand in salutation but was looking ahead.

Lisa had walked on, and Christiana had gone after her, towards an angler sitting on a stool, his rod resting before him on a stand. He was eating a sandwich, which between bites, he placed back in a plastic container beside him. Lisa walked slowly up to him and in a sudden movement, grabbed the sandwich and started eating it.

"Lisa." Christiana was just behind her. "Give it back. Naughty girl!"

"It's okay," the angler shrugged. "She's all right. It's only a cheese sandwich. She's welcome."

"Are you sure?" Shaun had caught them up and saw the incident.

"She's fine." The angler seemed relaxed about it.

They stood smiling for a moment watching Lisa eat the sandwich.

"Thank you" Christiana added. They walked on, but as soon as they were a distance from the angler, Christiana snatched the sandwich from Lisa and threw it into the lake. "Don't take food from strangers. It might have germs. Only eat food from your mummy." She tightened her grip on Shaun's arm and pulled herself closer to him. He looked at her and she held his gaze and smiled. "And I'll make your food tonight."

"Thank you. Don't go to any trouble. I'll make your lunch tomorrow, then."

"Okay." She kissed him on the cheek.

That evening, she made some pasta, mixing in a pesto sauce when it was cooked, and had already prepared a salad with dressing to go on the side. She served it up on three plates. Then she went to the living room and hovered at the doorway for a moment. Shaun seemed to be settled in front of the television, laughing at a comedy programme, so she returned to the kitchen and went to her handbag. She took out a packet of turquoise capsules, popped one out of the pack and sliced through the gelatine shell to reveal the powder inside. She looked round to see that Shaun wasn't about to enter the kitchen, and then sprinkled the contents of the pill over Shaun's pasta, but not over her own or Lisa's. Then she sprinkled grated cheese on top. She placed Shaun's plate on a tray and went to the living room with it.

"There. *Bon Appetit.*" She placed the tray on his lap and tousled his hair.

"Thank you so much. That's really kind of you."

Shaun ate the food, which was very tasty, most of his attention being on the television.

Shaun had expected to feel low with Pilar gone from the house, but by about 9 p.m., he was the opposite, feeling very good. Music from the television seemed to trigger little bursts of bliss in his head, like when he was very relaxed. It reminded him of being a teenager again, when the world was fresh and new, and there was nothing to worry about. By about 9.30, a slightly raunchy scene in the programme he was watching gave him a very hard erection. He wondered why his body was reacting in such a way.

Christiana had already gone up to bed early, to have a bath, and she hadn't come back downstairs. Shaun retired at his normal time, but was aware he felt different to usual, like he was energised. As he entered his bedroom, he knew immediately something was wrong. There was a dim light in the room, but he did not have a dimmer switch. Then he realised it was candlelight, gently flickering, and Christiana was in his bed where Pilar usually lay. She was naked and sat up in bed as soon as Shaun entered, revealing her ample breasts, which she massaged while blowing him a kiss.

149

"Come on, Shaun." Her voice was soft as she said it. "Ram it into me."

Shaun's penis was so hard, it was like it might burst. He hesitated momentarily, but he was so aroused it was not going to be possible to exercise any kind of restraint and after some quick, frenzied foreplay, they were copulating. For all his wild abandon, he was aware that Christiana had not used a condom like she had in Hamburg.

"What contraception are you using?" he said in her ear.

"It's okay, baby," she said tenderly, stroking his hair. "Just come now, come for me. Come inside me. That will be fine."

He finished as she had asked him to.

"Oh that was so beautiful," she whispered as she stroked his hair and kissed him. He fell asleep cuddling her.

When he came round the next morning, with a huge erection, he opened his eyes to find Christiana gazing at him.

"How long have you been awake?" he asked, still sleepy.

"Hello, big boy." She ignored his question. "Have you got something for me?" She put her hand on his penis and started kissing his mouth. He was soon above and inside her.

"Harder," she whispered in his ear. "I like it. Give it to me harder."

After a few minutes he was thrusting at top speed, her breasts bouncing against his chest with each inward penetration.

"Harder, you dirty man. I want it harder." She was saying it louder now.

He could not go any faster, but instead released his load and fell to one side, panting. She gently stroked his hair and rubbed his back as they lay together. She had a very contented smile on her face. Shaun went to pull out and clean himself up, but Christiana stopped him.

"No, keep it inside me. Just hold me close. Just lie here with me. I like it."

When he finally got up to wash and get dressed, Christiana lay quietly for half an hour with two pillows beneath her butt and a pad made of tissues against her vagina, to keep Shaun's fluid inside her. That night she made lamb curry and once again discreetly sprinkled the turquoise capsule onto Shaun's plate. The spices easily masked the musty taste of the pill's ingredients.

The days passed and they settled into a close, sensual relationship, with Christiana adding the turquoise capsule to his food every evening. During the day, they would do Pilates sessions together, Lisa joining in on a little mat of her own. They would take Lisa down to the park to play on the swings and feed the Canada geese and ducks. They also did some outings to the sights of London, and to theme parks. And they made love every morning when they woke up, and every evening when they went to bed. Shaun knew he was doing something wrong, and by mid morning always planned to stop that day, but by the evening, when Christiana had secretly sprinkled the powder onto his food, he always weakened. He wanted to discuss it with Pilar, but kept putting it off, because he couldn't work out what he was going to say and how he could explain it.

10

Rio de Janeiro – Part 1

It was unmistakably a flight to Brazil. The voices were loud and everyone was enthusiastic and excited, like it was a hospitality suite in the air. Pilar almost expected to see a carnival procession coming down the aisle of the aeroplane.

"Pleased to be going home?" She had an aisle seat and the steward paused for a moment beside her and asked in Portuguese.

"It's wonderful."

"Is there anything you'll miss about England?" he said, smiling.

She didn't have to think too hard. "Well I like the way they stand in line for things, you don't get all the pushing and shoving like you see in Brazil."

"I don't think you'll be missing the weather?"

"True."

"Nor the food?"

"Actually, I like fish and chips…. and my boyfriend makes me Shepherd's Pie, I like that very much."

The steward frowned. "You have an English boyfriend?"

"Yes, I've fallen in love with an Englishman."

"What's wrong with us Brazilians?"

"Nothing, but he's so wonderful."

* * *

Eleven hours had passed and the plane circled over the beautiful bay of Rio, the sea a luminous turquoise colour. Behind the beaches and downtown neighbourhoods, a semicircle of dark green forested mountains rose steeply, in which nestled the *favelas*. The white statue of *Cristo Redentor* (Christ the Redeemer), arms outstretched in the shape of a cross, atop the *Corcovado* (hunchback) mountain, presided over the whole bay and had given Brazilian Catholics a symbol of hope and faith since its construction in 1931. It could be seen from any point in Rio and had sometimes given Pilar strength during difficult times.

She took a Radio-taxi from Galeão airport, twice as expensive as a yellow cab, but considered safer because they were regulated and besides, what was the difference of fifty Brazilian Reais (£20) to her nowadays?

"Shall I put some music on?" the taxi driver asked before they set off.

"Bebel Gilberto."

"You like the queen of *bossa nova*?"

"I remember her first CD *Tanto Tempo* [Long Time] in 2000. We'd never heard of her, then suddenly she was everywhere you went."

Gilberto's soft, whispery voice came over the car speakers. Pilar felt a wave of joy to be back home. She started to sing along with Bebel:

If I could name a fruit for you
It would be jabuticaba
Blue black and small on the outside
And soft and sweet within

She saw the taxi driver looking at her in his rear view mirror.

"I'm happeeeeeeeeee." She pulled a funny face and grinned at him.

It was about 5 p.m. as she reached the edge of the *favela*. The taxi could not go in, as there were no proper roads. Pilar stepped out into the sunshine and squinted her eyes as she looked to the West, at the township rising steeply in front of her. It was so different from the grey overcast London she had left behind. But after just a few months in London, she had become used to the symmetry and orderliness of English architecture and the ugliness of the *favela* took her by surprise, sending her into shock. It was like looking at a big rubbish tip, functional, oblong concrete or brick bunkers, some with corrugated iron roofs, of all shapes, colours and sizes, randomly sited and crowded in on each other so closely, going up the very steep hill as far as the eye could see, the dwellings seeming to be piled on top of each other. She had also forgotten that distinctive smell that was already in her nostrils, even standing on the edge of the *favela*. It was a toxic mix of sewage, diesel fuel and cooking oil. She was surprised to feel a little nauseous; how quickly she had forgotten her hometown.

There had been talk of clearing the *favela*s before Rio hosted the 2016 Olympic Games, but it would have been too big and expensive a job. The authorities had instead settled for trying to contain the lawlessness and had driven out the gangs from some *favelas,* following which they replaced the violent military police with a more socially trained force called the Pacification Police Unit (UPP) which would be more likely to be accepted by the *favela* dwellers as part of the community. Pilar's township had yet to be pacified.

The cocaine baron's lookouts, wearing T-shirts and Bermuda shorts like LA rappers, spotted her immediately.

"Hey Pilar, taxi girl," one called out in an excited voice. "London has been good to you. Drinks on you later."

"Hey Pilar Fernandes," one from a different vantage point called, "I will tell Emilio his girlfriend is back!"

It reminded her of her childhood, the gangsters calling out like that. She was such a celebrity because of the scholarship she had won. Every day she had travelled downtown to be taught by the nuns and mix with the rich and well-to-do girls of the city, but when she returned at the end of the day, in her smart uniform of white shirt with school logo and electric blue skirt, the gangsters would delight in waylaying her, like a mascot, and show her their guns and let her take some target shots. The noise never worried them. They were proud of their guns and wanted everyone to know they had them. Over the years she became one of the best shots in the *favela*, able to shoot down six bottles or tins in a few seconds. How she loved the kick of the gun in her hand as the bullet discharged, the sight of the bottle breaking and the tang of cordite in the air. It was her turn on. 'That's fifty cents a bullet you owe us,' the gangsters would say afterwards, but she would just have to look at them with her cute face and they would always indulge her.

Her father and sisters had come down to meet her, prompted by her phone call and she disregarded the gangsters' shouts. They embraced, but then Pilar insisted they get moving. They hauled her cases through the irregular streets and walkways, her father carrying just a small bag, because of his weak heart.

"I've brought you some nice presents from London."

"Why didn't you bring Shaun?" her father asked, sounding a bit wheezy. "He seems like a wonderful man. I wanted to thank him personally for what he has done for us."

"Next time; maybe for the wedding." She smiled.

"Wedding? Oh, you will make your father a happy man before he dies."

"*Papai*, don't talk like that." Pilar stopped and put her arms round her father. Tears had come to her eyes. "Don't ever say that again; don't you dare."

They reached the house halfway up the steep hill. It was mid way along a single storey, brick built terrace, and they entered the front door straight from the rough path and went directly into the main living room, which had a small kitchen and two bedrooms leading off it.

"Pilar!" her mother cried out. "Thank God you are here. You naughty girl. Why didn't you phone more often?" She started to cry.

"*Mamãe*! I did phone you, lots." They hugged.

"Pilar, you've lost some weight and you've gone pale. You need some sun."

"Well, London isn't that sunny and I'm inside a lot nowadays, teaching salsa." She did the salsa wiggle of her hips. "This is me now," and then she samba'd over to her suitcase, making her family laugh. She started to unpack the presents purchased in London.

Pilar started to give out the gifts she had carefully selected. "*Mamãe*, I've brought you some perfume and soap and chocolates from Harrods." She kissed her mother again, and handed them over.

"They're so luxurious. You're such a thoughtful girl."

She turned to her sisters, who were teenagers aged seventeen and nineteen. "Look what I've got for you. I spent ages choosing them." She gave them some of the latest clothes from London's high street stores, still in their Primark and Matalan carrier bags.

"Oh Pilar. We are going to be IT girls," said Mariana, the elder of the two. They knew clothes would give them a

156

lot of status; you could even move up the social pecking order in Rio, just on the basis of your clothes.

"We can show off at *Posto 9*," said Luciana, the younger one. She referred to the lifeguard tower on Ipanema beach, where the young and beautiful people congregated.

"And I have some face creams and cosmetics for you." Pilar handed them over. She had left her father till last. "*Papai*, the English are great tea drinkers, and I know how much you like tea." She produced a giant pack of English tea and gave it to him proudly. Most *Cariocas* drank coffee, but Pilar's father had developed a taste for tea during his time working as a waiter in a five-star hotel. He could no longer afford to buy it. She hugged him once more. Most English people would never understand how close Brazilians felt to their family, how strong the tie of blood was for them. Pilar went to sleep happy that night, the sounds of the *favela*, including drunken arguments and gunshots, like a lullaby in her ears because she knew they would soon be living their dream in a quiet coastal neighbourhood.

Next day they made their way down as a family to the edge of the *favela*, in order to take a taxi to downtown Rio. Pilar noticed her father had grown weaker since she had been in London, so much so they had to keep stopping for him to catch his breath. "Stand back!" Pilar suddenly ordered to her family.

A convoy of motorbikes droned past, going up the hill, *Carioca* drivers with tourists riding pillion. It was still an incongruous sight. Tourists hungry for a new experience had always been attracted into the *favela* and a few years previously, they used to be in considerable danger of being mugged if they were male or of being mugged and raped if they were female. It had been known for tourists to be robbed of everything, clothes, money, credit cards, camera, phone, and to be dispatched at the edge of the *favela* in just their underwear. But recently, this had changed. A tour of the *favela* had become a must-do for any *gringo* (foreigner) visiting Rio. The tourists would be taken up to the top of the hill on motor bikes, to enjoy the panoramic views, and then they would descend on foot down through the township, all with the blessing of the cocaine baron. This was in return for some money being paid by the tour organisers to the local community projects such as schools and kindergartens. Pilar waved to the tourists in a friendly gesture as they passed, to reassure them that everything was safe, and then led her family down to the edge of the *favela*, where they hailed a cab.

They were soon in downtown Rio, which was a mix of old colonial grandeur and more modern, ugly office blocks. First they visited the *procurador* (solicitor) to sign the legal papers, and then to the bank to arrange the final payment for the villa. Administrative work took hours and hours in Brazil, the bureaucracy seeming to go back a hundred years, but Pilar and her family didn't mind because they were on the threshold of a new life.

By late afternoon, they were back home and doing final packing. Pilar had not been socialising much, because the priority was to stay focused on getting her parents relocated safely. She made a phone call.

"Hi Shaun! We're almost ready to move. Everyone's so excited!"

"Hi Pilar. That's great. So the money transferred, okay?"

"Yes… have you missed me?"

"So much."

"What have you been doing?"

He hesitated. "Not a lot so far. Just spending time with Christiana and Lisa, really."

"Shaun, you okay?"

"I'm fine."

"You sound a bit distant."

"What, like 6000 miles away, maybe?"

"No, the line's fine. I mean in yourself, you sound kind of, like you're curled up inside, like a tortoise in its shell. What's wrong?"

"Nothing, I'm fine." He sounded uncertain.

"Tell me what's wrong."

"Look, I'm fine."

"Shaun, I'm psychic. I can tell something's wrong."

"Even psychics have off days, Pilar."

She sighed. "Yeah, maybe."

"Shaun, your food's ready." It was Christiana's voice interrupting.

"What does she want?" Pilar sounded indignant.

"Oh, she's made me a meal. She likes me to eat it when it's hot. Look, can I catch you later?"

"Okay, Shaun, love you."

"Have a good move."

Pilar sat quietly for a few minutes. She felt something was wrong, but she had a lot of other things to think about and pushed it to the back of her mind.

* * *

A few days later, Pilar and her family moved out, ferrying the few pieces of furniture they were retaining and their personal belongings by cart to the edge of the *favela*, where a van was waiting. Pilar was the last one out of the house, having sent her parents and sisters on ahead. She gave all the keys to a friend who was trading up from a more rundown part of the township. They had not charged him as he was her father's old chum and title was in any case unclear.

The news that the Fernandes family had won the lottery, or some equivalent, and were moving down to Ipanema had spread quickly through the *favela* and many people had come to say goodbye that morning. A large young man, almost a giant, was hurriedly making his way through the alleyways, having woken up late after a night of heavy drinking, followed by some puffs of marijuana. People nodded to him deferentially or muttered a greeting such as, "Morning Emilio," or "Okay, Emilio?" He mostly ignored them in his rush.

As Pilar walked away from the house, she felt a touch of sadness, as this was after all where she had spent her childhood and this was the house she would always associate with her granny. But mainly she was pleased to be making a clean getaway. Suddenly, a heavy hand fell on her shoulder, the kind of contact you dreaded in the *favela*.

"Pilar, you're not going without a word to your old boyfriend?"

A *frisson* of fear went through her, but she released it from her body before she turned round so that she appeared calm as she faced him. She looked at him without smiling. A few seconds passed. He looked at her as though he expected her to say something. She finally broke the uncomfortable silence.

"Emilio," she said with a flat tone.

"Don't sound so enthusiastic!"

She continued to stand there, unsmiling. "What do you expect me to say?"

"Show a bit of enthusiasm for your old boyfriend."

"Boyfriend?" There was surprise and irritation in her voice. "I was never your girlfriend." She thought for a while, then she blurted out, "you raped me."

"Oh come on!" He seemed indignant. "Aren't you scared to talk to me like that?" He instinctively stretched his body up to full height and glared at her. It was an imposing sight.

"I'm not scared of you." She looked up at him, towering above her. "Why should I be scared? Are you scared of me?"

He admired her courageous spirit, he always had and he harboured feelings for her which he had kept hidden because he didn't want to appear weak. He was a big burly man, with a chubby boyish face, flanked by black curly hair. Many of the gangsters in the *favela* were Afro-Brazilian or mixed race, while Emilio was of pure Portuguese descent, but gypsy. It was hard to place him in the hierarchy of the gangsters. He was more of a loose cannon than anything, but people respected him because he was very big, a bit crazy and capable of anything. 'He won't make old bones,' some of the elders used to say, 'he'll be dead by twenty five.'

Pilar well remembered the night he had raped her. She and her sisters had been to a local rave, a *baile funk* (funk ball), and they had danced all evening, from time to time pushing their way through the gyrating bodies to sit on the side and sip from bottles of beer. Emilio had latched onto them in the last quarter of an hour as they took one of these breaks, seeming not to notice their fear and tension at the unwelcome attention he was giving them, or if he did he pressed on regardless.

"Aah, the Fernandes sisters. You okay?" had been his opening line.

"You alright Emilio?" Pilar had said nervously. "Will your excuse us? Come on girls." Pilar downed her beer in one big gulp. It had been a sweltering day and she had drunk far more alcohol than she normally would have. "Let's have another dance." She stood up and beckoned to her sisters to join her on the dance floor.

Emilio followed and hung around them, till the dance finished.

"Come on! Let's go for something to eat."

"We're going home." Pilar didn't look at him, as though half ignoring him.

"I'll come."

"No, that's okay."

"I'll walk you back. It's not safe this time of night."

"Seriously, it's okay. We'll be fine." She looked him in the eye, hoping the message would get through.

But he followed them home anyway, and as they opened the door to the house, he pushed his way in.

"You two girls go straight to bed. I need to discuss something with Pilar."

"If you've got anything to say to me, you can say it in front of my sisters," Pilar retorted in anger at the intrusion.

"Girls, come here." He beckoned Pilar's sisters to come to one side of the room and started speaking to them in a whisper, like they were conspirators. "I have some secret business to discuss with your sister. It's very confidential, to do with making Pilar *rainha* of the *favela*." He was referring to the election of a carnival queen to lead the *favela*'s drumming *bateria* (troupe) at the annual Sambódromo parade. "She's such a great dancer. But everyone will be so jealous of her, her life could even be in danger. It has to be between just her and me, you understand, yes?"

Her sisters nodded and went into their bedroom.

"Hey. Come back here." Pilar called out to her sisters as they disappeared, her speech slightly slurred from the alcohol, and maybe a touch of sunstroke.

"Go on." Emilio whispered as he stood in the doorway of the sisters' bedroom, gesturing with his hand that they should go to bed. Then he put his finger to his lips to indicate that they should say nothing of the secret. "I'll look after Pilar. Leave it to your uncle Emilio. She'll be fine with me." He winked at them and closed the door to shut them in.

The sisters consigned to their bedroom, he sat next to Pilar and put his face close, grinning. Within seconds, his heavy body was on top of her and the smell of rum on his breath was in her nostrils and the few days' stubble on his chin was rubbing against her face and body like wire wool. She hadn't bothered reporting it to the police afterwards as they never entered the *favelas*, except in armed Swat units, who came in to search for drugs and to have shoot outs. She also had never told anyone else what happened that night, as she wanted no comeback.

"I raped you, you say? I say no! Take care what you accuse me of. I seem to remember you enjoyed it." He grinned at her, revealing his misshapen teeth. It was as though he still relished the evening.

It is true that she had put a bit of enthusiasm into the coupling, because he was a big man and she was a small girl and if things went on too long there was a danger she would have got injured. He had not watched her face as he entered her or seen how her eyes and mouth opened in shock as he was much too large for her vagina. To make matters worse, she had become dry and he had got angry that he couldn't easily slide in and out to satisfy himself. He had shaken her roughly, and she became even more tense and scared of what he might do. She had to spit on her hand to get some saliva to apply down below for lubrication and had then been forced to whisper sweet endearments in his ear, such as "Come for me darling," in order to get the ordeal over with as soon as possible. He finished quite loudly and she gave a big sigh of relief. She had looked up at the picture of Christ, hanging on the wall above them and thanked God it was all over and that she was still alive.

"It was rape." She glared at him. "My family's waiting for me. I have to go." She turned and walked away, hoping that was the last of it. She did just sometimes wonder, as she had drunk rather too much that evening, whether she had given off some wrong signals. But she doubted it.

"So you are moving down to Ipanema?" he shouted after her. "Have you forgotten how I saved your sisters?" He referred to a time, following the rape, when some local gangsters had wanted Pilar's sisters to pretend to be prostitutes and lure sex tourists onto Copacabana beach at night, so they could be robbed. As soon as Emilio had heard, he had intervened and put a stop to it. Maybe he had wanted to compensate for his crime.

Pilar turned round. "I haven't forgotten." She sighed and looked annoyed that she had to concede something to him. "Yes. Thank you for that."

"So I'll come down and see you in your new house, right?" Pilar had already turned and was walking away. She didn't answer him. "Where did you get the money for the house? London's been good to you," he shouted as a parting shot.

The villa was fabulous, completely refurbished with freshly painted walls and new kitchen and bathroom. They had purchased mostly brand new furniture, bringing just a few items of sentimental value from the old house, such as Pilar's father's chair that he liked to sit on to watch television. Located a few blocks back from the beach, outside was a beautiful and secluded garden with scented flowers, shrubs and herbs, where they could sit in the evening and enjoy the cool breeze off the ocean.

They had only been in the villa two days and were still getting themselves organised, when a silver Mercedes pulled up outside. A tall, muscular man, obviously a bodyguard, got out and opened the rear car door and an elegant looking lady stepped out gracefully, allowing the bodyguard to take her hand and assist her. She was casually dressed in a brightly coloured floral skirt with a pink blouse. She opened the front gate to the garden and walked in.

"Pilar, you have a visitor," her sister called.

Pilar was helping her mother prepare lunch and went out to see who the stranger was. She was shocked but also delighted to see it was her rich auntie Maria Josefina de Alencar, who had visited her granny for a tarot card reading all those years ago. Pilar noticed she was older, more haggard and careworn with traces of botox or a facelift on her slightly puffed up face, but to Pilar it was exactly the same woman who had loved her so much. They hugged and Pilar became a little tearful.

"Auntie, how did you know where to come?"

"Shaun contacted me a few weeks ago; he worked very hard to track me down. He's so charming my dear and I feel he loves you so much."

"Me too. It's a two way street... oh! Aunt Maria, I miss him so much."

Maria sensed that Pilar was getting emotional so she changed the subject. "It's so beautiful here and so different from the *favela*. Come my dear niece," she put her arm in Pilar's, "show me round and let me say hello to your family. Then I'm hoping you'll come back with me to see the palace."

"Palace?"

"My husband inherited his father's business empire. We sell iron ore to the Chinese. We're more like billionaires now," Maria said in a rather matter of fact way.

"Auntie." Pilar shook her head, "we're just simple hard-working people. You must keep to your own kind."

Maria looked disappointed. "Please come, Pilar. I need to talk to you. I need to explain some things from the past."

Pilar looked at Maria's pleading expression. "Okay Auntie, but say hello to my parents and sisters first," Pilar smiled as she led her into the house.

It was a long drive to Petropolis. Pilar knew the place by reputation only, that it was a mountain resort to the north. Many super rich people had retreated there, away from the heat, dust and poverty of Rio. It was also the burial place of the pious Queen Isabel the Redemptress, who signed the Golden Law in 1888 to totally abolish slavery in Brazil. The car snaked smoothly up through the mountains. They chatted all the way, but Pilar had expected them to reflect on life a little and get onto deeper topics. Instead, Maria seemed only able to talk about her wealth. She spoke of the new boat they had built; it was the length of three buses and was now berthed in a local marina. It was cream and white, it had four en-suites, four guestrooms and a separate area for the crew, it cost twenty million Brazilian Reais (£8 Million) to build.

They eventually came to a walled garden, with tall security gates and CCTV cameras covering every angle. The car stopped at the gatehouse and a security man let them through. They continued up a long driveway, and Pilar noticed three German shepherd dogs sitting on the lawn. They appeared to be watching the car as it passed. They finally came to a halt at a beautiful Portuguese style palace, painted white, and descended from the car.

"You'll have to forgive all the surveillance; we have an alarm that goes straight through to a private security firm. You see we're now so rich, we've become a prime target for the kidnapping gangs. They got our neighbour a few months ago; they cut off his toe and sent it to his wife in a little coffin with a note asking for two million Reais (£1 Million)."

Pilar gasped in horror. "What did she do?"

"She came to me, asking what she should do. It was awful my dear, just horrible. She never usually came to see me… sit down please." Maria motioned to some chairs on the lawn just outside the front door, as though the story was so exciting that nothing should be allowed to break its flow. They sat and Maria continued. "She came in and said 'I'm your neighbour'. I said, 'I know who you are. Do you want some coffee?' Then she placed this little toy coffin on the table. 'This has been delivered to me,' she said as she opened it, and showed me the toe. I was trembling with shock and told her, 'you're bringing your trouble to me. I cannot help you, please go now. I don't want you here.' She said, 'I'm scared to be in my own house, can I stay here?' She begged me. All I could do was to call a security firm I knew, all ex-military, who specialise in snatching back kidnap victims. We then took the toe to the hospital, as we thought the doctors might be able to preserve it and would be able to sew it back on when the husband was returned."

"That's a horrible story; did she get her husband back?"

"Two months later. He'd lost a lot of weight, but he was far too fat anyway. It did him good, really." Maria chuckled. "The snatch squad ambushed the gang and shot them," she said in a matter of fact way.

"But Auntie, money should give you freedom, now look at how you're living. You're like a prisoner in your own home."

Momentarily, Maria looked confused, but quickly regained her regal composure. She continued. "We are good friends with the President of Brazil, my dear. I have met the U.S. President and his wife, and I even met Prince Charles and Camilla when they came to Rio." She looked at Pilar, who nodded, not really knowing what to say. "You know what I have to do when I want to wear my jewellery for a gala?" Maria continued, excited by her own stories. "I go to the bank to retrieve it and rendezvous there with the insurance company's security guard, who then stays with me all the time. He comes to the gala and then back to the palace to sleep overnight. The next day, we return the jewellery to the bank."

"Auntie," Pilar looked concerned and put her arm round Maria. "Do you own your possessions or do they own you? This is no life, you were better off when you had less money."

"What can I do? I can't walk away from my responsibilities." Maria frowned. "I help so many charities. I helped pay for a new hospital for the poor of Rio. It was me who made it happen."

Pilar sighed almost in desperation. "Like you helped me you mean, but on a larger scale?"

"You were different. I would have given my life for you." Maria's expression at last became more thoughtful and reflective.

"All you've talked about is your yacht, your jewellery, your money, all material things. What about how much you loved me, and how much I loved you? Isn't that worth far more? What price would you put on it?"

Tears suddenly welled up in Maria's eyes. "I never stopped thinking about you, even when your parents said I couldn't see you any more. The scholarship bursary for your education was something I set up especially for you. It was me who was paying your school fees for all those years. Your photo was always on my dressing table, and still is." She took Pilar's hand in hers and looked at her.

"Auntie, carry on with your charity work, and every day thank God you are blessed with so much money, and ask how it can best be used."

They hugged for what seemed a long time, and then Maria pulled away, smiling, but with tears rolling down her face. "I haven't seen you for so long. You've turned into a visionary, just like your grandmother. What a woman she was, and those piercing eyes!"

"I know Auntie Maria, I feel she's with me a lot of the time."

Maria took Pilar by the hand and led her into the house out of the heat of the evening.

Pilar returned to Rio late that night. Maria's household had three bullet-proof and armour plated Mercedes, one for Maria, one for her husband, and one for her daughters. But on this evening, one was being repaired and the other two were in use, so Maria had asked if Pilar would mind returning to Rio in the Volvo, which was normally used for collecting supplies. Pilar had replied, 'of course not.'

Alone in the back of the Volvo, without the bodyguard, who remained at the palace, Pilar remembered Maria had promised to visit her in London, which was kind, but she was a little sad at how Auntie was living. She secretly hoped that Shaun and she would never become that rich. After half an hour, as they reached the outskirts of Rio, the chauffeur's eyes were all over the place. He was looking in all the mirrors in sequence. Pilar was rather intrigued as it made him appear very anxious. She could see his eye motion flicking from left to right and centre, all the time keeping the car moving at a steady pace. Suddenly she felt a shudder from the back, something had hit the car and the driver became even more nervous and agitated.

"Stop the car. Something has hit us from behind," she insisted, but the driver ignored her. "Stop the car now please," she repeated, talking to him as though she had the authority of Maria.

"I can't stop, *senhorita*. This is a very bad part of town. It's not good for stopping. We must drive on."

Then it happened again, `Bang` and as she swung

round to look out the back window, she saw a motorbike with two men on it. They were dressed in old, dirty clothes, but she noticed they were wearing crash helmets. `Bang` they hit the car again, then they swung round to the side and the pillion passenger hit Pilar's window with a piece of pipe. The window shattered and the glass shards covered her, but she had instinctively raised her hands to protect her face. `Bang` the pillion passenger then smashed the driver's window and the car shuddered to a halt. The hot surface of the road made the tyres squeal almost in unison with the terrified driver. He slid over to the other door and opened it. As he fell out onto the road, he shouted for Pilar to follow him and to leave the car from the other side. She bounced across the seat and opened the door, exiting in a continuous motion, and landing in a heap on the dusty, hot and hard concrete road. The next thing she knew she was being pulled onto her feet with a tight grip on her wrist. Someone was dragging her at speed down an alley way. She struggled at first thinking she was being kidnapped, then she realised it was the driver and stopped resisting. They ran for a long time before he picked her up and threw her over a wall. He then followed her over. As he landed he put his finger to his lips and moved to cover her. They lay silent, puffing for air.

"Haaaah!" The motor bike driver had laughed as the two victims disappeared down the alley. "That was easy. I thought he might be armed and start shooting at us." His passenger got off the bike and removed his helmet. Tossing it into the back, he opened the driver's door and wiped the glass from the seat.

"Come Antonio, the cops will be here soon, get the doors." He pointed to the off side doors that Pilar and the driver had exited out of. The rider rode round the other side and knocked the doors shut. Just then a faint sound of a police car could be heard in the distance, and the rider revved up and zoomed off back the way they had come. The pillion passenger jumped into the car and sped off. It was all over in a few minutes.

A door opened behind them and Pilar and the driver looked round at the same time. A rather large lady beckoned them into the house.

"Come quickly, come, come. You're safe now," she whispered. They looked at each other for some sign that it was okay, then the driver picked her up and carried her into the house. Putting her down gently on the sofa, the driver took a mobile phone from his pocket and called the Palace to tell Maria what had happened. The host brought a tray of lemonade, some glasses and cotton wool with a steaming bowl of cloudy water.

"This has iodine in it, so it will sting a little," she said, reassuring Pilar as she cleaned the wounds on her arms and hands. Wincing at the stinging, Pilar braved the pain and thanked the lady. The driver came over and poured two glasses of lemonade.

"Do you have anything stronger? Vodka, whisky?" he asked the woman. Smiling she nodded in the direction of the kitchen. "Your auntie is sending a car and more security for us. We'll wait here," he said to Pilar.

Then handing the phone to the lady, he asked her to tell the man on the line exactly where they were. Pilar sat up and told the driver to sit down.

"You have a nasty gash; let me clean it for you, and thank you for not leaving me out there to the mercy of those kidnappers."

"They were only after the car I think. If we resisted, they might have killed us. It's my job, to look out for you."

An hour later two Mercedes pulled up outside to take

them back to the Palace. One of the security men gave an envelope to the lady. She wouldn't accept it at first, but Pilar took it and pressing it into her hand she said:

"*Obrigado*, please take this as a token of my appreciation." The lady nodded and smiled as she took the envelope. Then they were all gone.

Pilar spent the night at the palace, after having her wounds dressed at the hospital. She had phoned to let her family know what had happened, and returned to Ipanema the next day, this time with a bodyguard riding shotgun in the Mercedes.

"Pilar, are you okay?" Her mother came running out of the villa.

"It's nothing permanent, *Mamãe*. Just a few scratches on my arms. It will all heal. At least I'm alive."

Later on that day, she was sitting in the garden in the cool of the evening, looking thoughtful. There had been two bad things the day before, the disappointment that Maria had been changed so much by money, and the carjacking. Shaun's mother had told her that trouble came in threes. She took a call on her mobile. She wondered if it might be Maria, making sure she was okay.

"Pilar."

"Hi, how are you?" Pilar had recognized Christiana's voice.

"We're fine, thank you."

Something about the way she'd said, 'we're fine' made Pilar uneasy.

"Is Shaun okay? He's sounded a bit odd on the phone."

"Good that you've noticed. That's why I'm phoning you. I won't beat about the bush. Shaun and I are back together again. He couldn't resist me. We were lovers in Hamburg long before you came along. Fate just kept us apart for a

172

while." Pilar's mouth opened in astonishment. Her heart started to beat very fast. There was silence. "Pilar, are you there?"

"What do you mean?" Pilar laughed. "Are you having a joke with me? Put Shaun on!"

"Look, I'm sorry to do this to you because I can see you're a really sweet girl, but you're young and pretty, and you have your whole life ahead of you. Don't come back. Stay in Brazil. Shaun is mine."

At that the line went dead. Pilar phoned back, but all lines went to message.

She went straight to bed, hiding her pain from her parents and sisters and cried for an hour and eventually fell asleep, comforting herself with thoughts of childhood in the *favela*, when she had been happy. She remembered playing patty cake, where two girls face each other and bat their palms against each other's in various patterns, and jump rope, where two other girls stretch out a rope and Pilar would jump over making different shapes with her arms. She remembered watching her father and the men playing dominoes.... and above all, she remembered her granny speaking to her in the baby talk voice and carrying her everywhere so she felt safe.

Next day, she felt stronger and phoned Shaun.

"Is it true, Shaun?"

"I've been meaning to phone you. Christiana was an old girlfriend from years ago."

"Okay, but why is she saying she's your girlfriend now? Did you sleep with her while I was away?" There was a silence in which she could hear him trying to speak, but not able to get any words out. "So that's a yes then."

"I'm so sorry." He sounded very tender as he said it. "It was a moment of extreme weakness."

Pilar started to sob. "I really thought we had something special. Why did you do it?"

"We have got something special. I wish I could explain to myself, even, why I did it. I don't know what happened. I just couldn't stop myself. I'm so sorry."

"So why didn't you phone me to discuss it?"

"Because I can't get it clear in my own mind what's happening. I just can't get my head round it. It's like something's possessed me, like something external has taken control of me."

"Ughh! So you are like your father after all, a philanderer!" Shaun was silent, stunned that the comparison was now valid. Meanwhile, Pilar had closed her eyes. "Shaun, is she making your food? I'm seeing the kitchen."

"I do lunch and she does the evening meal."

"I can see something. My granny's showing me, like when I read the tarot cards. It's not very clear. Something's happening in the kitchen... come on Granny, give me a clear picture." She was silent for a while. "Christiana's mixing something together in the kitchen... come on Granny, show me... okay, now I can see it. She's got a blue pill. She's cutting it open. Oh my God, Christiana's mixing some powder in to your food, some kind of stimulant!"

"No! She couldn't be. She wouldn't be that irresponsible."

"Yes, she would. Where is she?"

"She's bathing Lisa."

"Go to her handbag and see what you can find. Phone me back."

Shaun phoned Pilar back a few minutes later.

"You're right. I've found something." He was holding a packet and his hands were shaking as he read the leaflet that was inside the box. "Herbal Viagra, all natural sexual stimulant, one hundred per cent guaranteed for rock hard erections. Money back guaranteed if not fully satisfied."

"She's a total bitch. I can't believe you let such a bitch come into our house." She said it with anger, but there was no reaction from Shaun. "Shaun, are you there?" There was silence. "Shaun, are you okay?"

Shaun was reading the leaflet, with a serious expression on his face. "I can't believe she would do this," he said at last. "All these ingredients, so many of them." He started to slowly read them out. "Rhodiola rosea, Siberian ginseng, schisandra chinensis, muira puama bark, saw palmetto fruit, damiana, chuchhuasi bark, guarana seed, cayenne fruit." His voice sounded miserable. "And they go on."

"Look what you've done, Shaun, letting that bitch into our house." Shaun was silent. "Shaun, are you okay?"

"We took her in off the street. This is how she repays us. I don't understand how she could do it…But we're okay aren't we? You understand what's happened?"

"Get her out of the house tonight. Then we'll talk about it."

"Of course I will. Let's talk later, when she's gone. I don't want to lose you, Pilar. I'm very sure of that. You have become my whole world. I'm really sorry."

"Right, of course you are. Whatever."

"You're upset with me."

"Of course I'm upset with you. Do you think I would be pleased about it?"

"What can I do to make things right?"

"Well, you can start by getting her out of our bed tonight and send her back to Germany tomorrow."

"Okay, of course. Maybe it's time for you to come back to London. Now you've made the move, tie up your loose ends and book your flight tomorrow."

Pilar knew this was the right thing to do. Shaun could

sometimes be much too easygoing. After all, look where she met him. She had to book her flight immediately. She resolved to fight for her man, even if he had wronged her.

The next morning, Pilar's father had got up for breakfast, but had gone back to bed, saying that he felt ill with a bad headache. Half an hour later, the family heard him moaning and when Pilar went into his room, he told her that he might need to vomit. She fetched a bucket to keep beside his bed. Pilar had noticed that his speech was slurred, like he was drunk.

"*Papai*," she tried to hide her concern as she placed the bucket down beside him. "Sit up for me." With some difficulty, she got him to sit up in bed. "*Papai*, smile for me. It's very important *Papai*, please make a smile for me." Pilar had trained as a nurse on leaving high school, but had abandoned the course halfway through, because her father had fallen ill and could no longer work, and in any case the eldest child of the family often had to go out to work and bring money in to help keep the younger siblings. Her father's smile was lopsided; she knew what it meant. "*Papai*, lift both your arms up for me. It's very important." He could not lift the right arm properly, just as his smile drooped on the right-hand side.

Pilar returned to the living room, out of earshot of her father and dialled 192 in a panic. It was the SAMU (*Serviço de Atendimento Móvel de Urgência*) number for medical emergencies. "My father's had a stroke; please come quickly."

The ambulance came almost immediately, something that would never have been possible if they were still in the *favela*, as the ambulance crew would never enter for fear of being attacked. At the back of her mind, Pilar knew that this was a double nightmare, because she needed to be on that plane going back to London.

A week later, Pilar's father was discharged from hospital and back home convalescing, manifesting all the typical characteristics of a stroke survivor. He cried a lot, was depressed and dragged the right side of his body around like it belonged to someone else. His speech was slurred and he seemed distant and vacant. He had once been a great football fan, but no longer watched the matches on television. Pilar was also depressed, but tried to hide it from her family. She wondered if it would be okay for her to return to London, whether her father could get better without her being there.

Quite a few people from the *favela* had already visited them to see the new villa and how Pilar's father was recuperating. This was in accordance with the *Carioca's* gregarious nature and the feeling that there was no need to make an appointment to drop in on someone. There had been no jealousy at what Pilar had achieved, more a pride that a *favela* girl could make good and a hope that others could do the same. Pilar was in the kitchen helping her mother prepare lunch when she heard her sisters laughing and joking with someone in the front garden. She suddenly realised it was Emilio, and then remembered his promise to visit.

"So what did you do to get the money for this place?" she heard him say. "You robbed a bank, right?" Her sisters laughed.

"No, it's Pilar's English boyfriend. He's a millionaire… multi, multi," said Luciana, the younger sister, keen to show off their new-found wealth, and believe that she had it made for life.

Pilar gasped. "*Puta merda*" (shit).

"Pilar!" Her mother was unusually forceful. "There's no need for that terrible language. We live in a respectable neighbourhood."

"I'm sorry *Mamãe*." Pilar tried to contain her panic. The very worst thing you could do was give people the idea you had money. Walking along the street, even in the affluent part of Rio, the rich tried to hide their wealth and not be ostentatious.

Pilar went out into the front garden to head Emilio off before he entered the villa, but when she caught sight of him, her mouth dropped open. He'd had his hair cut short, he'd shaved and he looked a lot more neat and tidy than before. He had swapped his casual gangster sportswear for a smart business look.

"Hello Pilar. I was so sorry to hear about your father, and I've brought this card signed by all his friends. I'm here to help." He was speaking more correctly and formally than usual. Pilar continued to stare at him, astonished at his transformation. "Pilar?" he said uncertainly.

"How would you be able to help?" she mumbled, looking confused and still unclear as to what had happened to Emilio.

"I want us to take your father to *João de Deus* (John of God)."

Pilar had vaguely heard of him. He ran a healing centre in the village of Abadiania, near Brasilia. "I don't like hippies."

Once again, like when they had met in the *favela*, Emilio looked wounded. "He's not a hippy." His voice was angry. "He's seen fifty million people. They make pilgrimages from all over the world to see him and he's on our doorstep. He helped my uncle from Sao Paulo; my uncle had only four weeks to live, and John of God saved him."

Pilar's father chose that moment to shuffle out from the villa. "I heard what Emilio said." His words were slurred. "Yes, I want to see John of God."

11

Rio de Janeiro – Part 2

Pilar accepted the fact that she was flying to Brasilia, with her father and Emilio, instead of returning to London to be with Shaun. They were met by an official John of God air-conditioned bus and journeyed through the tropical countryside. Pilar ignored Emilio as much as she could, but noticed he was on his best behaviour and kind in looking after her father, who remained quiet most of the time. He and Emilio managed to have a few discussions on their favourite topic of *futebol* (soccer) and whether Pelé was the greatest footballer of all time. Like Ronaldo and Rivaldo, Pelé came from the *favelas*, but only Pelé had been named the greatest athlete of the 20th century, which was a matter of great pride for all *favela* dwellers and gave them hope for a better life for their own children.

They finally reached the village of Abadiania just in time to see a wonderful sunset against a vista of open countryside and distant hills.

"It's so peaceful." Pilar took a deep breath as they stepped off the coach. The air was fragrant and the only sounds were birds singing, and the water sprinklers in the gardens. They passed through the little village, with its New Age style souvenir shops and cafes, to reach their *pousada* (guest house), a large, terracotta coloured bungalow with a tiled roof, surrounded by a spacious garden, which included an outdoor area for dining. The guesthouse owner came out to greet them.

"Good afternoon. I'm Carlos and I'll be looking after you during your stay."

He showed them to their rooms which were simply furnished with a bed, chair and writing table, the walls being painted a plain magnolia. Pilar appreciated the lack of clutter. She wished her life was as simple.

"When you've settled in, come and have a drink with me and I'll tell you a bit about what's going to happen."

Later, Pilar, her father and Emilio came and sat in the dining area in the garden. Carlos spotted them, took their order for drinks and came back with a fruit juice for Pilar, a tea for her father and a sugarcane juice for Emilio.

"It's so beautiful here. I can't believe it. I already feel so different." Pilar smiled at Carlos.

"It has that effect." Carlos nodded.

"What brought you here?"

"Mine is a long story, but an interesting one. I was a top litigations lawyer in Sao Paulo, which is a city of work, work, work, not laid back like Rio. I had slogged away all my life, always trying to do the right thing, always trying to make as much money as I could, so my family could have a better life. But when I reached my early forties, I found I was heavy with responsibilities, sickness and depression. I seemed to have everything wrong with my body and then my voice started to go, which I needed for my profession as a lawyer as I still made court appearances. I was diagnosed with inoperable throat cancer and was given a few months to live." He raised his eyebrows and paused for dramatic effect. Pilar imagined him in court putting a case. "I knew that juice fasts could sometimes help cancer, so I started one, alternating organic fruit juices with organic vegetable juices. I felt a little better for it, but ten days in, an acquaintance suggested I visit John of God."

"That's like what happened to my uncle!" Emilio interjected.

"Sshh!" Pilar put her finger to her mouth. "Don't interrupt."

"So I came here," Carlos continued, "and John of God cured me and now I'm completely well. So I gave up my lawyer's practice and spend all my time here."

"That's amazing." Pilar's face had lit up. "You're giving me hope."

"Yes, but hope is not a strategy for life. What you want is the real thing, something that will make tangible changes, like John of God's healing."

"So how does he heal?" Pilar gave Carlos a puzzled look.

"He's a psychic surgeon. He works with spirits, who detect the part of the body that's diseased, increase the vibration using John of God's hands and perform spiritual surgery, like a super laser, removing disease in the same way an orthodox surgeon would with his scalpel."

"I understand. My granny was a spiritual healer," she nodded. "You're so enthusiastic…I really admire you. You have given up so much materially."

"There's nothing to admire. I enjoy every moment here, much more than my old life.., so tomorrow I will give you breakfast at 7 a.m. and then you will go down to the healing centre for eight o'clock. While you are here, eat only the food I give you or that served at the centre, and no alcohol."

"What will the food be?" Emilio changed his posture from a slouch to one of sitting up.

"It will be light, spiritual food, to help you release your sickness and stress." Carlos could see Emilio's frown.

"Don't be scared. Craving for food is mainly in the mind, not the body. The meals will be mostly rice and vegetables." Carlos watched Emilio let out a big, weary sigh. "If you still feel hungry, you can always have spiritual soup, made of vegetables. Soup is very effective in taking away hunger."

* * *

"Hi Shaun. I'm in central Brazil, Abadiania, getting my father some special healing. I don't know how long it's all going to take."

"Brilliant! That's your priority. Get him better."

"So Christiana and Lisa will have gone by now?"

"They're still here."

"What? Shaun, no! I don't understand."

"She's pleading with me to forgive her. She says she hasn't got anywhere else to go, that she'll be killed if she goes back to Germany."

"That's not our problem. Just give her some money and kick her out."

"I can't just throw her out."

"She's not your responsibility."

"I'm trying to sort something out. I want to contact her brother-in-law, Hartmut, who I met in Hamburg, but she doesn't want me to. He was a very together chap."

"Is she in our bed?"

"No! Absolutely not." His voice was softer. "Don't you realise how much I love you?" He waited for her to her reply.

"Do you? That's what I want to hear you say."

"Christiana's gone a bit crazy, that's all. I threw her out of my room, as soon as I knew what she'd done. I was so angry with her. I've been all this time trying to restore my health. I've researched those Chinese herbs and they can attack the vital organs, particularly if you overdose on them."

"So why haven't you thrown her out of the house?"

"Look, I'll sort it out."

"You worry me. You're too nice, too easy-going."

"You do your job, get your father better and I'll do mine."

She sighed. "Maybe. So make sure you do. Next time we speak, I want her gone."

* * *

Next day it was Friday, and at 7.45 a.m. Pilar, her father and Emilio walked down to the end of the Central Avenue, where John of God's healing sanctuary stood, set back in a lush, green, subtropical garden. They entered the main Assembly Hall of the one storey complex, where they were greeted by the 'sons and daughters' or helpers, dressed in all white. They were then ushered to the right, through a series of rooms, called the Current rooms, where Pilar understood their energies would be cleansed and harmonised before they reached John of God, who healed in an inner sanctum, called the Surgery room as this is where he performed psychic or invisible surgery. Around the edges of the rooms, John of God's helpers sat with eyes closed, meditating. Pilar saw Carlos there and she wanted to wave to him, but he seemed to be in a different world.

Despite her grandmother having been a healer, Pilar was naturally sceptical about it and yet, unmistakably, as the line they were standing in worked its way towards the Surgery room, she felt the weight of the world on her shoulders, all the worries over her father and Shaun, drop away with every step, until by the time she was ten feet from John of God, by some magic she felt completely carefree. She noticed also that her father's face was much more relaxed, and his drooping mouth looked less twisted. As for Emilio, he seemed to have gone into a dream world of his own.

John of God was a middle-aged man dressed in all white, with a pleasant face, wearing glasses. On the photos Pilar had seen, he had a beatific smile, but performing his surgery, he was in a trance state and looked half asleep. He pressed a surgeon's scalpel into Pilar's father's face for about sixty seconds, performing psychic surgery. But he also gave a blessing to Pilar and Emilio. Pilar walked out, energised, uplifted, as though walking on air and she prayed that she could hold on to that feeling. Afterwards, they were given Blessed Spiritual Soup and told not to have sex for forty days.

* * *

Back home and over the next two weeks, Pilar's father made an impressive recovery and at last, Pilar could start to relax. There was a local saying, *Cariocas nao gostam de dias nublados*, (Cariocas don't like cloudy days.) and that was because young people especially would go to the beach every day. It was Sunday and Pilar had arranged to go to Ipanema beach with her sisters, who had a day off from their jobs in a local hotel. Mariana, the elder at nineteen, was a receptionist and Luciana, seventeen, was a waitress. They walked the few blocks down to the beach, and across the coast road, which was pedestrianised on a Sunday and given over to strollers, bike riders, roller skaters and skateboarders. They stepped on to the beach at *Posto 9* (lifeguard post nine) and removed the throws they had wrapped round their waists, revealing their bikinis. 'Tah dah,' Mariana would always say as she removed hers. Ipanema beach was divided into *postos,* each one comprised of toilets, showers and a lifeguard tower, upon which sat a lifeguard peering out to sea for swimmers or surfers in trouble. The lifeguards would enter the water, but if the waves were large they would instead call a helicopter, which would arrive within minutes, to winch swimmers in distress to safety. The helicopter might be called out five or six times on a rough day. The red flag was flying, which meant this Sunday was a rough day.

The beach was free to all and the great leveller of Rio society, but even so, each *posto* attracted different affinity groups, the surfers, the gays, the families, the in crowd, the playboys. *Posto* 9 was the most famous, being where the young and beautiful people, the in crowd, gathered. The trio stopped, taking in the abundance of tanned, muscular men in their Speedo trunks and the beautiful women in their tiny bikinis. They stood and watched a game of *footvolei* (foot volleyball), where the young men used their head, chest, feet, legs, but not their hands, to get the ball over the net, displaying an incredible coordination and fitness. They were world class.

"Come on girls, let's go down to the gay section," Pilar said after a few minutes of watching. "We won't get bothered down there."

"But we don't mind being bothered." Mariana said. "We want to be kissed, starting at our feet and working all the way up…" She looked at Luciana and giggled.

"That's enough." Pilar frowned "Let's just relax."

They walked down towards *Posto* 8 and stopped where a huge rainbow flag was flying. They set up camp and stretched out in the sun. They hadn't been there very long before Pilar heard a strong American accent.

"Where was my breakfast today?"

Pilar looked round to see two chubby, pale skinned men, in their thirties, smiling at Mariana and Luciana. She could tell by their Bermuda shorts they were *gringos*, as locals would only ever wear tight Speedo's on the beach, and anyway, their lack of muscle tone meant they could not be Brazilian. She realised they were staying at her sisters' hotel.

"Oh, hello!" Luciana started laughing. "Sorry about that. Are you hungry? Sit down and I'll get you something to eat, sir." Her English was unusually good for a *favela* girl, mainly due to Pilar's tutoring and the fact that she had also paid for her sisters to have private lessons from an American student spending a gap year in the *favela*.

The men needed no encouragement and instantly dropped down onto the sand. "I'm Dan and this is Jim." They both held out their hands to Pilar's sisters.

"I'm Luciana, which you know from my name badge in the restaurant and this is my sister Mariana, who you may have noticed on the reception desk."

"Sure thing. She checked us in, and we never forget a pretty face."

The two sisters shook hands with the men.

"And this is my sister Pilar who lives in London." Luciana added.

Pilar nodded to them and muttered a minimally effusive greeting, looking away almost immediately. She did not care for them. Rio attracted lots of older sex tourists looking for pretty teenage girls like her sisters. She did not want her sisters prostituting themselves, although lots of *favela* girls did, because it was such easy money.

The men chit chatted in a suggestive way, taking every opportunity to touch Pilar's two sisters, stroking their skin on the excuse of admiring their suntan, and then asking the girls if they would apply suntan lotion to their white, blubbery bodies, to which Pilar's sisters readily agreed.

"Hmm, that feels so good. You know just how I like it. You should do this for a profession," the one drawled as the beautiful, youthful Luciana spread the cream over his body.

There was sexual innuendo in all their conversation and Pilar could not stand to hear any more and said, almost unnoticed, that she was going in the sea for a dip. She walked down to the water, which looked much rougher than usual, but she entered to waist level. She flicked her hair, adjusted her bikini top and turned round to look back up the beach to see what her sisters were doing. To her astonishment, they were kissing the men. She stood transfixed.

At that moment, a huge wave came and took her from behind while she was off guard, rolling her over and over towards the beach, then sucking her back out to sea. It was like she had slipped into a new, unfamiliar dimension, a silent dark world, where she was powerless. She stood up gasping for air. She was not a strong swimmer. Before she could recover, a second, larger wave took her again, rolling her over and over towards the beach and then sucking her back out to sea. She seemed to be under longer this time, but managed to stand up and gasp for air.

Then a third, even larger, wave took her in the same way, and she seemed to be under for a very long time and did not know if she could hold her breath as this wave did not seem to want to give her up. It started to feel painful and she realised she was in trouble when suddenly, she was hovering above the sea, very calm and looking down on herself under the water. Time seemed to be expanded, going very slowly and she had the thought, 'so this is how you die. I always thought you would live a long time.' There was a golden tunnel of light above her and she started to walk up it. At the top end of the tunnel was a source of great goodness and love and just as she was about to be bathed in the love, her granny was there. She knelt and hugged Pilar round the middle. She then said:

"I love you. It's not your time. You have much more work to do. You must go back."

At that very moment, she was in her body again and lifted out of the water by a very tanned, muscular man. She was lying in his arms, like he had picked up a matchstick. She was gasping for air, a terrible sound like someone who had whooping cough. Her face was pale and her skin cold.

"It's too rough today. You shouldn't be here." He shook his head in admonishment. "Be careful next time."

She just looked at him, gasping for air. A helicopter swooped low across the beach and stopped to hover above them, its rotating blades creating a drumming sound over the sea and throwing up a lot of spray. The muscular man waved to the winch man, who was looking out of the helicopter's hatch, giving him a gesture of, 'go back, it's okay'. He carried Pilar out of the sea and on to the beach.

"Did you take in any water?" the muscular man asked as he lay her down on her side on the beach, in the recovery position. He crouched beside her.

She was still panting with a strained expression on her face, but shook her head. "Don't think so," she whispered her first words.

"I'm João, by the way."

"Pilar." She managed a little smile.

"I think you'll be okay. Just rest and get your breath back." He went over to where he had left his things and came back with a towel, which he placed over her. "Here," he started gently rubbing her back through the towel, "you seem to be very cold. Let's get your circulation going."

She said nothing, just lay there quietly. He rubbed her back and chest for a few minutes in silence. Then he lay beside her in a relaxed manner, without any fussing, just gazing at her from time to time. She was looking back at him. He noticed the colour start to seep back into her face and a sparkle return to her eyes. About ten minutes passed in silence, while João just enjoyed the rhythmic sound of the waves breaking on the beach, the light spray coming off them, the tang of ozone from the sea and the warmth of the sun.

"So strong," Pilar finally whispered, her little arm reaching out to squeeze his bicep.

He looked at her and realised he had just saved a beautiful woman from drowning. He didn't notice that she was sneaking a look at his body. He was very fit and toned, stronger than Shaun.

"I have to go back to work now, but can I buy you dinner tonight?"

"I pay." she whispered, nodding.

"We'll see. Meet me at *Posto* 8 at 8 p.m. That's easy to remember. You can keep the towel."

"Okay… may God grant you a long life." A little more strength had seeped back into her voice and she squeezed his hand and then smiled in farewell.

João disappeared up the beach and Pilar slowly got up and made her way back to her sisters. She sat down next to them. The two Americans had already gone.

"Did you see what happened to me?" Her voice still lacked its usual power.

"We saw you flirting with a very gorgeous man. What about Shaun?" Mariana asked. "And there's you trying to tell us how to behave!"

"That gorgeous man saved my life! I nearly drowned. I need to get back to London before anything else happens to me!"

"Was the helicopter for you?" Mariana suddenly looked concerned as Pilar nodded in the affirmative. "Are you all right? What happened?"

Both sisters reached out to touch Pilar, but she brushed them off.

"What did those two men want?" Pilar asked.

"Nothing. Just being friendly," Mariana replied.

"Why were you kissing them?"

"They said, 'do you kiss?' So we showed them."

"Stay away from men like that. They're creepy."

"They're rich Americans."

"They're not rich or they wouldn't be staying in your hotel. Stay away from them."

"But we want money, like you. We want a rich boyfriend like Shaun."

"Don't compare those creeps to Shaun. He's gorgeous looking. You two can do much better for yourselves."

* * *

It was the evening and Pilar was sitting opposite João in an upmarket restaurant. They were both eating grilled chicken with fries and salad.

"You look so different to the girl I pulled out of the sea earlier today. You're stunning."

"And you look like a young Julio Iglesias."

He started to sing, closing his eyes and pulling a face as though full of passion. *"When they begin the beguine."*

"Okay. That's enough, Julio." Pilar leant across and kissed him. Lots of kissing went on in Rio's bars and restaurants, but it didn't have much significance. "So where's your girlfriend tonight?"

"She's right here, opposite me." He widened his eyes.

"Seriously, where is she?"

"I'm between girls right now… and where's your boyfriend?"

"He's in London."

The smile dropped off João's face. "Oh! A long, long way away."

Pilar shrugged. She took João's hand. "Thank you so much. I owe you my life."

"You're welcome. Looks like we have a special connection."

"Maybe."

"Shall we go to a bar after this?"

"Okay."

The evening had been fun and at the end, Pilar insisted on paying. She felt she owed him much more than a meal. As they left, they passed an adjoining room of the restaurant and Pilar thought she heard a familiar laugh, Mariana's. She looked to the far corner and could not believe her eyes. Mariana and Luciana were having a meal with the two Americans.

"João, I'm so sorry. I have to go now." She kissed him again. "I have to go and see my sisters over there." She pointed them out to him. "Here, put my number in your phone. Call me tomorrow and we can do the bar." She gave him her phone number and walked off, picking up a spare chair en route to the far corner. "Hello, you two." She placed the chair on the end of the table and sat down.

"Oh, it's the elder sister." The two Americans giggled like a couple of cliquey friends who used their own secret language and excluded everyone else.

"What's going on?" Pilar asked her sisters, who just looked down at their plates in silence. She didn't really need to hear their answer. "I don't want to appear rude," Pilar looked at the two men, "but I think my sisters are much too young to be dating men of your age." Pilar gave the men a hard stare, but they just giggled again.

"Aaw! That's not a good attitude. In America, we try not to be ageist. We're young at heart," the one said.

"Yeah," said the other, who was more drunk, "we're two lonely men looking for some company. We have a lot of mutual interests."

"I don't think you've got much in common, have you?"

"I don't know," the drunker one continued, his speech slurred from alcohol. "I feel a strong connection to your sisters. I think we're on the same page here. We're only looking for OWO and CIM, followed by Swallow and bareback A to finish."

The two men exploded with laughter. Pilar frowned. She knew the terminology from her escort days in London. She spoke to her sisters in Portuguese, knowing the men would not be able to follow.

"Girls, all they are looking for is OWO, oral without, where you suck their dicks without a condom, followed by CIM, come in mouth, which they want you to swallow. Then they want to fuck your arse without a condom, which might just give you Aids." Pilar looked at the men. "If that's what you want, you should go to the *termas* of Copacabana. You'll fit in there." She referred to the massage parlours very popular with sex tourists, and local businessmen pretending to work late.

"That's where we were last night," the drunker one said.

"Sshh," said his companion.

They dissolved into giggles again.

"I think that's where you'll be again tonight." Pilar glared at the men.

"Hhmm," said the one who was more drunk. "But your sisters are far more succulent than the shrivelled old bitches in the *termas*."

"Come on girls, we're out of here."

"Have we missed something?" The one who was less drunk had decided to put up a fight and addressed Pilar as she went to stand up. "Were we wrong to think that your sisters are," he put on a theatrical Brazilian accent, "*garotas de programa* … and that we are doing them a favour?" The Brazilian phrase meant, 'goodtime girls', but it was an accepted euphemism for a non career prostitute.

Pilar's face was flushed. "Yes, you were completely wrong. We don't live in the *favela*. We're a respectable family, and you two should be ashamed of yourselves." She gave the man a hard look and then turned to her sisters. "Come on girls."

"Sorry, if we let you down, ma'am," the less drunk one retorted, in a sarcastic tone.

Pilar marched out of the restaurant, followed by her sisters, who had looked uncomfortable throughout the whole episode. They started to walk home.

"I told you to stay away from them!" Pilar broke the silence.

"But they were rich." Mariana retorted.

"I bet they weren't."

"They said they would give us a lot of money if we were cherry girls, if we still had our cherries… What did they mean?"

Pilar sighed. "Can't you work it out? The first time a girl has sex, the man pops her cherry and she bleeds. They wanted to know if you were virgins… well, are you?" She looked at them. There was a silence. "That means you're not. Who took your virginity?" There was another silence. "Who?" Pilar insisted. There was still silence. "Who? Tell me!" She stopped and stood in front of them, holding their arms. "We don't go home till you've told me."

"Emilio." the two sisters said in unison.

"No! No! *Filho da Puta!*" (son of a bitch). Pilar's face became distorted, and she started to cry. "*O que eu fiz para merecer isso?*" (Why do I deserve this?) She repeated the question a few times, banging the palm of her hand against her forehead. Then she continued through her tears. "So Emilio raped you and you said nothing?"

"He didn't rape us." Mariana spoke for the two of them. "When he scared off the gangsters who wanted to be our pimps, he said we owed it to him. He said it was like protection money. It was a debt we had to repay."

"So it was like rape. He bullied you into it." Pilar was crying and her face was red.

"But we agreed to it."

"Where did he do it to you?"

"At home, when our parents were out."

"I'm not sure how much more I want to know, but were you two together, when it happened?"

"Yes, he said he would make it a threesome. He said he would spear me first because I was the eldest."

"Ughh! He makes a pig look human. I'll kill him." She scowled.

* * *

Pilar had calmed down by the next day. Many *favela* girls had lost their virginity by the age of fourteen, and not always in a romantic manner. She decided that she had done enough to help her family for one trip, and that she would book a flight back the next day, before any more bad things could happen to her. But the same afternoon she received a phone call from Christiana.

"Pilar."

"Oh! My favourite person. You're in Germany, by now?"

"Pilar, I need to tell you something."

"What? That you're sorry?"

"I'm not sorry for anything."

"What then? What are you after this time?"

"I'm carrying Shaun's baby." There was a silence. Pilar was stunned. "You shouldn't come back sweetheart. You're

194

better off staying in Brazil. Shaun is very happy with me; don't spoil it for us. If you love him and want what's best for him, stay away."

"You're a bitch. You date raped him. We could go to the police about you."

"No. I'm still in the house and Shaun is in love with me now, and I've got his child in my womb."

"You could have made that up. I wouldn't trust you with anything."

"Shaun's seen the pregnancy test results."

"We'll see when I get back. Don't think I'm not coming back. Shaun is mine, not yours."

"We'll send you a hundred thousand pounds. We'll make an electronic transfer into your bank account. We can get a value date of the day after tomorrow. Think about all that money. That will go so far in Brazil; you can set yourself up for life. You're young, and the whole of your life is ahead of you; you'll soon find somebody else. You can pick and choose. Your UK mission will be accomplished."

"It's not all about money with me. Shaun and I will give you a hundred thousand pounds for the baby. That must sound good to you. I would want Shaun even if he had nothing."

"That's not true. You're just a gold-digger; that's why you came to London. You're an economic migrant, Brazilian slum dog. You're trailer trash."

"I'm flying back tomorrow, and I want you out of my house when I arrive," Pilar shouted.

"Stay where you are, Brazilian whore," Christiana shouted back as she cut Pilar off.

It was a while later and Pilar was sitting in the cool of the evening in the front garden of the villa, rather tearful, wondering whether to phone Shaun or to leave it till the next day. She let out a weary moan as Emilio came up the garden path. He was still looking much smarter.

"How is your father doing?" he asked in his effected gentlemanly manner, but she sat there in silence, not answering. "Pilar… what's wrong?" He looked puzzled. They had achieved a certain amount of familiarity, during the visit to John of God.

"I know what you did to my sisters." There was an indignant tone in her voice.

"There's something I've been wanting to say to you for a while." Emilio hesitated. "I want to sincerely apologise for what happened to you that night in the *favela*. I'm really so sorry. As for your sisters, they agreed to it, but I'm also sorry about what happened to them."

"I'd like you to go now, please."

"Hear me out." As a gangster in the *favela* he had become brazen. "I can't go back and change what I did. I can only look forward and try and make things right."

She shook her head. "Save your flowery words. I'd like you to go now, please."

"Listen, when we had the healing from John I realised, you can dance with the Devil or you can walk with God. I've changed. I don't want you and Jesus to think bad of me. I'm a good Catholic now." The words rolled off his tongue quite effortlessly, and he looked to see if Pilar was convinced. "I'm not the old Emilio anymore. You have to believe me. I know I haven't been a saint, but I want to make everything up to you. I want to go to London with you. I want to see if I can make some honest money, better myself, follow your example, become a good person and a role model for the youngsters of the *favela*. I want to open a mission to save young souls."

"Don't involve me… I'd just like you to go now, please."

"I won't be any trouble. I can look after myself. Just give

me somewhere to stay for a couple of nights and show me how to get started there."

"Please will you leave?" Emilio just sat there in silence for about a minute and Pilar was starting to become annoyed at the situation. "So not only must I and my sisters suffer being raped by you, you think I should put up with you as a travelling companion as well?"

"Please, Pilar? Please forgive me for what I did. Please believe that a person can change." Suddenly, the giant of a man seemed meek. There was another minute's silence where he just sat there.

She shook her head. "No. Definitely not." She had a fixed, stubborn look on her face.

"Please, Pilar. Give me a chance. You are blaming me for the sins of the world." He looked again to see if his words were having the desired effect, but Pilar had her eyes closed. She was distant, as if in a little reverie, like when her granny was talking to her. She was whispering for a minute or two, while Emilio just sat there, looking ahead. He thought she must be praying. He could make out a few words. She was repeating, 'are you sure?' quite a bit and shaking her head, like in disbelief, as she whispered it. She finally opened her eyes, looking confused. Emilio spotted uncertainty in her expression. "Come on, Pilar. I want to make lots of money and come back and fight the evils of the townships. I'll use prayer, the Bible, free food and my size to win people over. Help me, Pilar." She had closed her eyes again and was whispering once more, speaking to her granny. After a few moments, she opened her eyes and looked at Emilio. "Come on, Pilar. This is God's work. Don't throw Emilio on the rubbish tip." She was looking at him in silence. He could see the whispering had changed her stance. She was looking as though she might agree to letting him come. "Please, Pilar."

"My granny says you can come. There's some purpose in it. You'll repay a karmic debt." She said it in a flat tone.

"What?" Emilio screwed his face up.

"You can come. Book your ticket today. You'd better do it quickly before I change my mind."

Her family saw her off at the airport the next day. Her father had insisted on coming, so they had hired a special people carrier. Emilio's parents came too, quite excited about their son's impending adventure. His father towered above Pilar, but his mother was Pilar's own height and pushed her face in close.

"Take care of him," she demanded.

"Isn't he big enough to look after himself?"

* * *

"Shaun, I'm just about to board."

"Great. Have you had a nice holiday?"

"Not entirely… not with my father's stroke and me nearly dying twice, once in the carjacking and once off Ipanema beach."

"Oh my God, no! We're going to spend lots of quality time together, when you get back and we're going to talk all this through."

"Yes, lots of time together."

"And you'll need some pampering?"

"Lots of spoiling, like when I first moved in with you. You remember all the nice things we did? That's what I need right now."

"Of course. It's going to be wonderful to have you back. Our lives are going to be so much fun from now on. I've decided we're going to do some weekends to Paris, Rome, see a bit of Europe. We can go to Lisbon. You can see where you Brazilians come from."

"Oh Shaun, I'm feeling so happy… what about… she phoned me last night…"

"Christiana is still here."

"Shaun, no!" Pilar raised her voice. "Why?"

"Look, it's complicated. She says she's having my baby."

"She's lying."

"She showed me the pregnancy test results."

"She can have an abortion."

"I can't force her to do that. Anyway, it's against my religious principles, and yours, I think."

"I thought we'd been through all this. Why is she still in the house? You've had lots of time to get rid of her."

"We're almost there with it. My parents have agreed to put her up, until we can work out what to do with her long-term. But she just needs to stay with us for two more nights as my parents have got my uncle and aunt over from the States right now."

"I'm not happy with her being with us. Put her in a hotel for two nights."

"Try and be a bit understanding. She seems to have lost her balance of mind. She must have, to do what she did to me. I'm not even sure I believe the gangster story she told us. Maybe she came to get money out of us. It might even be worth giving her some, just to get rid of her."

"You're too kind, sometimes, Shaun. It scares me how nice you can be. People can use you. Look, I have a surprise for you also. I'm bringing someone who wants to get started in London… Emilio."

"Who is he?"

"He's a gangster from the *favela*."

"Woah! Hang on. Is that a good idea? Do we need a gangster in our lives right now?"

"I'll explain when I see you, but let's say that he can stay two nights like Christiana, and then he has to leave. They can both leave together... my plane's boarding now, Shaun. See you soon."

Pilar had been nervous about an eleven hour journey with Emilio next to her, but she needn't have been because it was in any case, a night flight and he slept all the way, the result of partying till dawn the night before. It was a Saturday morning when they touched down in London, and she was relieved to be back. She knew things could only get better.

12

London – Part 3

Cupoeira is an Afro-Brazilian dance derived from fighting, where sparring pairs wear white and play-fight with fluid acrobatic sweeps, kicks, handstands, cartwheels and rolls. Musicians make a circle around the pair and play instruments such as drums and the *berimbau*. Pilar had brought a *berimbau* through as hand luggage all the way from Rio. It was like a long bow, about three foot in length, with a gourd attached about a third of the way up to form a sound chamber and bridge. The player would strike the wire with a stick to give a percussive accompaniment, resting the gourd against his stomach.

"Hello sweetheart." Shaun met them as they emerged from airside. "Cor, what you got there, Pilar?"

"It's your present. You rest the gourd against your stomach." She shoved it into his middle as hard as she could.

"Ow! That hurt." Shaun grimaced and then looked up at Pilar's companion. "Hello Emilio. Pilar told me you were coming. Nice to meet you. Hey, you're tall."

"Hello *amigo*," Emilio said, smiling, in halting English. "Your country is cool." He had learnt to smile a lot to reassure people, as their initial reaction on meeting him would otherwise be fear.

They trundled their way to the car park, Shaun pushing

the trolley laden with the cases, the *berimbau* sitting precariously on top.

"Aaah!" Emilio exclaimed as they reached Shaun's Porsche Carrera, "I see why you like England, Pilar. It is a very good country. People are rich!"

"Not everyone, Emilio. Only if you work hard, you will get the rewards. There's no other way of doing it." She said it like she was talking to a child.

They put the bags in the boot and got in the car. Emilio squeezed his huge frame into the back and Pilar sat in the front passenger seat.

"Well Shaun, you look pretty washed out. Looks like it's been a draining experience." Pilar said it calmly and quietly so as not to involve Emilio. "What have you been up to? I'm hoping you can give me some answers face-to-face as to what it's all been about. Sounds like you've had lots of fun."

"Don't worry. We'll sort everything out. It's not a problem."

"What, it's not a problem? You don't think sleeping with Christiana behind my back is a problem?"

"We've been through all this on the phone. She drugged me."

"But these drugs only work if you have some desire in the first place. Who do you want to be with?"

"You."

"Are you sure?"

"Perfectly sure."

Pilar's expression looked a little more relaxed. "I'm a strong girl, and I've taken lots of knocks in my life. But I don't expect to be cheated on."

"You won't be. I promise. It's just you and me. I just made a little mistake. Don't give me a hard time."

"Little mistake?"

"You're blaming me for things that aren't my fault. You're not being fair. We'll talk about it later." Shaun let out a sigh, as though slightly exasperated and then looked in the rear view mirror at Emilio, who was sprawled across the back seat, half reclining. "So what are you hoping to do in London, Emilio?" Shaun asked.

"Oh, I want to find somewhere cheap to live, and then find work and earn lots of money as quickly as possible." He pulled himself up into a less supine position.

"Are you hoping to see some of the sights of London?"

"Yes, I want to go up in the London Eye so I can see all of London from it. I want to see the London Dungeon. I want to see the Tower of London where people had their heads chopped off. I want to go clubbing. I would like to see a film premiere where all the film stars walk on the red carpet. But my favourite thing is to go paintballing."

"Really?" Shaun laughed. "That sounds quite an anti climax to end your list on. You don't have paintballing in Rio?"

"We do. But I would like to see how you do it here." Emilio suddenly looked sly. He wasn't mentioning that he had been banned from all the Rio paintballing sites for not playing according to the rules and, when challenged, beating up anyone who confronted him.

"We've got a venue very close to where Pilar and I live. Maybe we can go this afternoon, as you won't be staying with us long."

"That would be great."

"Pilar, will you come?"

"Maybe." She pouted.

When they got back to the house, Christiana was sitting with Lisa on the sofa in the living room, watching television and sipping a cup of tea.

"Shaun, take Emilio upstairs to his room, so he can

unpack his things." Pilar pulled up a chair so she was directly facing Christiana, while Shaun and Emilio disappeared up the stairs. "Let's talk." Pilar was looking Christiana straight in the eye. "You tricked me. You come in to the house, tell us you're a fugitive, I help you and this is how you repay me."

Christiana shrugged. "I've known him much longer than you. You went home, and our love was rekindled. Is that my fault? And now I'm carrying his baby."

"SHAUN!" Pilar had stood up and was calling up the stairs. "Leave Emilio to unpack, and you come down." A minute later, Shaun entered the room, looking uncertain. "Let's have the truth." Pilar looked at him. "She's saying you're together and she's having your baby. But you're telling me that you want me. So where do we go from here? Tell her that we're together."

Shaun sat on the sofa next to Christiana. "I know it's been a tense time for you, not knowing whether Ralf is dead or alive, Christiana." Shaun was speaking in his soft voice. "It must be terrifying, but you know I only slept with you because you tricked me with the Viagra."

"Tell me you didn't enjoy it," Christiana interrupted.

"A moment's lust isn't the same as loving someone, the way I love Pilar."

"I'm giving you a baby."

"Pilar can give me babies. She would be a wonderful mother to my children…"

"But I've got one right now, and it's yours."

"Look, you're going to stay with my parents two days from now, until we've got your situation sorted out. There's no more to say on the matter."

Christiana held her head down and tears started to flow. Emilio entered the room at that moment. He already knew something was wrong, having overheard quite a bit in the car from the airport, but as he looked at the scene in the living room he immediately saw the triangle relationship and the tension between the two women.

"I'm taking Emilio out to go paintballing. We have to go now to catch the afternoon session." Shaun beckoned Emilio to follow him. "Pilar, are you coming?"

"No, I don't feel like it."

"You okay?"

"I suppose so."

"Would you rather we didn't go?"

She thought for a moment. "No, I don't want to spoil your fun. You go," she said, looking miserable.

* * *

Shaun and Emilio stood next to the paintball fields for their safety briefing, wearing camouflage pattern overalls and ammunition belts holding their canisters of paintballs. There were other groups there, teenagers, companies, stag parties, mainly young men in their twenties and just a few women. Shaun and Emilio were added in to a stag party team.

"For those of you who are just starting for the afternoon, these are your goggles." The instructor held up a helmet that had a large visor at the front, covering the complete face. "Number one rule is, you never, never ever under any circumstances lift your visor once you go through that gate." He pointed to the entrance gate to the fields, which was underneath a high netting designed to contain any stray balls. "We have ten games you can play, each with its own field or area, but you've only got time for five this afternoon, so you need to choose. Now come and collect your helmet and gun and then go through to your chosen scenario field."

"We played this morning already." The leader of the

stag party team looked at Shaun as he was less intimidating than Emilio. "We have Urban, Tank Convoy, Aeroplane Wood, The Wild West and Radar Station to play this afternoon."

"That's fine, sounds great. We'll just fit ourselves in with you." Shaun smiled at the leader. Emilio just looked at him with a blank expression.

Their first game was Urban.

"You have to rescue the man sized dummy which you can see in the middle of the field and carry it to the evacuation point without getting shot. If you are shot, then you must withdraw to the wounded zone on the side and you no longer play for the rest of the game." The instructor pointed to a netted off area on the edge of the field. "Now each team go to opposite ends and, when you're in place and I give the word, let battle commence." He withdrew to the sidelines.

The scenario was mainly old cars and tractors scattered across a field but, adjoining, there was a red bus, a wooden fort and a hay barn. When the instructor shouted the start of the game, Emilio moved with surprising speed, running up to the bus before the other side could shoot him and using his vantage point to fire off lots of shots, picking off four of the enemy within a couple of minutes, who all withdrew to the wounded zone, in accordance with the rules. Every few seconds were punctuated with the pop of a paintball being released under air pressure. It was as though Emilio had been injected with adrenalin. He seemed to move at twice the speed of everyone else. Having thinned the opposition down, he made a dash for the dummy, which was lying in the middle of the field, and started to run to the evacuation point with it, laughing like an excited child. Despite his speed, one of the enemy team caught him on the arm with a paintball, clearly visible on his overalls. But Emilio kept running as though nothing had happened.

"Hey mate, you're out," one of the enemy team shouted.

Emilio ignored it and everyone came to the evacuation point as though the game was finished. The opposition team were muttering to themselves that the game had not been played fairly but, looking at Emilio's size and general demeanour, they said nothing. Emilio was still laughing with excitement, clutching the dummy as though it was a prize he'd won. He had all the volatility of a child, but he was a supersized version.

"Hey, I got caught by a paintball." Shaun was rubbing his thigh. "Painful aren't they?"

"I haven't felt anything." Emilio shook his head.

The other games were similar, capturing a laptop in the middle of some tanks, retrieving a briefcase from a crashed aeroplane, saving a dummy from the hangman's noose in the Wild West town, and disabling a radar station. And Emilio's strategy was the same for all of them, to run at top speed to the objective and to ignore getting shot. The opposing teams were different for each game, and they just accepted that Emilio was a bad sport and had cheated. But, as they came off from the last game, one of the opposing team didn't want to let the matter go.

"Hey mate, why do you have to cheat?" He was a wiry man in his twenties, quite tall, with curly ginger hair. Emilio ignored him. "I say, why do you have to cheat?"

"It's a game, just a bit of fun, *amigo*." Emilio turned to look at him. "It's not something you need get upset about... you want me to feel bad about it?"

"But the way you played, no one else had any fun." The wiry man was now standing fairly close. Emilio raised his gun and shot the man three times in the groin. The man fell over, crying out in pain.

"Now everyone's having fun." Emilio turned and walked away and the wiry man's team mates gathered round to laugh at him as he rolled around on the ground in agony.

Ten minutes later Shaun and Emilio were driving home.

"Did you enjoy that?" Shaun asked.

"That was great." Emilio grinned. "Do you think we could come back again with Pilar?"

"I don't think it's her sort of thing."

Emilio said nothing. He realised that Pilar hadn't told Shaun everything about her life in Brazil.

As they got back home, Shaun could see that Pilar was glum, like she had been brooding all afternoon, but at that moment Pete phoned. Since Pilar had become his live-in girlfriend, Shaun saw very little of Pete.

"Shaun, is that you lad?"

"Hi Pete, it's so good to hear from you, stranger. Sorry I haven't been down the pub."

"That's why I'm phoning. The landlord's pushed the boat out and hired a large screen. They're showing a friendly football match, England versus Brazil, tonight. Do you fancy it?"

"Perfect! I've got two Brazilians in the house. We'll definitely see you down there. It'll be great to catch up with you again." When he put the phone down, he went to the hallway and shouted through the house, "Brazil versus England football match tonight. Compulsory attendance for all Brazilians."

Later that evening, when it was time to go, he found Christiana in the kitchen, making some food for herself and Lisa.

"Christiana, we're going out to the pub. You'll be staying in to look after Lisa?"

"Sure sweetheart. Have a nice time. I'll keep your bed warm."

"Don't be silly. I'm with Pilar, you know that." Shaun sighed as Christiana hung her head low, looking sad. "Look, I can't discuss it any further now. We're going out. I'll chat to you later."

"I want you back, Shaun. I miss you." She grabbed his arm.

"Just stop it. I'm going out now." He shrugged her off and walked away.

* * *

The trip to the pub had been a success and, late evening, the trio returned to Shaun's house quite merry. Christiana had stayed up and she could see that the three had bonded as a result of their outing.

"I'm going up now." Shaun said fairly soon after arriving back, having forgotten his promise to talk to Christiana. A few minutes later, Pilar followed him, with Christiana hard on her heels, not noticing that she herself was being trailed. As Pilar went to enter Shaun's bedroom, Christiana suddenly got her in a bear hug from behind and started to drag her away from the bedroom door.

"Shaun is my man now. I'm carrying his baby." Christiana hissed.

"Go and sleep with Lisa, you mad woman." Pilar retorted.

Suddenly, a heavy hand fell on Christiana's shoulder. She looked round to see Emilio, towering above her. "Christiana, sleep with your daughter. Shaun is Pilar's man."

"Shaun, Shaun." Christiana cried out, but nothing happened, and Emilio guided her to the spare room where Lisa was sleeping, shutting the door behind her.

Shaun and Pilar lay in bed together.

"Oh, it's so good to have you back. I see you changed the bed sheets while I was paintballing."

"Of course. I wanted to cleanse that bitch's influence from our bedroom."

"So that we can make love?" Shaun snuggled up closer to her.

"No Shaun. It's too soon. You've got some grovelling to do."

He sighed. "I know I don't deserve you. I was weak and selfish. But I'm going to make it up to you. I'm going to win you back."

"No, you don't deserve me." Pilar snapped. "Why didn't you come to the door when you heard the commotion? Why did I have to fight Christiana to get in here?"

"I heard Emilio take care of it… I must say, when I first saw him, I thought he wasn't your type, but actually he's a bit of a laugh. He must be a good friend of yours?"

"Not really." She hesitated. "I've never told anyone before, but you should probably know, he raped me a few years ago."

"Hey! What?" Shaun sat up in bed, suddenly completely awake. "What's he doing in our house?"

"Let it go, Shaun. I'll explain when he's gone. It's complicated." She remained lying down, looking up at him.

"I can't let it go."

"Don't spoil our moment." She propped herself up on one elbow.

"I'm sorry. He can't stay here. I'm not having a rapist in the house. Who knows what he might do? It's the kind of thing you read about in the newspapers. I'm responsible for the safety of you all."

"Please, Shaun. Do it for me. Trust me. I'll explain everything when he's gone."

"No! He can't stay here. I'll be nice about it. He's a big guy in any case. There's a posh hotel just down the road. I'll pay for a few nights for him, sell it to him as a better arrangement, that he'll be more comfortable there. He won't have gone to bed yet."

"Please, just leave it," she said, but Shaun got up and walked across to his clothes. Pilar jumped out of bed, and rushed over to him. "Shaun, will you let it go?" She got in front of him and pinned his arms to his side.

"Why? What's the problem? You don't need him in the house, do you? What's going on?"

"Shaun, stop and just listen to me." She looked at him with a serious expression. "Do you feel you owe me anything after all the bad things you've done to me, after you've hurt me so much?"

He was silent and his face suddenly had a dejected look. "Yes, I do. You don't have to keep going on about it."

"Okay then, indulge me. Please, just let it go... let's make love."

"You said you didn't want to do it."

"Well, I've changed my mind. Come on."

She pulled him back to the bed and took his pyjama top off. She started kissing him gently, caressed his hair and he was quickly reacquainted with the tenderness and purity of her touch, so different from Christiana's sensual passion. He fell asleep in her arms, happy that soon the visitors would have left, and everything would be back to normal.

Meanwhile, Christiana had sat on the bed, where Lisa was fast asleep beside her, and started to sob uncontrollably. She could no longer deny Shaun's rejection. She had somehow hoped against hope that Shaun would choose her over Pilar, or that Pilar might not return from Brazil. She had felt certain that carrying

Shaun's baby would have clinched it. Her face was contorted with emotion. She remembered the last time she spoke to Ralf, just half an hour before she fled Berlin, seven weeks previous. She wondered if he was still alive or whether the gangsters had tracked him down and finished him off, because that's how powerful they were. His last words to her had been, 'Phone me on my mobile only if you're in a life and death situation. If I don't pick up, leave a voicemail. My phone may be monitored, so only phone in a real emergency.'

She decided to phone his number. The ringing tone went for twenty seconds and then stopped, like someone had picked up the call but was saying nothing.

"Ralf… is that you?" There was silence. "Ralf?"

"Err…" The voice seemed distant and lethargic, unfamiliar to Christiana.

"Ralf?"

"Yeah?"

"Ralf, is that you? You sound different."

"I told you not to phone unless it's life and death," he snapped in a harsh tone.

"Oh Ralf! What's wrong? You sound strange. I've been so worried."

"What do you want?"

Christiana hesitated. "Have you been on the marijuana? You sound really weird."

"What else am I supposed to do stuck here like a prisoner?"

"Oh Ralf! I needed you to stay strong."

"Why? What's happening?"

"I wanted you to come and join us in London. I'm staying with my friend Shaun."

He chuckled. "I'll come. I need a change from this place. Nice one."

"I thought I wanted you here, but I don't need you full of drugs. Stay where you are and get yourself clean."

"No, I'll come. I'm staying with Fritz. He'll sort out the arrangements for me."

Christiana thought for a moment. "I'm really not sure…"

"Christiana." It was a more assured, clearer voice. Christiana knew Fritz from Berlin, but he'd moved off to Munich.

"Fritz, so Ralf was with you. A right state you've got him into. I wanted him to join me in England, but he seems completely wasted."

"He's been here too long, that's the trouble. You can't keep a big man like Ralf caged up. Give me your details. I'll get him over to you."

Christiana sighed. "Okay. Get him on the afternoon flight, tomorrow. I'll give you the full address and postcode. Tell him to get a taxi to the house. I'll be waiting for him. Have you got a pen?" Christiana gave Fritz the address.

She had no idea that her capricious act would bring so much danger into their lives.

13

Berlin

It is interesting to consider which country produces the toughest men in the world, who would win an international Last Man Standing contest. As the Germans discovered in World War II, Siberian Russians would be serious contenders for the title. Siberia is life in the raw. It could be minus forty degrees on a winter evening and a foreigner might freeze to death just taking a fifteen minute stroll, even while wearing outdoor winter clothes. But not the locals. They would even take a dip in ice cold water.

Sergei Patrushev sat in the living room of his spacious home in the Kreuzberg district of central Berlin. Once the artists' and students' quarter, it was now home to Turkish immigrants, with whole streets where hardly a German shop sign was to be seen. Despite that, Yorkstrasse, where Sergei lived, was one of the most expensive streets in all Berlin. His house was well furnished, if a little grimy, like the day after a party, with the smell of stale vodka and beer hanging in the air. There was also a whiff of tea, as in the middle of the living room table sat a gold samovar, an ornate version of the English tea urn or water boiler, except that, in the samovar, the tea was kept as a concentrate in a pot on top, and diluted with the hot water, ten parts to one. It was well suited to tea-drinking in a communal setting over a protracted period, but Sergei never partook himself. He provided it for visitors and the gangsters' women, and to give himself a reminder of the Russia of his childhood and how a samovar had sat on his grandmother's table.

Sergei was a big man with a bald head that seemed to emerge straight from his torso, with no neck to connect the two. There was some quality of a hornless rhinoceros about his face and body. In his prime, he had looked indestructible, like a life-size version of a plastic monster children might collect in their morning cereal, but middle age had crept up on him unawares, and he had developed a paunch and a heavy, sluggish demeanour.

Sergei liked living in Kreuzberg among the Turks. His grandfather had died in the Great Patriotic War, fighting Nazi Germany and, for this reason, Sergei loathed all Germans. Atrocities had been committed by both sides on the Russian front, in what was generally accepted as being the deadliest conflict in human history, with over thirty million killed. Hitler referred to the campaign, codenamed Operation Barbarossa, as a 'war of annihilation' in which the Slavic people were to be destroyed or enslaved. Sergei's grandfather was one of the million Russian prisoners of war who had died after being captured by the Germans. He had been executed for trying to escape. Under the Geneva Convention, he should have been given a maximum of thirty days solitary confinement as punishment. By chance, his execution had been photographed by a German Army photographer. Sergei's grandfather, looking tough and defiant, was standing in a trench, with a German officer in a long coat and peaked cap standing behind him, above the trench, pointing a gun at the back of the condemned man's head. To make matters worse, a second photo had been taken of the corpse, with the officer smirking at the camera, while pointing at the body, as if to say, 'See what happens to Russian dogs'.

Sergei might never have seen the photos if they hadn't been presented in 1965, the year of his birth, in a book called 'A Photographic Record of the Great Patriotic War'. There was no mistaking the family resemblance. Sergei and his grandfather looked like twins separated by history and he had treasured these photos since childhood. Encouraged by his father, who was also full of bitterness, they gave him a purpose in life, to take revenge on all Germans. He had tried to trace the executioner, so that he could eliminate the officer's children and grandchildren. That might have satiated his bloodlust, but he'd had no luck in his search. His favourite film was made in 2001, 'Enemy at the Gates,' a cold, harsh, authentic depiction of the close quarter fighting for Stalingrad, in which half a million Russian soldiers died. The Germans looked smart in their blue grey, serge uniforms and had vastly superior firepower. The Russians, like the underdogs, looked drab and poor in their dark brown battledress, made of a coarse blanket material but, even so, they won the fight against all odds. Sergei never tired of watching that film.

His father had died when Sergei was young, in a shootout with rival gangsters in his native Siberia, but the lack of a father had not stopped him becoming one of the most feared and respected young thugs, having single-handedly taken on a gang of twelve on one occasion, and achieving legendary status as a result. He moved to Moscow when he was eighteen, cleaning office windows and cars to make money. Those who did not require his services would find their windows broken the next day. He did this for a few years, but his first chance of making really big money came in 1988 when Gorbachev's policies of *glasnost* and *perestroika* triggered a mass emigration of

Jews to Israel and the States. They were in such a hurry to leave, Sergei found he could do a deal with them to take their possessions, sell them at a good price on their behalf, and send the proceeds on to them, minus his commission.

He never did send any money and, a few years later, relocated with his small fortune to Berlin, where he thought the demolition of the Wall and the reunification of Germany would offer a lot of opportunity to a Siberian gangster like himself. It would also allow him to work through his hatred of Germans. He wondered whether, if he killed enough, it might slake his thirst for their blood. It was only five years after his arrival in Berlin that he had come to dominate the city's cocaine, prostitution, card cloning and protection rackets. He also did contract killings.

It was late, and all seemed quiet in his criminal empire, and Sergei was thinking of having an early night.

"We've got him, Sergei." Igor came running in to the living room. He was a giant of a man with arms and legs like the thick branches of a tree and a head that looked as though it was hewn from a block of wood. To see him running was an awesome sight, like some great metal robot brought to life. In his youth he had been part of the Russian Olympic weightlifting team but, in an earlier era of history, he would have been a brutal warrior or knight, or a hooded executioner who chopped off heads. He was the gang's main enforcer and married to Sergei's eldest daughter. "Kurt has just phoned." He referred to their informant who worked in the phone monitoring section of the German police. "He didn't have authority to ping the mobile and Ralf didn't answer any calls, but he's just taken a call from his wife. It routed through a mast in Munich, but we know where he'll be tomorrow, with his wife and child and we even have the postcode. But it means travelling to London."

"Aagh!" Sergei's eyes widened and he roared his approval. "How did I know my favourite son-in-law would bring me this news?" He walked over to the large photo of his brother on the wall, its frame still covered in wilted flowers from the funeral five weeks previous. "My dear brother, your killer will die like a dog, and his wife and child with him."

"Really?" Igor looked surprised. The *Vory V Zakone*, the original Russian *Mafiya*, formed in the Siberian labour camps in the 1930s, had a strict code of conduct in which women and children had always been exempt from blood feuds. Igor knew that, in recent years, Russian gangsters had become far more indiscriminate about who they killed. Some had even sprayed an entire restaurant with bullets, just to get their single target. "But we don't kill women and children. It will give us a bad name."

"I decide what is right and what is wrong. This is for my brother. Ralf's wife and child will die first, before his eyes, then him." The photo of Sergei's brother suddenly fell off the wall and crashed to the floor, the glass front smashing to pieces. Sergei's mouth dropped open in shock; then he started to laugh. "You see. My brother approves… this is a great day for us."

The incident between his dead brother and Ralf had been one of those unfortunate misunderstandings. It had appeared that Ralf had started to source cocaine directly from Colombia and Sergei's brother had been sent to dispense the ultimate punishment. The reality was that Ralf had remained a loyal distributor of Sergei's cocaine. It had been a case of mistaken identity, where Ralf had been framed by the real culprit, who had since been eliminated by Igor. But it was too late now. The damage had been done. Even if Ralf had only acted in self defence, Sergei still had to avenge his kid brother's death. When Sergei had identified his brother's body for the police, they had asked if he had any idea who had committed the murder. Sergei had replied yes, but, when the police asked who, Sergei had said he would take care of the matter himself.

"We need to drive through the night to France, to be in London in good time for tomorrow evening." Sergei swung into action and set the strategy. "We'll take the Volvo, it will arouse less suspicion than the BMW as we go through British Customs… and bring Kateryna." He referred to one of his gangster's wives. "She looks harmless. She can drive on and off the ferry and we'll go as foot passengers."

"What weapons shall we take?"

"Four Baikals, four silencers and sixteen clips of ammunition." He referred to the small, snub, black handgun that looked almost like a toy cap gun and yet was made of solid steel and performed its function with great reliability, made in Russia to fire teargas pellets and expertly converted in Lithuania to shoot live bullets. "Hide them in the compartments beneath the car… and not too much vodka. This needs to be a neat little operation. I owe it to my brother."

Sergei's wife, Valentina, gave them *kolbasa* (salami sausage) and white bread, which she had packed in a small holdall, to keep them going through the night. Sergei had her as a drudge, to shop, make his food, wash and iron his clothes, keep house generally. She had also borne him three daughters. It was late when they set off an hour later, four men and Kateryna. The men were wearing dark clothes, and Sergei had on his favourite black leather jacket. As they had stepped out of the house onto Yorkstrasse, a black cat was sitting on top of their old black Volvo S40 sport model and, when they opened the doors, it ran across the roof of the car and the bonnet, scowling at

Sergei as it did so. It echoed with the dark, insecure world they inhabited, where mistrust and death were never far away. They left Berlin and were soon speeding along the autobahn, the great legacy to the infrastructure bequeathed by Nazi Germany. They took turns to drive. Due to his size, Igor sat in the front passenger seat when not driving, and Kateryna, who was not expected to drive except onto the ferry, sat behind him.

"Put the Red Army choir on." Sergei commanded from the back seat, as they sped west towards Hanover. It was his favourite CD and he liked to play it before a job. The first track was Kalinka, the most famous Russian song ever, particularly after Roman Abramovich bought Chelsea FC and it was played at all the London club's important matches. Sergei would not interrupt the opening chorus, sung by the whole choir:

Kalinka, kalinka, kalinka moya! V sadu yagoda malinka, malinka moya!
(Little snowberry, snowberry of mine in the garden, raspberry, little raspberry of mine)

But he would always sing along with the solo tenor on the verse, as though it befitted his position as the gang leader:

Akh, pod sosnoyu, pod zelenoyu, Spat' polozhite vy menya!
Ay-lyuli, lyuli, ay-lyuli, Spat' polozhite vy myenya
(Ah, Under the pine, the green one, Lay me down to sleep, Ah, lully lully, ah lully lully, Lay me down to sleep)

As the song accelerated in speed, Sergei would stamp his feet and clap his hands. It was done with the abandon of a child, and he looked deceptively benign when the CD was playing. Nikolai let the first track go with no comment, although he did think, 'I'd like to lay you down to sleep, Sergei.' He had a permanently sour face, with a mouth that turned down at the corners and was the smallest in stature of the four gangsters, but all the more ruthless, as if in compensation. As the track faded, Nikolai spoke.

"Do we have to listen to this CD all the time?" Igor looked round at Nikolai, who was sitting in the back between Sergei and Kateryna. Viktor, the fourth gangster, who was driving, looked at Nikolai in the rear view mirror. They would never have dared to challenge Sergei. "Why can't we have Alla Pugacheva for a change?" Nikolai referred to Russia's equivalent of Edith Piaf.

"This is Russia how it used to be." Sergei said it calmly, as though enjoying the opportunity to share his wisdom with the younger men. "A great country where the state would care for its citizens, where old people would be warm in the winter and well fed, where children didn't live on the streets, where our athletes, artists and scientists were the best in the world."

"The good old days." Nikolai put on a shaky, old person's voice. "How much vodka have you drunk today?"

"Sergei is right. He knows what he's talking about." Viktor's voice was high pitched and whiney. He was the dimmest of Sergei's henchmen, but very loyal.

"Don't patronise me," Sergei yelled at Viktor, slapping the back of his head to reinforce the message. Then he continued his lecture in a calm manner. "We think we gained freedom under Gorbachev in the early 1990s, but what did we really gain? No one has a sense of moral duty any more. Yes, in the good old days, Nikolai, you worked for the common good. Now everyone is out for themselves."

"Well, you've done all right out of it, Sergei." Nikolai interrupted.

"Have I? You want to know the happiest time of my life?" Sergei waited till Nikolai made some kind of affirmative gesture.

"Go on then," said Nikolai finally, in a weary tone.

"When I moved from Siberia to Moscow at the age of eighteen. I drove all the way with a friend in an old Mercedes. We pooled our money to buy it." Sergei hesitated, as though hit by a wave of nostalgia. "At night we slept in the open, under the stars and all we had to eat was rye bread, cucumber and onion."

"You ate like a peasant!" Nikolai scoffed.

Sergei ignored the slight. "Sometimes, as we travelled across Russia, we worked as *shabashniki* (casual labourers) on the farms, in return for a meal. We had nothing, but I have never been happier, because I had hope of a better future." He quoted an old Russian saying, "*Mechtat nye vredno; Nadezhda umirayet poslednei.*" (It is not harmful to dream and hope is the last to die.)

"You seem to forget that Stalin killed millions of innocent people in the *gulags*." He referred to the penal labour camps and salt mines in the remote and sometimes frozen wastes of Siberia, where millions died from the harsh conditions.

"Ordinary people were housed, fed and kept warm. As long as you stayed out of politics, you had nothing to fear... When we came to Moscow, we went to *Krásnaya Plóshchad*, (Red Square), like any other tourist. We queued thirty minutes to see the body of Lenin. We looked up at St Basil's Cathedral, its domes like brightly painted onions. And we went into GUM, more like a palace than a store. We had never seen a shopping mall like it, never seen so many luxury goods. We had our first taste of coca-cola. It was the most wonderful time for us."

"I think we should turn back." It was said softly, the first remark Kateryna had made on the whole trip. "I've got a funny feeling about this journey."

All of Sergei's henchmen were Russian and most of them had Russian wives or girlfriends. Kateryna, Nikolai's wife, was no exception. She was from the seaside resort of Odessa, now in the Ukraine, and had picked up something of its warm, sunny atmosphere, her cheerful disposition seeming to be an antidote to Nikolai's sadness and cynicism. It was hard to believe that she had made her life with someone as ruthless and cruel as Nikolai. For one contract killing of a man who frequented saunas, he had sealed the man inside and turned up the heat to roast him alive.

"What's wrong, Kateryna?" Sergei always felt a little sorry for her, being married to Nikolai, and showed her more patience than he would normally display.

"It's like you're giving us your farewell speech. You know your brother was a madman, you said so yourself. Just let it go. Let's turn back."

"I can't do that. That's the man I am. I never back down. Once I've made a decision, I never turn back."

"But Sergei, you did turn back once," Viktor interrupted in his whiny voice, trying to be helpful. "That Christmas when you had a party on your yacht and the police came to arrest you and you jumped in the water to escape. You swam back and climbed back onto the yacht, so they could get you."

"Stop talking shit." Sergei slapped Victor on the head once more. "It was too cold that night, idiot. It gets into my bones now I'm older. Just drive."

"I think we should turn back," Kateryna continued. "The black cat crossed our path."

"Did it?" asked Sergei.

"You saw it. It scowled at you."

"I suppose I did see it. You don't expect Sergei Patrushev to turn back because of a cat?"

"Isn't it time you retired? Do some things you want to do?"

"You should go to Miami, St Tropez, Goa, Pattaya, like the oligarchs," Viktor whined, thinking he was being loyal and helpful.

"You think I want to sit outside some poncey cafe, with a coffee, wearing sunglasses and watching the beautiful people go by? You think I'm a poser? I will never lose my Russian culture." Sergei's voice was angry, and he slapped Viktor across the back of the head one more time. "Just drive, oaf, unless you want me to throw you out of the car." His tone changed back to one of calmness, as he addressed Kateryna. "So what do I want to do?"

"There are so many things: photography, reading, skiing, travelling, playing chess, spending time with your grandchildren, going to your *dacha* (country house)… failing that, you can just go out for meals, go to the theatre, go to see shows, watch soap operas on the television."

Sergei laughed. He didn't often laugh with all the responsibility he shouldered. "Enough! People will say I've gone soft. People would think the lion has become a pussycat."

"You can't hold onto it for ever, no one can. You have to…"

"Kateryna" Nikolai sensed that Sergei was enjoying bantering with her. "Stop interfering."

"She's fine," Sergei interjected. "Where did you get such a clever wife?" Sergei thought for a few moments. "Do you agree with me, Kateryna, the old Russia was better?"

"I grew up in Odessa. It was beautiful."

"Odessians always reply to a question with another question, don't they?"

"Who told you that?"

Sergei laughed. "I've never been to Odessa."

"It has lots of famous sites. You can see the Potemkin Steps, 192 of them, that take you from the town down to the sea. I would storm down them when I was young, like a naughty gremlin on the rampage!"

Sergei laughed again. "So you had a good life there?"

"I was always outdoors as a youngster. I would be on the beach. I could swim for miles. Or else I would be on long hikes or camping in the forest. I loved the Young Pioneers camps. I still sing some of their songs." She sang a catchy children's tune:

Poost vsegda budet solntse, (May there always be sun)
Poost vsegda budet nebo, (May there always be sky)
Poost vsegda budet Mama, (May there always be mama)
Poost vsegda budu Ya! (May there always be me!)

"We sang that when I was a boy. I always thought they left out father because they knew mine was dead." Sergei looked across at Kateryna, his eyes a little watery. She was stirring up feelings that had been hidden for decades.

"It must have been hard for you, growing up, having no father." She said it with compassion in her voice. Normally, Sergei would have snapped at someone who implied he had any kind of weakness, but he didn't this time.

"It was, but it made me tough. I had nothing to lose, because I'd already lost everything, so I didn't care what happened."

"The legend is that you fought off a gang of twelve single-handed."

"It's true. I was seventeen. I took out the leader first, then the next hardest. It was as though I was much stronger, indestructible. By the time I got to the remaining eight, it was like fighting spaghetti. There was nothing to them. They just ran off. They wanted to keep their noses in shape and their teeth intact."

"How did you come to live in such a hostile place as Siberia?"

"My great great-grandfather was exiled there in Tsarist times, before the Revolution. He led a peasants' uprising."

"So he was brave like you?"

"Braver. Ploughing and sowing wasn't the same in Siberia. They nearly starved most of the time." Sergei smiled. He was enjoying Kateryna's conversation. He wished he was married to her, instead of his own wife. Kateryna made him happy. "You know, I think you might be right about retiring, Kateryna. I'm going to make this my last trip. I've made enough money. Perhaps I'll go legitimate, open a casino or restaurant. Or maybe I'll dedicate myself to good causes. Give something back. You see. People won't recognize the new me. Just one last job to do… I must avenge my brother's death. I know he'd gone a bit crazy, but I remember him when he was a little boy. I was ten when my father died and my mother was pregnant with my brother. I was like his substitute father. I taught him to ride a bike, to tie his shoe laces, to tell the time, to tell left from right. I used to pull him on a sledge in the winter time and we would stop and play snowballs. We used to play cards and dominoes in the long winter evenings. I remember when I left for Moscow at the age of eighteen. He was just eight years old. He came out of the cottage, crying '*Ne uhodi*' (Don't go). Those words haunt me still. He ran alongside the car for a while. I'll never forget that, looking back at him in the distance, still crying. I was the hardest man in Siberia, but that broke my heart. It was eight years before I saw him again." A tear

226

had come to Sergei's eye and a wave of fatherly sentiment overtook him. He reached behind for the holdall his wife had prepared for him and gave it to Kateryna. "Here, you can be mum. Give the boys some *kolbasa*, they must be hungry… and, when we get back, I'll throw a big party, a banquet, with caviar, salami, smoked salmon, goulash… and enormous cream gateaux."

"I'll bring my accordion and we can have a sing song." said Nikolai in a sarcastic tone.

Sergei knew Nikolai couldn't play the accordion. "That's a good idea. I'll get Vladimir and his troupe for the evening." Sergei referred to a band of Russian musicians he'd hired for his daughter's wedding. They wore the traditional Cossack peasant dress of baggy trousers tucked into boots and embroidered shirts, and sang folk tunes such as The Song of the Plains, The Volga Boat Song and Kalinka. Kateryna took out the salami sausage and bread in silence, cut it up and handed out pieces to the men.

SatNav guided them to Calais, where they arrived by mid morning the next day. To save time, they decided to take the Eurotunnel, rather than the ferry; thirty minutes rather than four hours. Kateryna and her charm got the car through British customs with no problems and she was reunited with the four men in Folkestone.

14

London – Part 4

By 4 p.m., Sergei and his team were waiting up the hill from Shaun's house, keeping as low a profile as possible, with one of them looking through binoculars from time to time, to see who was coming and going. They had retrieved the Baikals from their hiding place, and now had them stowed under their seats.

"Pass the piss pot." Sergei said to Viktor with an aggressive tone. He was in the back seat and Viktor could feel him poking his neck as he said it.

"Piss pot, huh! It's just a pickling jar." he fired back.

"Pass me the piss pot now, you peasant." Sergei insisted, as he again poked Viktor.

"Okay, Okay, stop with the poking." Victor was getting irritable, feeling that he had done most of the driving through the night and that he was the whipping boy for the other three. He handed the pickling jar backwards. It was an old KGB secret service trick that surveillance teams used in the days of the Cold War. The idea actually originated from taxi drivers and chauffeurs, who always had a pickling bottle stowed beneath the driver's seat, particularly those working in Siberia, where the weather could be forty degrees below. Leaving the warmth of the car to take a leak could lead to frostbite in a very sensitive place.

"Kateryna, avert your eyes, please," Sergei said, hoping she would do the opposite and look.

Viktor felt a bit queasy as Sergei filled the bottle, loudly, and then passed it back to him. He opened the car door and emptied the contents onto the road, then replaced the screw top.

"What about you, Kateryna. Are you sitting on a sponge?" Sergei said, in an effort to get a reaction.

She gave a false little laugh. She was starting to realise that her friendliness may have been misinterpreted. "I'm fine, thank you," she said.

Nikolai frowned; he was irritated with Sergei chatting to his wife in that tone. He seemed to have been flirting with her from the outset of the trip. "Why are we waiting out here, you don't want to go in and wait?" Nikolai asked, thinking this was the obvious option.

"No need. They have no idea we're here. How could they know we're staking them out? Better to surprise them when Ralf arrives," Sergei replied, and then nodded at his own wisdom.

"There's a small Latin woman and a big man, looks like a gypo, just gone in." Viktor surreptitiously observed Pilar and Emilio through the binoculars. "The man looks quite useful."

"Will he still be useful with a bullet in him, dummy?" Nikolai asked with a sneer and a sarcastic laugh.

Inside the house, the uneasy truce had been maintained, with Christiana keeping out of the way, brooding in her bedroom. Only she knew that Ralf would soon be arriving. Shaun was in his bedroom and, from force of habit, was surveying the panorama from the window. His house was halfway up the hill. 'From *favela* to *favela*," Pilar had joked when she first saw it, to which Shaun had replied, 'Hardly, although it does have good views of London if you look west.'

There was a black Volvo further up the hill to the east, which had been there a few hours, and Shaun thought it looked out of place with its German number plates. He looked through the binoculars he kept handy on the windowsill.

"Ow!" he cried out as he hit the floor with a thud. He was hyperventilating. Up until that moment, he had been inclined to not believe Christiana's story that she was a fugitive from Russian gangsters. He thought she had probably come to London to try and get as much money as she could from him, and the ruse with the herbal Viagra and getting pregnant seemed to support his hunch. He had been thinking it was going to be a relatively simple matter of having to pay a high price for a sexual indiscretion. An awful new reality had just come crashing in.

"Christiana," he finally managed to call out, his voice shaking.

"What?" she said sulkily as she entered the room, but, when she saw Shaun lying on the floor and she could see the panic on his face, her attitude immediately changed. "What's wrong?" she cried out, trying not to look scared as a huge wave of fear started to well up inside her.

"The gangsters who are after Ralf, is there any way they know where you are?" he said breathing heavily. He was obviously in pain.

"Aah! Oh no... shit! Possibly." It came out of her as though she had been physically wounded. "Why?" Her face was contorted with fear.

"Oh my God, no. What have you done?"

"What's wrong? Tell me."

He just lay there in silence for a while, trying to steady his breathing and compose himself. "There's a car full of heavies up the road," he had an air of extreme anxiety, "and they've got binoculars trained on the house."

"No! No! Please God, no." She sat on the bed and held her head in her hands as the tears streamed down her face. "Maybe you're mistaken. Let me see." She stood up and moved towards the window.

"Don't look," Shaun shouted. "Stay away from the window." He stood up and pushed her back towards the bed. "The car driver had the binoculars in his hands, but he wasn't actually looking at the house."

"Maybe they're looking at another house."

"Of course. That's it. They're staking out someone else's house, not mine... God, we're sitting ducks, you idiot." Shaun was becoming angry.

"Are you sure?" She looked at Shaun in a childlike, desperate way, as if he might somehow be able to make the problem go away.

"I'm very sure. We're like mice caught in a trap, waiting for the man to come and get us."

Christiana let out a howl and her heart started to beat very fast as reality sunk in. She immediately heard a rhythmic clomping on the stairs. She knew it would be Lisa, who had been playing with Chimbo in the hall, coming up to see what was happening to her mother. Lisa slowly ascended, using hands and feet, step-by-step, like a fully grown person would climb a ladder rung by rung. Christiana did her best to compose herself, to shield her child from the unfolding horror.

"Lisa, it's alright sweetheart!" Christiana's hands were shaking as Lisa came through the bedroom door. "Go down to your auntie Pilar please, while I talk to Shaun... go now, it will be fine."

"Mummy crying," Lisa said.

"No, Mummy's fine, Lisa. Please go down to Pilar. Good girl."

Lisa reluctantly went out, looking back to check if her

mother was all right, and descended the stairs in the same manner that she had climbed them, like going down a ladder. Christiana was hyperventilating, and she looked as though she was going to vomit. Shaun was peeping out of the corner of the window, watching to see if the car had moved.

"I'm sorry. It's all my fault," Christiana said slowly and quietly. "Last night I was so upset I phoned Ralf and told him to come here to get us. They must have picked up the call. Ralf said they might."

"Shit! Shit! Shit! Fucking great, well done." The anger was clear in his tone. "What a brilliant night's work that was. Haven't you caused enough havoc in this house?"

"I'm sorry. I'm so sorry. I was wrong; I'll call the police now." His anger had unnerved her and there was terror in her voice.

Shaun was by now also sitting on the bed, and holding his head in his hands. He was thinking of a way out and quick, the process impeded by the rapid thumping of his heart. He was tapping his foot on the floor as a kind of outlet for his tension.

"They probably don't know we know they're there." he said, after a few seconds thought. "They've been there quite a while, so they must be waiting for Ralf to arrive." Some strength came into his voice. "Phone him and tell him not to come to the house. Let's get everyone together quickly."

"Shaun, you don't understand, these men are monsters. Don't play with them," she pleaded, "call the police now… Please." She was shivering, like the temperature had dropped to freezing.

"I'm not playing with them. Just call Ralf and tell him not to come here."

Christiana ran to get her mobile, returned to the room and speed dialled Ralf. Fifteen seconds elapsed.

232

"He's not picking up; it's gone to message. Maybe he's still on the plane."

"Try again. Keep trying... Let's get everyone together in the living room." Shaun said, trying to reassure her that he was back in control, although his voice was still trembling.

They went downstairs and Shaun called out to Pilar, who was in the kitchen making food, and Emilio, who was playing computer games in the home office.

Within a minute, they were assembled in the living room. Pilar knew something was wrong, because Shaun had an agitated look, and his voice was emotional. He was usually the cool guy.

"Pilar, Emilio... Christiana was upset last night and she phoned Ralf." His voice was still breathy with panic. "The call was picked up and now there's a car full of Russians waiting up the hill for Ralf to arrive."

"You stupid bitch!" Pilar shouted out, giving Christiana a look of contempt. "What an idiot!" She shook her head in disbelief.

"I know, I know... I'm so sorry. Look, just call the police now. Please, don't waste any more time." She was still shaking.

"We don't need the police," Emilio said in a steady voice. He showed no trace of fear. "We can take care of it ourselves."

"They have guns, Emilio," Christiana replied, as she gave him an angry look. "Do you have a gun?... No, I didn't think you had."

Emilio shrugged in answer. Pilar glanced at him. He looked strong, fit and relaxed, like someone about to go out and play a game of football. Suddenly, she was glad Emilio was there. She knew that life involved compromise.

"But we don't know how the police will respond." Shaun

said, shaking his head despondently. "What if they bungle it? They'll probably just cordon off the whole area till the shooting's finished."

"That's right." Pilar became agitated. "Look at what happened to Jean Charles de Menezes."

"Don't be silly! British police are the best in the world." said Christiana as she gave Pilar an angry look. "You have to call them now. Please... I'm scared for Lisa and for my unborn child." She tapped her belly. "It's alright for you, you haven't got children." She stared at Pilar.

"Shaun, what shall we do?" Pilar asked with urgency in her voice.

Shaun was starting to look calmer, as if, by assuming leadership of the group, he no longer had time to be scared for himself. He looked at Christiana.

"Is Ralf answering?"

"He's just not picking up. It keeps going to message. Maybe his battery's flat."

"Look, I have a Porsche Carrera, top speed 185mph. They have a Volvo S40, top speed 130 mph. We could outrun them, and I know the streets better than they do."

"Yeah!" Emilio nodded and raised a clenched fist, sensing that Shaun was suggesting a chase.

"I also have a weekend house by the sea two and a half hours from here." Shaun referred to the main indulgence he had allowed himself after the sale of his business. He had bought an Edwardian house in a little seaside town on the north Norfolk coast. "Okay, here's what we'll do; we'll arrange to meet Ralf at the airport... and we can phone the police when we're safely out of this area."

"But what if Ralf doesn't pick up?" Christiana looked at Shaun as she said it, a sour expression on her face.

"Then we go without him. We have to get ourselves

away from this area. While they can get to Ralf through you, none of us are safe here… Sorry."

"Don't apologise to that stupid cow. It's all her mess anyway." Pilar scowled at Christiana.

"So if he comes here and we're gone, it's certain death for him." Christiana's face had become very tense. She looked older. She was wringing her hands, as if trying to shake off the tension.

"Okay, we get out of here now and we phone the police and tell them to catch the Russians before Ralf arrives."

"No, I don't like it." Christiana was staring at Shaun. "If it doesn't work, this plan sacrifices my Ralf. I told him to come here and that he would be safe. I can't leave without him."

"But why shouldn't it work?" Pilar looked annoyed. "You think the British police are so wonderful. We'll tell them what's happened and they'll come and catch the Russians. Problem solved." Pilar raised her eyebrows as she looked at Christiana.

"Ha Ha, aren't you funny? And what if they don't catch them? My Ralf will be at the front door wondering why he can't get in, and the Russians will pick him off like a little pigeon."

"Well, I think we should all go except you and you can wait here for Ralf," Pilar continued.

"Look, you two." Shaun interrupted, "We're starting to lose time here. This is urgent. I say we take a vote… All those who want to leave the house now, phone the police when we're out of the area and try to contact Ralf on his mobile, raise your hands now." Shaun raised his hand as he said it, and Pilar and Emilio followed suit. Christiana scowled at Pilar. "I'm sorry, Christiana." Shaun continued, "We're going now. Let us take Lisa."

Christiana shook her head. "You're not taking my child.

She stays with me. Come here, Lisa." Christiana pulled Lisa, who had been lying on the floor with Chimbo, on to her lap and clutched her.

Shaun looked at her. "Why not? It's for her own good. Look how many Jewish families sent their children out of Nazi Germany before the war. Thousands were saved."

"Don't talk to me about the fucking war," Christiana shouted, "what's that got to do with anything? You're not taking my child."

Shaun held his hands up like he was giving a benediction. "Then we go without you. We'll phone the police for you as soon as we're out of this turning."

At that moment, a taxi pulled up outside the house. It caught Shaun's eye from the bay window and he recognised the muscular frame and blonde hair of Ralf. He was sitting in the back of the taxi, leaning forward to settle his fare with the driver.

"Everyone through the kitchen and into the car… Now!" Shaun shouted with panic in his voice, but, at the same time, as the man who was in command.

"Shouldn't we call the police?" Christiana sounded terrified, and she started to howl like someone who was helpless, now that the moment the Russians were waiting for had arrived. She stood up, looking shaky and weak, like she was about to collapse, but was still wailing. Shaun slapped her face.

"Pull yourself together, woman. Just do what I say and we may just make it out of here. Go, will you… for God's sake. Emilio, will you help Christiana? Pilar, you take Lisa." Shaun's adrenalin had kicked in, just as it did when he used to play rugby at school. He felt no fear, just a rush of excitement.

The others went through the kitchen to the side door, which opened directly onto the garage. Christiana seemed frail, like a walking wounded, but she was hustled along by Emilio. Pilar had picked up Lisa and Chimbo, one in each arm, and followed Emilio into the garage. They got into the back of the car. Meanwhile, Shaun opened the front door and waved his hand in an urgent beckoning motion to Ralf, who was just ambling up the driveway. He looked surprised and confused as he stepped in to the hall.

"Ralf, I'm Shaun. We're in great danger. Quickly, come through." Ralf had assumed he was coming to a safe haven, and just stood there looking shocked. Shaun grabbed his arm and pulled him towards the kitchen. "Hurry. Christiana and Lisa are waiting for you in the car."

They ran through the kitchen and into the garage. The others had already squeezed into the back seat of the car. Shaun and Ralf threw themselves into the front and Shaun started the engine. Christiana leaned forward and put her arms around Ralf.

"Ralf, we've been so worried." She started to cry.

"Not now, Christiana. Get down low. Everyone stay down below window level. Get right down into the foot well," Shaun shouted above the roar of the powerful three litre engine.

He opened the garage doors with the remote control and shot out at high speed on to the road, stopping momentarily to turn and point the control at the doors to close them. He then accelerated down the hill at top speed.

The Russians had seen Ralf arrive and were just pulling up outside the house at the same moment Shaun emerged.

"They're getting away," Igor shouted in a panic. They had watched the Porsche zoom out and start to rapidly disappear down the hill as it reached sixty miles an hour within five seconds.

"Shall I chase, Sergei?" Viktor asked.

"What's the point of chasing, idiot? No, don't chase. There's only the driver in the car," Sergei said in a relaxed manner. "We want a quiet, discreet hit, not a mad chase. We're in London, not Russia. If we chase, we'll have half the British police after us. They have helicopters in the sky. I've seen their television programmes, 'Brit Cops Frontline' on satellite. They're a very sophisticated force." Sergei said it calmly, like he was a wise old man who had seen everything before. "It's the most watched country in the world; the people are CCTV'd everywhere they go."

"But why was he going so fast?" Nikolai interjected, as though challenging Sergei's judgement. "The bastard knew something. I'll kill the smart arse fucker if I get hold of him."

Ignoring his remark, Sergei quietly said, "Nikolai, you and Kateryna go over and see who's in. You look the least intimidating."

They went over, knocking and ringing the bell together. They waited for a minute, but there was no answer. They returned to the car, shaking their heads.

"They knew. They knew we were waiting." Sergei banged his fists on the back of the car seat. It looked as though the charging rhinoceros in him might emerge, but then he grew calm and thought for a minute. "How could they have worked it out?" he mused and thought for a while longer. "It's okay." He suddenly gave one of his rare smiles. "I like a challenge." He had obviously hatched a plan.

Kateryna knocked on Shaun's neighbour's door.

"Hello. Can I help you?" the middle-aged lady asked, with a polite smile.

"I'm sorry to bother you," Kateryna said in a little raspy voice with her foreign accent, as if she was a harmless nuisance. "I'm looking for my friend and her daughter who're staying next door. I'm just calling on the off chance while I'm in London."

"Are you a friend of Christiana and Lisa? Such a sweet girl."

"Yes she is. I'm worried that I might have just missed them."

The lady gazed outside. "Have you tried phoning them?"

"I'm not getting any answer on her mobile. Have you any idea where they might have gone?"

"Well, Shaun often goes to his weekend home in Norfolk. You could try phoning there."

"Do you have the phone number, I can try on my mobile?"

"I'm afraid I don't have any phone numbers for Shaun... silly really, given that we're such good neighbours." the lady said almost apologetically. "You could phone directory enquiries and they will give you the number."

Getting her mobile ready, Kateryna continued, "Do you have the address, then?"

Shaun's neighbour sighed. "Really my dear, I'm in the middle of preparing dinner at the moment... wait a minute, he did invite us to a housewarming party there. We didn't go, but I might have kept the invitation." She invited Kateryna into the hallway and rummaged in the drawer of a sideboard that stood against the wall. "Ah!... You're in luck." She gave Kateryna the invitation with Shaun's Norfolk address on it.

The Russians turned out of Shaun's road, just as the police car turned up, responding to a phone call from Pilar. The armed response vehicle drove up and down the road slowly, and then they sat outside Shaun's house for a few minutes.

"All Quiet on the Western Front, Bob. It looks like a false alarm." the driver said to his colleague. "But I'll just take a quick look." He got out and knocked on Shaun's door, peered through the window and after a minute returned to the car. "It looks deserted, like it's a hoax. Do you want to make door-to-door enquiries on the neighbours?"

Their police radio crackled into life at that moment.

"All cars in the vicinity proceed to a serious knife incident on the High Street, at the King's Arms pub. Immediate deal requested."

"Forget door-to-door. Let's attend this next call." Bob said, and they zoomed off, lights flashing and siren blaring. "I love the rush of this job," he said, as the driver nodded his head in response.

15

North Norfolk, England

"We'll call on my uncle on the way. I just want to pick something up." Shaun said, as they drove at top speed towards his weekend villa in Norfolk.

"You never told me you had an uncle in Norfolk." said Pilar.

"I had no reason to. He's my mother's brother, a farmer. She grew up on a farm. That's why she's such a good cook. Farmers are hungry people."

"But all those evenings we've sat together and you've been very quiet, and you never told me this before… What are you going to pick up?" Pilar asked. She was sitting in the back, behind Emilio, with Chimbo at her feet. Due to his size, Emilio was in the front. Lisa was asleep on her father's lap in the back, with Christiana in the middle, leaning against Ralf.

"A gun, just in case we need it," he replied in a matter of fact way.

"Yeah! Now you're talking. *Viva os companheiros.*" Emilio raised his clenched fist, turned and grinned at Ralf. They recognised the gangster in each other but, in his more fanciful moments, Emilio also saw himself as a latter day Che Guevara, liberator of the oppressed, although, in reality, he was more just a thug, rapist and thief. "So what troubles are you in *amigo*, that we have to help you out now?" Emilio looked round at Ralf, as he asked.

"It was a misunderstanding, completely stupid, quite funny if you weren't in the middle of it." The words had come out awkwardly, with a gap between phrases, like someone who wasn't used to speaking. He gave a big laugh.

"Ralf, you've been smoking." Christiana slapped him across the arm.

He continued, oblivious to her disapproval. "The Berlin cocaine baron Sergei Patrushev, he thought I'd double crossed him, and so he sent his crazy kid brother after me. His brother was a madman, but that saved my life. It was well known that he didn't like to use a gun. He got a thrill from feeling the blade enter his victim's flesh... so he confronted me." Ralf held up his hand, acting out the scene, pretending to hold a knife, "And I saw the blade in his hand, so I shot him. The police didn't do anything. It was good riddance. I'd helped them."

"So that's how you made your living then, drug dealing?" Shaun butted in.

"Normally I'm a cage fighter. It was a temporary thing. Christiana wanted a new apartment."

"Don't blame me," she interrupted with an angry tone. "Don't you dare try to put the responsibility on to me." She slapped Ralf across the shoulder.

It was with a huge sense of relief that Shaun had seen the Russians disappear in the distance in his rear view mirror, as he sped away from the house and left them stationary outside it. By now, he had driven north from Essex for a few hours, putting a comfortably large distance between him and his pursuers. It was dark by the time he reached the Norfolk border and they drove through the flat, featureless countryside, field upon field of cereal, sugar beet, onions and potatoes, with just the odd one of sheep or free range pigs, now and again. The only illumination came from the headlights of the car, which occasionally caught a rabbit darting across the road. Half an hour later, they reached Shaun's uncle's farm and drove up the long driveway to the house. They could see the barns to the right-hand side and a few tractors, with the all-weather protection cabs on top. Shaun knocked on the farmhouse door, having already phoned his uncle to warn of his impending arrival.

"'Ello there young Shaun. 'Ow are yuh, boy?" Shaun's uncle had a strident voice that carried across fields and could be heard above the sound of farm machinery. He still spoke the old Norfolk dialect. "Your friends comin' in? Everything all right, Shaun? You look a bit edgy, that's all."

"Hello uncle. We need to get up to my weekend house as soon as we can, but I just want to borrow something from you."

"If I can 'elp you boy, you're welcome to what I 'ave."

"I need your shotgun for a day or two."

His uncle frowned. "You sure you know what you're doin'?"

"I'll explain when I return it, but I just need it quickly now."

"Whatever you're up to boy, it implicates me if I supply the gun. I'm not sure about this."

"It's just a precaution. I'm sure I won't need to use it." Shaun replied, trying hard to sound convincing.

His uncle disappeared into the house and came back with a shot gun and an ammunition belt of cartridges.

"Er's old, boy, but er's a good un. Er's a twelve bore so you take care of the rebound. You load it like this." He broke the gun at its breech and inserted a cartridge, then snapped it shut. "You don't aim a shotgun, you point it.

Fire it like this, from the shoulder, tuck it right in and lean forward as you fire."

"How close do you have to be to stop someone?"

"Ooh! This sounds serious… five feet to kill, ten feet to maim, but ten feet could also kill. Go for the chest to kill and the legs to maim, but in any case the shots will spread out, it being a scattergun. Each cartridge contains a hundred birdshot pellets."

Turning away, Shaun's uncle fired into the darkness towards the barn. A great crack resounded through the night air and there was a scuttle of nocturnal wildlife in the surrounding fields and trees.

"Nice gun." Emilio had emerged from the car with a big grin on his face and grabbed the weapon. He took some pretend pot shots with it. "So devastating if your target is close." His grin widened.

"And who might you be?" Shaun's uncle looked up at Emilio, who was by now wearing a red bandana, making him look like a swashbuckling pirate.

"This is Emilio from Brazil, Uncle."

"I don't know Shaun, your mum told me about this little Brazilian girl you've taken up with… You seem to be walking on the wild side nowadays, and you were so quiet and studious when you were a lad."

Wanting to get away before he changed his mind, Shaun started to walk towards the car. "Thanks Uncle. I'll return the gun in a few days." They drove off waving.

They reached the coast half an hour later. Shaun's turning curved off from the main road down to the sea, with Edwardian houses on both sides. His was down the beach end. Marram was the name of the house, it meant beach grass, and it was one of the finest houses in the road, set back in large grounds with trees, bushes and lawns, and even a tennis court on one side. The house itself was built of brick, but covered with white, rough cast render, into which black wooden beams had been sunk in mock Tudor fashion. The windows were small paned and leaded and, in the upstairs rooms, were dormer style, like a Swiss chalet, protruding from the steep, tiled roof. Shaun got everyone out of the car, then parked it in the garage, which he padlocked, so that their presence would be inconspicuous. He had felt safe in the cocoon of his fast car, but now they had arrived, he had started to sweat again and his mouth had gone dry. In the darkness, the others didn't notice.

"Come in, come in." he put on a jaunty voice as he opened the front door. "We're safe and sound now. Welcome to Marram."

He gathered everyone in the living room at the back. He wanted to leave the front in darkness. "Pilar, can you come here?" he said, leading her into the Edwardian kitchen with its original white painted shelving and hooks for pots, pans and utensils. "You get everyone a drink and then make some food. Keep everyone on the back of the house. I'm going to keep watch at the front for a while, just in case."

"Is that necessary? Why are you so tense? Aren't we safe here?"

"Of course we are, but I don't want to take any risks. You know me, leave no stone unturned." He gave her a grin, but it looked a bit forced.

Shaun settled in an upstairs bedroom overlooking the front garden. He sat on a chair by the window, with the lights off. It gave him a good vantage point up the road, and he kept to hand some binoculars he'd bought for bird watching. All was quiet and it reminded him that, since it had been built, this house had only ever been used as a holiday home, for rest and recreation, and that, normally, a feeling of relaxation permeated the rooms. For decades, it

245

had soaked up children's chatter and laughter, the sound of seagulls, the healthy exhaustion of long, sunny days, playing in the sea and sand. But this night Shaun felt only tension and fear. His escape plan had been conceived in haste, and he was now starting to realise it was potentially flawed. He knew that, if the Russians were very clever and had the right contacts, and tracing Ralf's call suggested they did, then they might just work out where he was hiding. If they had someone who was an expert in computer systems, a hacker, then Shaun and his party were at risk. Staying in a hotel might have been a safer bet, or even seeking refuge at his uncle's. But Shaun was never one to make a fuss and had always been a bit of a risk taker. After about five minutes, he could hear the chinking of glasses from down below and excited chatter. Emilio was telling a story in a loud voice, punctuated by laughter from the others. Suddenly, he heard light footsteps on the stairs and Pilar calling to him.

"I'm in here, Pilar."

She entered the bedroom, holding two glasses. "We've opened some champagne. We're having a little party, now that we're safe." She pressed one glass into Shaun's hand and leant over him with her arm round his neck.

"That's great. You keep everybody happy. Think of me as the captain of the ship, and you're my number two, keeping the crew occupied for me. I'm going to phone the police now and see if the Russians were caught from your phone call."

She frowned. "What if they haven't caught them?"

"I'm sure they will have. If they haven't, then we'll have to stay here for a while."

"Are you okay up here on your own? Isn't it lonely?"

"I can't relax just yet. You go back down, and I'll join you soon."

"Don't be long, then." She kissed him. "Ready for some fun tonight? Hmm?" She went back downstairs.

He was feeling a bit easier. The lightness of Pilar's mood had lifted him and he took a few sips of the champagne. It had been a long and draining day. He closed his eyes. Now he was starting to feel relaxed. Maybe he was being overcautious, with all his worrying. He started to think about the good times in the house. He chuckled as the tree incident came to mind. A local builder had bought a dilapidated old house that bordered the far corner of Shaun's land and demolished it, squeezing two new houses onto the plot in its place. When they were completed the builder had knocked on Shaun's door.

"Hi. I'm your neighbour." He pointed to the new builds. "Would it be okay if I cut down those two trees?" He pointed to two very tall trees, that stood in the corner of Shaun's garden and were quite close to the nearest of the newly built dwellings. "I'm worried that if there's a storm they might get blown onto my house." He stood staring at Shaun. He had a big frame and looked very fit and strong.

"Hmm, well, I see the problem." Shaun looked at the man. He was giving Shaun a confident, aggressive stare. "It's a shame to chop them down, but… yeah, I suppose so."

Pilar had overheard and came to the door to stand beside Shaun. "I like the trees. Why did you build your house so close to them?"

"It was the only way I could get two houses onto the plot."

"Well, you should have discussed it before you built them."

"Well, I can't unbuild them now, so is it okay if I chop the trees down?"

"No. I like the trees."

The builder had looked shocked, but then a sneer came onto his face as he looked down at Pilar. "It's been a waste of time talking to you." He turned and hurried off.

Shaun had started to laugh. "That was too funny, Pilar, the look of shock on that guy's face with this little girl, telling him what to do. I get the impression he's used to getting his own way."

They had returned to London that night, and the next weekend, when they came up to Norfolk, the trees had been chopped down in their absence and piled up as logs in the corner of the garden. It was a half finished job, because the stumps were still there and Shaun would need to employ a tree surgeon to root them out. Pilar was furious and wanted to confront the neighbour, but Shaun persuaded her to let the matter drop, because they wouldn't be able to prove anything and being away so often, they had to keep on good terms with the locals.

He opened his eyes to take another sip of champagne. Still chuckling at how Pilar had dealt with the man, he thought he should make that call to the police, to get reassurance that the gangsters had been apprehended in the vicinity of his house in London. He glanced up the road. He blinked and then his mouth dropped open in astonishment. A black car was slowly making its way down the road. He looked through the binoculars. It was the Volvo with German number plates. He started to panic. He slid open his mobile and dialled 999.

"Emergency, which service?"

"Police," he said with emotion.

After a few seconds he was connected. "This is the police. What's your emergency, caller?"

"I have an armed gang outside my house." His voice was shaking as he gave the address.

"Can you stay on the line caller?"

"I can leave the phone on, but I've got things to do right now, like evacuating the house, so I won't be talking to you," he replied, sounding desperate.

"Our advice is to stay inside the house with all the doors locked."

"I can't have a conversation with you right now, but I'll leave the phone on for the time being."

He ran downstairs and found everyone in the living room, including Pilar, who was serving drinks from a trolley, like she was an air hostess and everyone was on holiday. The atmosphere was light and jolly, like a party was just getting going. "They're outside," he shouted. "I don't know how, but they're outside."

"No! How did they find us?" Christiana started to cry. She had relaxed since the reunion with Ralf, but her face went pale and tense in an instant.

Shaun shook his head. "I can't tell you. They're cleverer than I thought."

"Let's go out onto the beach." Christiana was shaking with fear.

"I don't run. I fight like a man," shouted Emilio. He had nursed the shotgun and ammunition belt ever since leaving Shaun's uncle's farm, but he threw them down on the sofa and dashed into the kitchen. He returned a minute later with a knife block that contained eight knives. He had also found a sharpening gadget, which was poking out from his trouser pocket. He took the largest knife for himself and tucked it underneath his belt. He then offered one to the others. He exuded a strength and confidence that everyone else lacked, although Pilar still looked composed. They all accepted a knife apart from Christiana, who waved Emilio away with her hand.

"Here, you can take the shotgun to protect Lisa." Emilio grabbed the gun from the sofa and pushed it into

Christiana's chest, forcing her to clutch it. "Hold it against your shoulder when you fire."

"No, you keep it." She tried to give it back. "You shoot them. I can't do it."

"I only need the knife. You go upstairs into a bedroom. Shoot them as they come through the door. It will take all of them out, with one shot; inside the cartridge is a hundred pellets. I'll finish as many as I can down here."

"You're very brave." Despite the panic, Christiana looked up at Emilio in awe.

"Better to live one day as a tiger than a hundred years as a sheep," he said as he calmly ran the blade of his knife up and down the sharpener, like he was a craftsman busy in his workshop, going about his normal business.

Lisa was asleep in Ralf's arms, oblivious to the pandemonium. Christiana looked at them, and pondered for a moment. She thought Ralf should take the shotgun and she should hold Lisa, but Ralf seemed to be in a dream world of his own and turned into a passive observer by his extended abuse of drugs while hiding in Munich. Christiana found herself swept along by the moment and was fastening the ammunition belt round her waist, as though that was a normal thing to do, while Emilio held the gun. He showed her how to reload it, but said it wouldn't be necessary as one shot would kill them all. Then he handed it back to her.

Pilar had observed the scene without comment. "Come with me." Pilar said it quietly and took Shaun's hand. "This isn't our argument. Let Christiana look after herself and let Emilio do whatever he likes."

"Switch off all the lights," said Shaun, as Pilar led him out of the back door and into the garden to hide in a thick clump of bushes nearby. She was clutching Chimbo, who seemed to sense the danger and was shivering.

Meanwhile, Sergei and his men sat in the car with the lights out. It was 9:30 p.m. on a Sunday night, but Shaun's road was very spacious, and everything was still, with no activity. There was something very incongruous about this genteel, middle-class holiday enclave having a visit from a car full of the toughest gangsters in Europe. But that was the reality that had unfolded.

"Looks quiet, maybe they've gone somewhere else." Viktor whined.

"There's no sign of them, but that doesn't mean they're not in there. We've already seen how devious they can be." Sergei spoke with the voice of experience. "Let's take a look… put your silencers on. Kateryna, you're going to knock on the door."

They got out the car and the men placed the silencers on their guns. Low clouds were being blown across the sky, hiding the full moon, as they slowly walked up the path in the darkness. Only the crunch of the gravel gave away their movements in the silence of the night. First Nikolai tried the garage door. He rattled the padlock.

"Shall I shoot it open?" he whispered, looking at Sergei.

"*Nyet!* Too noisy, let's carry on searching," Sergei whispered back.

They reached the front door and Kateryna rang the bell, which chimed through the house, while the men stood to one side, out of sight. There was no answer. They waited. Igor left them and crept stealthily round the side of the house, looking for the backdoor. He stopped suddenly halfway round. He thought he'd heard a noise from the bushes. It sounded like an animal whimpering. He trained his gun on the thick clump and prepared to release a round of bullets. Pilar was inside the bushes and busy stroking Chimbo, trying to calm him down. At that moment, a hedgehog slowly scuttled out onto the lawn.

Igor relaxed and lowered his gun. He continued round to the back of the house.

He opened the backdoor slowly. It creaked eerily, like it needed some oil. He stood there, looking inside and listening intently while holding his gun in front of him. He was scared but his heart was racing with excitement at the same time. He had done this sort of thing many times before and he was used to success. It was his bread and butter business. He usually killed with guns or knives. If the victim wasn't too large, he had a technique of picking them up by the throat with his left hand and stabbing them through the heart with his right hand. Witnesses had seen him do it quite often, but they were always too scared to testify. Where he had the time, he had also squeezed the life out of quite a few people with his huge hands round their necks. He had found that fascinating, to literally have their lives in his hands. Sometimes he had released his grip to open their windpipe and give them a few more seconds of life, only to close it again and extinguish them. Strangulation was his favourite method of execution. He enjoyed the intimacy of the moment, being close to his victim as their life ebbed away. Over the years, he had come to see himself as the invincible predator, and yet, this night felt different.

The back door being already open, seemed like a trap to him, so he stood his ground listening for any unfamiliar sound. A few seconds passed, when suddenly the clouds parted and the full moon shone a bright light into the kitchen. It was a surreal moment, taking Igor by surprise and he looked behind, almost expecting to see the searchlight of a helicopter zooming down on the scene. Most people would have been terrified of the big, muscular giant, but Emilio was also supersized and, like a fighting dog, capable of a huge surge of energy when aroused. It was at exactly the moment Igor looked behind that, in one powerful movement, Emilio sprang out from inside the house. He rushed at Igor so fast that the Russian, caught off guard, froze and couldn't fire his gun. Emilio ran to one side of him and stabbed Igor through the throat, twisting the knife as it pierced the soft flesh as easily as if it was a pat of butter. The blood gushed out with such force that Igor lost consciousness almost immediately, but as he fell to the ground his finger instinctively fired the gun in rapid motion. He jerked like someone having a fit, as the blood shot up like an oil strike from the gaping hole left after the knife was removed with a strange sucking sound. Emilio fell backwards into the house, caught by Igor's bullets.

Sergei, Nikolai and Viktor heard a gasp from Igor and the clicks of the silenced bullets. Leaving Kateryna, they ran round to the back of the house to find Igor's great frame sprawled across the ground.

Viktor bent down over Igor's body. "He's dead," was all he could muster for his comrade.

"See, I told you the big gypo was useless with a bullet in him," added Nikolai, kicking Emilio's lifeless body.

Sergei's face tensed and his eyes narrowed. He hadn't expected to lose a man on this trip, particularly not his main enforcer. Igor had been such a cold, ruthless killing machine, and above all, loyal and reliable, able to carry out orders without any questions. There was also the matter of Igor's wife and children. Sergei would now need to explain to his daughter that her husband and the father of her children was dead, and he would now be obliged to provide some kind of widow's and orphan's fund until she remarried. He had been lax in allowing Igor to go off on his own and he had underestimated the cunning of his prey. He resolved that Ralf would be tortured as punishment before he died, and his suffering prolonged as long as was practicable, even though the error of judgement had been Sergei's.

"We take no prisoners," whispered Sergei to the other two.

Emilio had fallen with his head into the kitchen, his middle on the doorstep, and his legs in the garden. So his body was now blocking the entrance to the house and the three gangsters had to step over him in their search for Ralf. Nikolai was the last to pass Emilio by and he gave him another kick, harder this time and in the shins. Emilio's eyes opened. He was down but not out. He kicked Nikolai's legs and the smaller man tripped and dropped his gun as he fell onto Emilio, their heads facing in the same direction. Emilio grasped the little Russian in a bear hug. Nikolai cried out, '*Na pomoshch!*' (help), but Sergei, maybe shaken by the death of Igor, stared blankly at the scene. Emilio rolled Nikolai to one side, so that he was wedged between Emilio's huge body and the door frame. Nikolai cried out with pain at the pressure being exerted on his chest. Slowly, Emilio worked his hands up Nikolai's torso and reached his throat. He then started to throttle him. Sergei continued to survey the fight impartially, as though interested to see who would win. Rasping noises came from Nikolai, and he appeared to be getting weaker with every second. Suddenly, just as Nikolai seemed to be fading away, a silenced shot rang out and Emilio's body slumped and went lifeless. Blood poured from his head where Viktor's bullet had entered. Viktor had waited for a signal from Sergei that had never come, and had eventually fired on his own initiative. Nikolai got up, massaging his neck and catching his breath.

"You took your time," Nikolai wheezed as he glared at Sergei.

Sergei shrugged. "Not you losing your edge, are you? We wouldn't want that, would we?"

They searched the downstairs of the house, creeping from room to room in silence, giving each other cover with their guns, Nikolai still massaging his neck.

Outside, Pilar waited a few minutes in the bushes, and then handed Chimbo to Shaun.

"Hold him," she whispered.

"What are you going to do?" Shaun whispered back, sounding nervous.

"Stay here."

She emerged from the bushes with Shaun trailing behind her. She went over to where the two crumpled bodies lay. She picked up Igor's gun and removed the silencer, tossing it on the lawn, aware that it decreased the gun's accuracy. Her little hands moved across the body of the dead Russian giant, fumbling in his pockets for his ammunition clips. Finding them, she saw the clips contained eight bullets and having heard Igor fire only three, she did not reload, but pocketed two clips just in case. She felt no remorse and stepped over Emilio's body, which was still blocking the doorway. Shaun had watched in amazement at the certainty and authority of Pilar's actions. It was like she was in a movie, a secret agent living a double life, housewife by day, assassin by night.

The Russians meanwhile had crept up the stairs, and continued searching every room in turn, switching on the lights as they went. They found nothing until they came to the furthest bedroom, where Ralf, Christiana and Lisa were cowering in a corner. Christiana was shivering with fear. Sergei's mouth dropped open in surprise to see Christiana had a shotgun and he retreated back onto the landing to take cover behind the half open door.

"Don't move bitch." He had his gun trained on Christiana. "Now drop the gun and put your hands up."

Christiana was standing protectively in front of Ralf, who had Lisa on his lap.

"Shoot, you fool. What's the matter with you?" Ralf hissed.

She was pointing the shotgun directly at Sergei. She was supposed to have fired as the gangsters came into the doorway, but she had missed her moment and in any case her hands were shaking so much the gun was moving around. There was terror on her face and her teeth were chattering.

"Oh, look what we have." Sergei was peeping round the edge of the door, and suddenly relaxed. He laughed and stepped into the bedroom, with Nikolai and Victor following. "We have a little German…Boo!" he shouted. Christiana let out a cry and the gun started to shake even more. As much as she tried, she couldn't pull the trigger. Sergei was enjoying the situation. "You're little pussycats really aren't you?" He stood in front of her and stared, confidently smiling. Her gun continued to shake, but she still couldn't pull the trigger. "Go on shoot… show us what you're made of," he goaded her. "You see, you can't."

Ralf, who was sitting in the corner, with Lisa asleep on his lap, made a move as though he was going to get up.

"Stay where you are or I'll kill you," Nikolai shouted, aiming his gun at Ralf.

Ralf stayed put.

"I'm going to kill you and your daughter and your man, but still you can't kill me." Sergei sneered. "You haven't the courage to pull the trigger. Isn't that a strange thing? What would your German intellectuals, your philosophers, make of that, eh! You know you couldn't even run your own concentration camps to kill the Jews? You got the vanquished East Europeans, the collaborators, to do that for you. Pathetic." He continued to stare at Christiana. "Get me the girl," he shouted at Nikolai, who took Lisa from Ralf at gunpoint. Lisa, who had been fast asleep, woke up and started to cry. It was a harrowing sound to anyone with humanity, the plaintive weeping of a two-year-old girl, like a child in hospital realising something bad was about to happen. But to Sergei it was just an aggravating reminder of his own pain. "I'm going to kill your daughter first and still you can't shoot me." He knelt on the floor and pulled a wailing Lisa onto his lap. He put the gun to her head. Christiana shook even more and now realised that the shotgun was useless, because Lisa would also be hit by the spreading pellets. She had to find a new strategy to save themselves.

"Get on with it, Sergei and let's get out of here." Nikolai was the only one that would challenge Sergei in that manner.

"What's the matter with you?" Sergei turned his head and scowled. "Got shit in your pants after what your wife said?"

"We're wasting time. Finish the job and let's get on our way. What if they've called the police?"

"Can I hear a police siren?" Sergei stared at Nikolai. "Or have I gone deaf suddenly? Shut up, miserable peasant, I'm saying important things here." Sergei turned back to Christiana. "You will watch your daughter die, rather than kill me." He changed his posture to one that was more upright. "My dear brother, Alexei, watch now as I avenge your death. This is for you. Three Germans in return for one Russian."

He held the barrel of the gun against Lisa's head, just above her ear.

"Please." Christiana pleaded.

"Please, what?" He rested the gun back down by his side, happy to squeeze more fun from the situation.

"She's just an innocent child. You don't want to be a child killer. Please spare her life."

"So what if she's a child? She'll grow up to be a German."

"Please, she's done nothing to you. Please don't touch my baby." As she said it, Christiana could see Sergei's leathery face was impassive and that she was having no impact on him. She suddenly found a bit of courage. "You'll never get away with it." Her voice was suddenly full of contempt. "The British police will hunt down a child killer wherever you go. However long it takes, they'll never give up. They'll never close the case. They'll find you."

Sergei shrugged, knowing that he planned to burn down the house in order to destroy the evidence. He decided he had played with his victims long enough.

"You will watch her die, your husband will watch you and her die. Then he will die." Sergei shouted it, having worked himself into a frenzy. He was full of hatred for the Germans that had killed his grandfather in the war. It was time to add to his long list of executions. He was now about to pull the trigger on Lisa. Viktor and Nikolai were standing with their backs to the bedroom door, their guns pointing at Ralf and Christiana. Sergei was kneeling as he held Lisa, his gun at her head. Christiana was standing in the far corner of the room, holding the shotgun, but unable to use it. Ralf was crouched behind her.

Stealthily, Pilar had climbed the staircase, with Shaun following. She could see the light coming from the far bedroom and heard their voices and Lisa's crying. Silently she crept along the upstairs landing. Then she saw the backs of the three Russians. She could see Sergei had a gun to Lisa's head. Slowly kicking off her shoes, she moved quietly towards the open doorway. How many times, had she shot down a row of bottles or tins in the *favela*, to the cheers and applause of the gangsters? She was the crack shot, the champion marksman, but she had never shot a human target. Would she freeze, like Christiana, unable to kill another human being? She stepped into the doorway. Ralf and Christiana looked at her. The Russians started to look round as Pilar fired. Sergei was the first to get it and did not have time to realise that the Patrushev dynasty and its reign of terror had come to an end, or that he ended his days with a bullet through the back of his head, just like his grandfather. He slumped forward on top of Lisa, who started to scream. Viktor, who was on the left, got it next, with a bullet in the middle of his back, delivered with amazing accuracy and cutting his spine in two.

But Nikolai, who was on the right, had time to swivel round and instinctively fired a shot, which went wide and hit a picture on the wall. Simultaneously, Pilar had aimed for his spine, but missed, because he had become a moving target, and her shot hit him on the side of the chest, so that he fell to the floor wounded. Nikolai aimed again, and this time Pilar felt the rush of air from his bullet, as it passed her face and exploded into the half open door behind her. She finished him with a shot to the forehead, between the eyes, a large red hole appearing, like a Hindu woman's bindi, his sad, cynical face in repose at last. Pilar was standing barefoot at the doorway of the bedroom, the gun in her hand, the tang of cordite in the air as the smoke leaked out of the muzzle, and a red weal across her cheek, where the gunpowder residue from Nikolai's bullet had burnt her. Three corpses were sprawled across the floor.

"Whoa! Where did you learn to shoot like that?" said Ralf.

Pilar gave him an intense look and swallowed. She was about to say something, but they had come surreptitiously, without sirens and at that moment, a voice came over a loudhailer from outside.

"Armed police. You're surrounded. Come to the front door of the house with your arms held out to your side. Leave any weapons in the house. Do not attempt to leave by any other exits. I repeat, do not bring weapons with you."

"Let's go. Do exactly what they say," said Shaun as he took the lead, his hands still shaking from shock at seeing Pilar shoot the three men dead. He motioned to them all to drop the weapons on the floor and put their hands on their heads. They went downstairs and as he opened the front door, he could just make out a wall of transparent shields, with heavily armoured policemen crouched behind them, and standing above them, a second row of police marksmen who were resting their rifles on the top of the wall, aiming towards the house.

"Don't shoot." Shaun shouted, his voice shaky and charged with fear. He knew it was still possible that a nervous police officer, scared for his own life, could loose off a bullet in error. "The men you want are dead."

"Turn around." The voice on the loudhailer resumed impassively. "Do it now. Lie down on the floor with your arms out."

They all complied and Christiana motioned for Lisa to lie beside her. Two police officers came from behind the shields to check them for weapons. A female frisked Pilar, Christiana and Lisa; a male searched Shaun and Ralf.

"They're clear," the female officer called to her colleagues.

The interviews lasted a few hours, their version of events being accepted in full, with no further action to be taken. Pilar and Shaun identified Emilio for the police, Pilar crouched over him crying.

"Why are you crying for that rapist?" Shaun asked.

"He's still somebody's son. How am I going to explain this to his mother? She's going to blame me."

Shaun put a comforting arm round her and she leaned her head into his shoulder. "Let it out." He rubbed her back. "Let it all go."

16

On the Beach

"Pilar, you were so amazing." Ralf grinned at her the next day as they crossed the sand dunes. "Who taught you to shoot like that? It was like, bang, bang, bang, bang and then there were these corpses all over the floor." He gave a big laugh.

"There are lots of guns in the *favela*. But I was the gangsters' favourite when I was a girl. I could take as many practice shots as I liked."

"You never told me about that side of your life." Shaun studied her, like she was someone new. The red weal on her face glistened with the soothing jelly ointment the hospital had prescribed.

"There was no need to tell you."

The five survivors looked like they'd been to an all-night party, short on sleep, but exhilarated as they stepped onto the beach, dodging the pools of water and clumps of seaweed. An ice cream jeep, specially converted for the sand, came speeding by.

"Ice cream, mummy." Lisa tugged at Christiana's sleeve.

"Let's get some coffee and croissants over there." Shaun pointed to a cafe with a terrace, on the edge of the beach. They sat outside it with their refreshments, enjoying the smell of the sea. Life was suddenly very sweet. "What will you do now?" Shaun looked at Ralf and Christiana.

Ralf shook his head and sighed. "We can't go back to

Berlin. The police say there was a fifth gangster who escaped. We may face retribution in Berlin, from the rest of Sergei's gang." Ralf was referring to Kateryna who, seeing the flashing lights of the police cars the night before, had driven off in the opposite direction, abandoning the car at Folkestone and crossing to France as a foot passenger. She then went into hiding in her native Ukraine, knowing that she was liable to prosecution as an accessory to murder. "We'll have to start somewhere new," Ralf continued.

"Maybe Hamburg," Christiana interjected.

"Or further west, Cologne, or maybe even Amsterdam."

"We can go around on bicycles." Christiana smiled.

"I'd like to help you." Shaun gave Christiana a surreptitious wink that no one else noticed. "You know I have a few pennies in the bank. I would like to buy you somewhere to live in your new adopted city."

"Shaun." Pilar looked shocked and grabbed his arm. "Can we afford that? It's no good giving all our money away."

"Why should you help us?" Ralf screwed his face up as he looked at Shaun.

"We've been through a lot together. This has been such a trauma for Lisa. I want things to be right for you as a family."

"Thank you, Shaun. We'll accept your help." Christiana said it softly, kicking Ralf underneath the table. She understood what Shaun was doing.

"And as for you, Missus," Shaun turned to Pilar, "how does Pilar Johnson sound to you?"

It took a moment to sink in. She looked blankly at Shaun, then started to smile. She had imagined this event previously and was expecting something more romantic, but she put her arms round him.

"I think Pilar Fernandes Johnson sounds better, but I'm giving you a 'yes'"

Epilogue

It was the first evening of their honeymoon in Búzios, an idyllic beach resort one hundred miles from Rio de Janeiro. As they came out of the hotel looking for somewhere to eat, Pilar heard a distant drum beat, and immediately recognized the slow, quick quick, slow, quick quick rhythm.

"It's the sound of the Rumba, from Cuba. Come on Shaun, let's go and see." Pilar ran through the strolling tourists with Shaun following. They arrived at an outdoor seafood restaurant which had a dinner and dance evening. Its name stood above the entrance, silhouetted in green neon against the sky: *Maldita Corvina* (Naughty Sea Bass). Pilar had already started to move her body to the beat of the music.

"Oh Shaun, let's eat here tonight and we can dance as well."

"Perfect. My favourite, seafood, and a dance floor for you!"

The waiter greeted Pilar. "*Boa noite senhora*. A table for two?... please come this way."

As the waiter ushered them to a table, Pilar was shaking her hips. She seemed to have even extra energy on this evening. Their table was overlooking the beach and sea. It was one of Pilar's favourite times of day, the setting sun making everything golden, and it was pleasantly warm with a light, fresh breeze. They ordered locally caught fish and some wine.

Shaun looked at the scar on Pilar's cheek, the skid mark from Nikolai's bullet, and leant across the table to gently touch it. "Does it hurt?"

"No. It's fading. It will go eventually."

"I don't mind if it stays. It reminds me what a brave wife I have. I think I must be the luckiest man in the world to have got you. What have I done to deserve it?"

Pilar reached across the table to take Shaun's hand. "You didn't have luck. You had pluck. It's you who were brave, to have me considering how we met. I'm so glad you were that bold. A Brazilian man would have wanted to kill me. Shaun…" She fixed him with an intense stare. "I see something so beautiful in you. I really hope we can have lots of children and stay together forever."

"It's strange." He looked thoughtful for a moment. "With other girls, I always felt a separation, even when we were together. But with you, it's like we're in the same place. It's an amazing feeling. It's like, I'm right where you are."

"I've got some news. You know how your mother always wanted grandchildren?"

"Oh my God… Pilar! Really?"

"Is it good news?"

"It's brilliant, and you know the sex already?"

She nodded. "A little girl came to me in a dream. She looked like me when I was young. I said, 'who are you?' She said, 'I'm Daniella.'"

"*Two girls for every boy.*" He sang the riff from the old Beach Boys number.

By the time their fish were just bones on their plates in front of them, the sun had set and the moon had come up, throwing a beam across the sea towards them, like a shining, silver ribbon that got wider as it got closer.

"See how it's coming across the sea to where we are?" Shaun pointed to it.

Pilar looked. "Isn't it beautiful?" She turned her head back to face Shaun. "Tonight is so special." Her eyes looked a little watery.

Shaun reached across the table to take Pilar's hand. "May I have this dance, Mrs Johnson?"

"Mrs Fernandes Johnson... and the answer's yes," she squeezed his hand, "and don't tread on my toes."